LICENCE TO DREAM

Recent Titles by Anna Jacobs from Severn House

CHANGE OF SEASON
CHESTNUT LANE
THE CORRIGAN LEGACY
FAMILY CONNECTIONS
A FORBIDDEN EMBRACE
AN INDEPENDENT WOMAN
IN FOCUS
KIRSTY'S VINEYARD
LICENCE TO DREAM
MARRYING MISS MARTHA
MISTRESS OF MARYMOOR
REPLENISH THE EARTH
SAVING WILLOWBROOK
SEASONS OF LOVE
THE WISHING WELL

Anna is always delighted to hear from readers and can be contacted:

BY MAIL

PO Box 628
Mandurah
Western Australia 6210

If you'd like a reply, please enclose a self-addressed, business size envelope, stamped (from inside Australia) or an international reply coupon (from outside Australia).

VIA THE INTERNET

Anna has her own web page, with details of her books and excerpts, and invites you to visit it at http://www.annajacobs.com

Anna can be contacted by email at anna@annajacobs.com

If you'd like to receive an email newsletter about Anna and her books every month or two, you are cordially invited to join her announcements list. Just email her and ask to be added to the list, or follow the link from her web page.

LICENCE TO DREAM

Anna Jacobs

This first world edition published 2010
in Great Britain and in the USA by
SEVERN HOUSE PUBLISHERS LTD of
9–15 High Street, Sutton, Surrey, England, SM1 1DF.
Trade paperback edition first published
in Great Britain and the USA 2011 by
SEVERN HOUSE PUBLISHERS LTD.

British Library Cataloguing in Publication Data

Jacobs, Anna.
    Licence to Dream.
    1. Women accountants – Fiction. 2. English – Australia –
    Fiction. 3. Widowers – Australia – Fiction. 4. Landscape
    Design – Fiction. 5. Love stories.
    I. Title
    823.9'14–dc22

ISBN-13: 978-0-7278-6934-0   (cased)
ISBN-13: 978-1-84751-265-9   (trade paper)

All Severn House titles are printed on acid-free paper.

Severn House Publishers support The Forest Stewardship Council [FSC],
the leading international forest certification organisation. All our titles that
are printed on Greenpeace-approved FSC-certified paper carry the FSC logo.

Mixed Sources
Product group from well-managed
forests and other controlled sources
www.fsc.org Cert no. SA-COC-1565
© 1996 Forest Stewardship Council
FSC

Typeset by Palimpsest Book Production Ltd.,
Falkirk, Stirlingshire, Scotland.
Printed and bound in Great Britain by the
MPG Books Group, Bodmin, Cornwall.

Dear reader

I sometimes wonder how my heroes and heroines have turned into the sort of person who steps out on to my pages.

This time I've indulged my curiosity and explored Meriel's and Ben's childhoods. Then I've watched them as adults pursuing their dreams.

I hope you enjoy reading this story as much as I enjoyed writing it.

Anna

One

Nine-year-old Meriel Ingram walked home from school, shoulders hunched against the rain, backpack bobbing against her shoulders. She slowed down as she got towards the house. Once she went inside, she'd be trapped indoors because her mother never let her play out in the rain. It wasn't fair.

The Ingrams had one of the two best houses in the long terrace, with three bedrooms instead of two. The smaller bedrooms were built over the arched passageway which led through the middle of the row to the narrow lane between the backyards at the rear. It was wide enough for a horse and cart to pass through and Grandpop said in the old days coal had been delivered that way.

With a sigh she opened the front door, calling, 'I'm back, Mum!' and went through to the kitchen at the rear.

Her mother greeted her with, 'Just look at you! Covered in mud again. Where do you find it? Get those socks off this minute and I'll put them to soak.'

Meriel removed the socks and trailed up to her bedroom, lingering by the window to stare down at the row of small oblong yards to the rear. Theirs was completely covered in black tarmac, which she hated. The next door neighbours had made a little garden with all sorts of flowers, but her mother said a garden would make the yard untidy and get in the way of her washing.

But the flowers were so much prettier!

When her father got back, her mother had the food on the table within minutes. As they began to eat, she announced, 'Mrs Perley next door's got herself a job. It's not right, mothers working. I'd never let my children come home to an empty house.'

Dad murmured something and concentrated on his food.

Meriel looked at him. Grey. He was nearly all grey: hair,

pullover, trousers. Today the teacher had been talking about what jobs their fathers did. Boring jobs, all of them. Hers worked at the Town Hall as a clerk. She was going to do something more interesting than that when she grew up: become an artist, or an astronaut, or a pop singer. Not work in an office, whatever her mother said.

The thing she kept coming back to was being an artist and painting pretty pictures for people to put on their walls. Her favourite Christmas present had been a big box of paints. She loved mixing new colours and trying to make her pictures look real. Art lessons were the highlight of the school week, as far as she was concerned.

After tea she dried the dishes then got out her paints.

'That's the only thing you're tidy about,' her mother grumbled. 'Did you put your clean clothes away? Are you *blind*? They were sitting on the bed. You couldn't miss them.'

'Sorry, Mum.'

'You're not fiddling with those paints till you've gone upstairs and put your clothes away. You'd live in a pigsty if I let you!'

With a sigh Meriel did as she was told.

When she went downstairs again, her father was sitting reading his newspaper, which he did every evening unless it was fine enough to go out for a walk. Her mother was knitting and watching a favourite TV programme. Her sister was doing homework, sneaking glances at the television.

Meriel had no homework tonight, so for an hour or so she was free to let her imagination roam. Bliss.

When Meriel was twelve her father suggested getting a computer. 'It's about time our girls learned to use one.'

Denise pulled a sour face. 'They're expensive.'

'They're the coming thing. We want to give our girls a good start, don't we?'

'Where are you going to put it?'

'We hardly ever use the front room, so a computer wouldn't be in the way there. I thought we could put it in the back corner.'

Meriel held her breath. She was learning how to use

computers at school, but you didn't get a turn very often and she desperately wanted one at home.

Denise got up and walked into the front room. 'It'd mean getting rid of Auntie Janie's table.'

'Well, we only use that for standing ornaments on.'

'Those are my great-grandma's ornaments. I care a lot about them. No. There just isn't room.'

'Then we could put it in a corner of the bedroom,' her father suggested.

'What, and spoil the look of my new bedroom suite!'

For once Frank tried hard to get his way and quarrels raged through the house, but Denise won, as she always did.

Wanting to help, Meriel suggested they put the computer in her bedroom. 'I wouldn't mind, Mum, and—'

'Don't you start. I'm not having one of those horrible things in the house and that's that.'

That same year Meriel's Grandpop retired and bought a little house in the next street with the money from his endowment policy, which had matured after forty years of payments.

His move across town meant he could see more of his only daughter and her family, but Meriel knew she was his favourite. Well, he was her favourite person, too.

From then onwards she was able to escape from her mother more easily. Grandpop had a workshop in the cellar and he let her help him with his woodwork. She loved making things.

Her grandmother was a quiet woman, very house proud like her daughter, except for Grandpop's cellar workshop, where no one was allowed without his permission. Not that it was messy. He wouldn't have stood for that. A place for everything and everything in its place, he always said.

Mum went out shopping with Grandma sometimes, or they sat gossiping together, drinking tea and eating biscuits.

Dad took up walking to get fit and spent even less time at home.

No one seemed to mind what Meriel did as long as she was safe with Grandpop.

And *he* was thinking of getting a computer.

'I'd have to go to classes first and learn how to use one,

mind. I'm not having anything in this house that I don't understand.'

'I know how to use one. We have them at school.'

He smiled down at her. 'Then you'll be able to help me. Once I've got the house shipshape I'll look into it.'

The town's campaign of beautification of the older suburbs spread to Meriel's area. Cul-de-sacs were created in some streets, with strips of garden at the blocked-off ends, though the trees and bushes planted there by the council always seemed to be struggling to survive.

Meriel was in the thick of this mania for revitalization because Grandpop had got a grant to modernize his home, which had a narrow downstairs bathroom, very old-fashioned, in a lean-to.

A builder created a tiny new bathroom over the stairwell, then a plumber installed the bathroom fitments, but after that Grandpop turned to Meriel. 'How about you help me tile the walls and paint the woodwork?'

He had to coax Denise to allow her daughter to participate in such mucky activities, and buy his granddaughter some special overalls to protect her clothes, but Grandpop was one of the few people who could make her mother change her mind.

By the time the work was finished, Meriel could use all the tools that had been too big for her before. Afterwards, she made her first solo piece, a bookshelf to stand on the chest of drawers in her bedroom.

Her mother pulled a face. 'It's crooked and I don't know why you didn't paint it white instead of polishing up the bare wood like that.'

'It's not crooked. The grain tricks your eye. See how the lines flow and curl.' She traced them with a fingertip.

'It's old-fashioned, plain wood is, but it's too late to change it now you've put the varnish on. Still, it'll keep your books tidy, at least.'

Her Dad said, 'It's lovely. You're a clever lass. I like the wood better, too.'

But he said that quietly, after a glance over his shoulder. Her Dad spent a lot of time avoiding his wife these days, which was beginning to worry Meriel. A classmate's parents had just split up and were getting a divorce. He had to spend alternate weeks with each of them, which he hated.

Surely her parents wouldn't divorce? She lay awake worrying about that sometimes, wishing her mother would be kinder to her father, and go out and have fun like other mothers did, instead of fussing about the house all the time. Her mother was stuck in an old-fashioned rut. Even Grandpop was more with it than his daughter.

Meriel wasn't going to be like her when she grew up.

'It's unnatural for a teenage girl to hang around with an old man like that,' her mother grumbled as she grew older. 'Why don't you go out to the cinema with your friends, our Meriel?'

'I don't want to.' She didn't want to spend the money, either, because she needed all her spending money for extra art materials.

'Well, what about joining a youth club, then?'

'Youth clubs are for people who have nothing better to do,' Meriel explained – reasonably, she thought. 'I've got plenty to do.'

'You should have grown out of all that painting and drawing rubbish by now. It's for little children not teenagers. A girl as pretty as you should have a boyfriend, but you don't make the most of yourself. Lovely blond hair like that and you scrag it back with a rubber band.'

But Meriel paid less and less attention to her mother because the art teacher was giving her extra lessons after school and talking about the possibility of her studying art at college.

She hadn't told her mother about that yet, though. Her mother had a way of destroying dreams, smashing the glowing rainbow hopes into dull shards of disappointment.

When Ben Elless was seven, his father died suddenly of a heart attack and his mother moved from Perth to the country. York was very small, like most country towns in Western Australia, dusty in summer, greener in winter, surrounded by low hills. His uncle Johnny lived there and had invited them to go and live with him, which his mother said would be cheaper till they'd sorted themselves out. Johnny said he could get her a job because he knew everyone in town.

'I miss my father,' Ben confided in his uncle one day.

'We all do, lad. But there's no way of bringing him back so we have to carry on without him.'

'Mum cries at night when she thinks I can't hear. I don't like her crying.'

'She'll get over that gradually. She's a strong woman. Now, no use moping. How about I take you out walking on my block and show you the little flowers that hide away, and the little animals too? There's a lot more than kangaroos to see. I've left the bush untouched so that as many animals as possible can still have a home.'

'I'd like that.'

'You need to wear shoes, not sandals, and sturdy jeans. I don't want you getting bitten by a snake, or spider, or picking up a tick.'

Once he'd got to know the block of land, Ben was allowed to roam through the bush on his own. He was so interested in the plants, he got books out of the library, thick ones which listed every single plant, with photos or drawings of each stage of their development.

His uncle bought him a big botany book for Christmas and his other presents lay ignored as he sat on the veranda studying the pictures.

After the meal was over, his mother came and sat with him. 'You seem to love plants, Ben.'

'Yes, I do. Look how beautiful that flower is.'

'Perhaps you'd like to help me start a garden here, once the hot weather is over? We could grow vegetables and herbs. I'm missing my garden.'

They worked together on that and he learned more about the tamer plants, proving that he'd inherited his mother's green fingers.

But it was the wild plants he loved most, especially the tiny orchids, so many types that he lost count. The bright yellow Hibbertia was so cheerful he always lingered to smile at it, and there was something about the intense blue of the leschenaultia that made his breath catch in his throat.

★ ★ ★

When he was eleven, his mother met a new guy. Ben was cool with that because Tom was fun to be with and made his mother happy. His uncle had explained this was likely to happen when a woman was as pretty as Louise. It didn't mean she'd forgotten his father, only that she enjoyed being married.

One day his mother came out to join him in the garden. 'Tom's asked me to marry him.'

'Me and Uncle Johnny thought he would.'

'The trouble is, Tom's been transferred to Queensland so we'll all have to move over to the other side of Australia.

'Uncle Johnny too?'

'No. Your uncle likes it here. He'll never leave York. But we can come back and visit him.'

'But Uncle Johnny will be on his own.'

'You can visit him in the summer holidays.'

'I suppose.'

'And you'll be able to learn about a whole new set of plants and animals.'

It was no consolation as Ben had begun to share his uncle's love of the area round York. It took him a while to settle down again because they lived in the suburbs of Brisbane and he missed the country. He spent a lot of time outside in the garden and in the end he took over because Tom wasn't interested in gardening, even if he'd had time for it. His Mum said Tom was a workaholic and sighed.

With her encouragement, Ben remodelled the garden completely, making some quite big changes to the layout. It looked far better when he'd finished.

As he said to his uncle on one of his visits to York, there was usually something interesting to do in a garden.

Johnny grinned at him. 'I think you were born with a happy soul, Ben Elless.'

'What does that mean?'

'You're always cheerful. That's good. I'm a bit that way myself. I think you take after the Elless side of the family physically too. You're going to be tall like me and your father.'

Ben grimaced and looked down. 'With big feet.'

'All the better to stand on.'

Two

Just after Meriel's fifteenth birthday her life changed overnight. She went home from school as usual and was sitting eating a biscuit before doing her homework when there was a knock on the door.

Her mother got up. 'I'll go.'

When Denise returned she looked puzzled. 'It was a courier. He brought this.' She held out a bright yellow envelope. 'It's addressed to me.'

Helen looked up. 'Well, why don't you open it?'

'I suppose I'd better. I'm sure it's a mistake.'

Two minutes later she screamed and began to sob, the letter clutched tightly to her ample bosom. 'He can't! I won't let him! He can't *do* this to me.'

It took a few minutes before Denise could be persuaded to stop sobbing. When she did, she thrust the letter into Helen's hands.

'Read that! See what your father's done to me.'

The two girls read it together.

Dear Denise

I'm sorry but I can't live with you any longer. We're nearly in the twenty-first century now and yet you live like someone from the 1940s. You even refuse to get a job so that we can buy our own house. I've always wanted that, as you well know.

Most important of all, I'm a man, with all a man's normal needs, which you deny. So I'm leaving you and I want a divorce.

You won't change my mind about this because I've met someone else, someone kind and loving. She's come into an inheritance so we'll have a house and garden of our own.

I'll still provide you with money, of course, but it won't be as much as before.

By the time you read this I'll have moved to another

*town. You can communicate with me via my lawyer, James
Benton of Benton and Bowles in the High Street.*
I wish you well, Denise, and the girls too.
Frank Ingram

Meriel gasped and stole a quick glance at their mother,
who was still sobbing.

'Fetch Grandpop and Grandma,' whispered Helen. 'They'll
know what to do.'

With great relief Meriel hared off down the street and
gasped out her story.

To her surprise it was her grandma who spoke first.

'I told her she was a fool to deny him her bed,' she said.
'She's never been easy to live with but that must have been
the final straw.'

'We'll come round straight away,' Grandpop said.

'Better if I go,' Grandma said. 'She won't want to see a
man at a time like this. She'll talk more easily to me, Arthur.
You stay here, Meriel love.'

'Did you have any idea your father was seeing someone
else?' Grandpop asked when they were alone.

'No. He used to go for lots of walks, so I suppose he saw
her then.'

'It's not often someone pulls the wool over our Denise's eyes.'

Meriel hesitated, then said what she'd been thinking. 'I
don't blame Dad for leaving, not really. She'd never let him
do anything he wanted.'

'He should have stood up to her, not run away. Frank
made his promise in church. I don't hold with breaking
promises.'

'She made promises too. *Love, honour and obey.*' Meriel didn't
agree with the 'obey' bit but the loving was important and
she'd seen no signs of love between her parents, not even
mild affection. They'd simply tolerated one another, living side
by side. She'd often felt sad about that, because some of her
friends' parents were happy together and it showed.

Marriage seemed to be a very chancy thing. She didn't
think she'd ever risk it.

What upset her most was that her father was moving
away, discarding his daughters as well as his wife.

But when she went to bed that night, she found a letter from him under her pillow, apologizing and promising to do all he could to help her in the coming years. He'd have her and her sister to stay with him and Linda, once they'd settled in together.

That made Meriel feel a bit better but she didn't really miss her father because he'd never played with them or taken them out, like her friends' fathers did. It was Grandpop she'd always turned to, still did.

Over the next few months Meriel learned to bite her tongue at the things her mother said about their father – and about men in general. She tried to discuss it with her sister.

Helen just shrugged. 'It's better for her to let off steam. Ignore it.'

'How can I? You're always out with Peter. You don't get half as much haranguing from her as I do.'

Helen smiled. 'Get yourself a boyfriend, then. It's about time.'

'I would if I fancied anyone, but I don't.'

'Has anyone asked you out?'

She shrugged. 'One or two.'

'And?'

'I didn't like them kissing me. All sloppy. Ugh.'

'You're too busy with your drawing. How do you expect to find a husband if you never go out and meet guys?'

'Maybe I don't want a husband.'

Helen gave her another knowing smile. 'You will one day. You're just a late starter.'

Meriel wasn't sure she even wanted to start if it made you smile as dopily as Helen did sometimes.

'I've got myself a job,' Denise announced two months later. 'The money your father's paying me isn't nearly enough to manage on, not if you've got standards.'

'Good for you, Mum!' Helen said. 'What as?'

'A receptionist.'

'You'll be good at that.'

'It's all I'm fit for without qualifications. You devote your life to a man, running his house *perfectly* and how does he repay you? He runs off with a floozy, that's what he does.'

It soon became obvious that Denise enjoyed going out to

work, though she wasn't admitting it. She grumbled for days about having to learn to use a computer but for all her protestations, she coped and was soon made permanent at her job.

Their father made one or two phone calls, but didn't come to visit and didn't invite his daughters to visit him. It turned out that his new wife was expecting a baby. He sounded excited about that.

Her mother grew rather tight-lipped for a while and Meriel had to tread carefully.

When Ben was seventeen, his stepfather was diagnosed with pancreatic cancer. He watched his mother care for Tom, staying cheerful and supportive through the operations and the chemotherapy.

Nothing worked and Tom died nine months later.

They came home from the hospital together and she went to make a cup of tea.

'I'll do it.'

She nodded, her eyes brimming with tears, and then suddenly she was crying against him. He was much taller than her now, so he held her close and patted her back, not knowing how to comfort her.

After a while she pulled away. 'Sorry.'

'It's all right. I'm going to miss Tom, but not as much as you will.'

'You're a bit young to be facing all this.'

'You shouldn't have to lose two husbands.'

'No, it doesn't seem fair.' She swiped away a stray tear. 'I'll get through it. Those who're left behind don't have much choice, do they?'

He didn't go to visit Uncle Johnny in Western Australia that summer, he stayed in Queensland. It was the first time he hadn't spent the summer in York since his father died. He missed it, missed being alone in the bush. But his mother needed him. He couldn't have left her alone so soon after losing Tom. Uncle Johnny understood.

Denise looked at her younger daughter one evening. 'I see it's the careers night at your school next week. You are still intending to go on to A Level, aren't you?'

'Yes, of course.'

'Good. You need to choose your subjects for the sixth form, it seems.'

'I've already chosen them.'

'Oh? You didn't ask me.'

'You were busy.'

'I'm not too busy to make sure you start on the right track. It's too late for your sister to have a decent career. She's as trusting as I was, thinks the sun shines out of her Peter's backside. It's not too late for you, my girl.'

'But—'

'I'm going to make sure you have a good profession behind you, so that you never have to be dependent upon a man. And if I have to take your father to court to get the money for your training, I will. What subjects are you doing?'

'Whatever I need to get into art college.'

Denise made a scornful noise in her throat. 'When are you going to grow up? You can get the idea of studying art right out of your head. You're going into something with security.'

'You know I've always wanted to study art.'

Denise gave her daughter the same sort of look she'd given her husband when he tried to go against her. 'I'll not support you if you study art, so how will you manage it?' She began to tick her points off on her fingers. 'You'll need somewhere to live, money to pay the tuition fees, money to live on. You don't think your father will provide all those, do you?'

The quarrels raged for days, but in the end, thanks to Grandpop's intervention, they compromised. Meriel agreed to keep up maths and computing for her two final years, in exchange for being allowed to continue studying art.

'But you're not studying art at university,' Denise said flatly. 'I shan't change my mind about that.'

Like her mother, Helen Ingram married young, with seventeen-year-old Meriel sulking along the aisle behind her as chief bridesmaid in a long pink dress – absolutely the wrong shade for someone with silver-blond hair and green eyes! It had been touch and go whether her father would be allowed to give Helen away, but face-saving prevailed, as it always did with

Denise – and besides, he'd offered to help pay for the wedding, so you could hardly tell him to stay away from it. But he didn't bring his wife.

After Helen left home, Meriel found it even more difficult to bear her mother's moods alone. Since she was to continue at school until she was eighteen, she was allowed to use the spare bedroom as a study and even to have a computer there, bought by her father. She got a weekend job in a café so that she could buy extra art materials, because her mother refused point-blank to pay out good money for that sort of thing.

Less than a couple of years, Meriel told herself, and I'll be away at art college. I can put up with it until then, and afterwards, once I've got a job, I'll find a place of my own to live, even if it's only one room.

When it came time to think about a career her teachers encouraged her to study art, making comments like 'promising' and 'raw talent'.

The battles were fought all over again during her final year at school.

'I've told you before, you're not studying art,' Denise said. 'There's no security in art.'

'But Mum, I'm *good* at it. Really good. Just ask my art teacher.'

'I'm good at home-making, too, and a fat lot of help that was to me.'

'But it's all I've ever wanted to do!'

'Did you hear me? You're *not* studying art.'

The row lasted only a few minutes, but bitter things were said on both sides.

For the next couple of weeks Meriel wept and pleaded, argued and threatened, shouted and sulked, but all in vain. Denise remained adamant.

'You're good at maths. All your teachers say so. The obvious thing for you to do is become an accountant.'

'An *accountant!* I'd rather *die!*'

Her mother ignored that remark. 'It's a nice safe job, respectable and clean. That matters. No one respects those who work with their hands.'

'Well, I like getting my hands dirty and making things.'

'I blame my father for that. I should have realized where all that do-it-yourself stuff was leading and put a stop to it years ago.'

In the end, after the arguments had raged for weeks and Meriel had become thin and drawn, her blond hair as brittle as dried straw and her eyes cloudy green pools of unhappiness, Grandpop took the girl aside. 'You'll never win, lass.'

'But I'd go mad stuck in an office all day.'

'There are times in life when you have to recognize you're beaten, love. If you don't train as an accountant, your mother won't support you in anything else, so you won't get your art diploma, either way. You'll have to leave school and work in a shop or a factory. That'd be even worse for someone with a good brain like yours. And don't think your dad will stand up to her.' He patted Meriel's back and stared out of the window, allowing time for his words to sink in.

After a few minutes she sniffed back an angry tear and slipped her arm through his. 'But I love art so *much,* Grandpop. You don't know how much.'

He put his arm round her. 'I can guess. But you sometimes have to go the long way round to get what you want. And even then, some of us never get it.'

She stood mouse still. She knew from chance remarks how much he had hated his job as an insurance salesman, and could only guess how he chafed now at the restrictions which age and living on the pension had set upon him, though he never complained.

'Things are better nowadays than when I was a young fellow,' the gentle, loving voice went on. 'You can get a second chance at life nowadays, what with the Open University and all. So you just go to university, love, and do what your mother says. Become an accountant. *But only for the time being.* Once you've got your independence, you can study art at night school.'

'I shall hate doing accountancy.'

'You'll enjoy it if you set your mind to it. Bear in mind that it's only for a few years. And in the meantime, no one can stop you from having a hobby, can they? In fact, you should tell your mum that you'll only agree to study accounting if you can still enjoy painting and such in your spare time. Once you agree, she'll give you back your art things.'

Her mother had confiscated all her art materials and locked them up in the big cedarwood chest at the foot of her bed when the dispute first erupted. Meriel sighed and brushed away a tear. She looked at him in a final mute appeal but he shook his head.

'I can't work miracles, lass. No one can. She's got the money, however much she pleads poverty, and your father needs all his brass for his new family now. Two young sons, at his age!'

Meriel's shoulders sagged and tears trickled down her cheeks. 'Well, I'm going to get away from home as soon as I graduate, as far away as I possibly can so she can't interfere in the rest of my life. And one day I *will* make my living from art.'

'I'm sure you will. I'll come to your first exhibition and boast to everyone that you're my granddaughter.' He stood up, easing his stiff joints into movement. 'I'll go and have a word with our Denise now, tell her I've persuaded you to study accounting on condition you can keep on with your art as a hobby. I'll make her see that she has to give way on that, at least.'

'It's not fair, though,' Meriel swiped away another tear.

'No, lass. It's not. But give her a year or two and she'll be so wrapped up in being a grandmother and telling your Helen what to do with her children and husband that she'll stop trying to live your life for you.' He hesitated, then added, 'She was upset when your father left her, more upset than you'll ever realize. In her own way, she loved him.'

'She had a funny way of showing it, then.'

'Aye, well, that's our Denise for you. She's not one to flaunt her emotions. But she loves you, too. Never doubt that.'

'Hah!'

Three

Meriel went to study accounting in Newcastle, because it was further away from home than Manchester. Once she had started the course, she followed her Grandpop's advice and focused on gaining good grades. She took a variety of part-time jobs during the holidays so that she could continue to buy the necessary art materials.

The situation suddenly became more relaxed during Meriel's second year, because Denise found herself a man friend. She was oddly coy when she told Meriel about Ralph. 'You don't mind, do you?'

'Of course not. I'm glad for you. Especially about the dancing. You always used to love dancing.'

'Yes, I did. But your father – well, he was born with two left feet. Ralph and I are going to classes. We're learning Latin American.' Denise twirled round then blushed and laughed self-consciously.

After that, she didn't nag quite as much about anything.

Most of Meriel's spare time at college, what little she had left after studying and her part-time job, was spent drawing and painting. She managed to fit in one or two evening courses and read a lot of self-study books about various techniques, trying them out as best she could in the privacy of her bed sitter.

She emailed Grandpop several times a week and he emailed back – warm, loving messages, with occasional pieces of sensible advice proffered tactfully.

There were guys at college, and dates – but not as many as there could have been.

'What's wrong with Jim?' a girlfriend asked one day.

'He's a faker, always trying to sound better than he is.'

'And Luke. Surely you can't have anything against him? He's very good-looking.'

'Yes, but he just doesn't—' Meriel shrugged. 'There's no spark between us.'

'Oh, you're hopeless.'

'Yes, I am.' She laughed, but she was beginning to worry about that. Was she hopeless? Why wasn't she attracted to the guys who fancied her? She pulled a face. Because she wasn't into quick gropes, because she wanted someone who would talk to her, really talk to her.

Only once did she progress to intimacy and that turned out to be rather a disappointment. She'd expected . . . more.

She wasn't going down that path again.

Just before she graduated, Meriel received a letter from her mother.

I thought I'd better warn you that my father isn't well. It's cancer, I'm afraid. He's bearing up bravely, as you'd expect. He's only got a few months, the doctors say . . .

All Meriel's escape plans evaporated overnight. When she graduated, she found a job with an accounting firm in her home town and went back to live with her mother.

Grandpop was much thinner, his colour poor. She tried to swallow her anguish at the sight of him but knew she hadn't hidden her feelings well.

'Come down to my workshop and let me show you a new piece I'm working on,' he said quietly.

Her grandma nodded and turned to her knitting again, but Meriel saw her blinking rapidly.

In the cellar, Grandpop looked at her with a wry smile. 'I see your mother's told you.'

Meriel tried to speak and burst into tears.

He gave her a hug then put his hands on her shoulders and held her at arm's length. Looking her in the eyes, he said quietly, 'We all move on, lass. It's only natural. Save your worritting for something you can change. I've had a good, long life – and I've had you. You've brought me such joy. A man couldn't have asked for a better grand-daughter.'

And of course, that made her weep even more.

But after that, she didn't weep in front of him again.

A subsidiary benefit to living at home was that Meriel was able to start saving money, money she intended to use one day to achieve her heart's desire, but of course she didn't tell her mother that.

'Why don't you buy some new clothes?' Denise would grumble, 'Something more colourful.'

Or, 'I can't think why you still mess about with paints. Honestly, at your age, you should be focusing your efforts on attracting young men.' She smiled at herself in the mirror, smoothing out her skirt. 'Ralph always says how smart I look.'

'Mum, for the millionth time, I don't care about keeping a man interested. And anyway, I've been out with Grant a few times, haven't I?'

Denise pulled a face. 'That one's no use to you. He's been on the dole for months.'

'He's an artist.'

'Exactly. It's not possible to make a living as an artist. I told you that years ago and I was right. I don't like to think of my taxes going to pay for lazy so-and-sos like him.'

'He's a brilliant artist and one day he'll be famous. I envy him the freedom to pursue his dream. One day I'll do the same.'

Denise let out an exaggerated sigh. 'I thought you'd grow out of that art stuff, but you haven't, have you?'

'No. And I never will.' Meriel stared steadily at her mother. 'You should have let me study commercial art, at least.'

'I did what I thought right at the time and I still think it was the best choice. You have a really good job and the wages you're earning are far more than I get.'

'And look how bored I am by that sort of work. I'd better warn you that I'm going to art classes at the local college next semester.'

'You can have any hobby you want, especially now you've got your degree.'

Meriel sighed and gave up trying to discuss things. Her mother would never change. But Meriel hadn't changed, either. She was still determined to make a future for herself in art. She didn't know how she'd do it, but she would.

She'd stay at home, though, as long as Grandpop needed her.

No one was surprised when Ben opted to study plant science and landscape design. In the first year at university in Sydney he met Sandy and that was it. The two of them were instantly inseparable, living together in the final year and getting married soon after they graduated, laughing at how poor they were.

They moved back to Queensland to live, because Sandy's family came from there, too. He'd enjoyed Sydney, but it just wasn't home. If there had been any way of making a living, he'd have gone back to York, in Western Australia, which still felt like home to him. But it was too small a place for what he and Sandy wanted to do.

A year later they set up a small landscaping business together in Brisbane. Ben did the design and the grunt work while Sandy did the paperwork and helped out with the lighter jobs.

'We were going to have babies,' he said ruefully as they worked through the accounts one evening – or rather Sandy worked through them and he explained what his scrawls meant and hunted for receipts.

'We can have babies later, once the business is on its feet. How's the new design going?'

He beamed at her. 'I had a brilliant idea.' By the time he'd finished explaining his design it was time for bed.

'You should go away for a holiday, love,' Grandpop said suddenly.

Meriel pulled a face. 'I'd rather stay here and take you out for day trips.'

'A week or two won't hurt. You know I'm in remission after the latest course of treatment. Look, I saw this online.'

He'd found a special offer on a package tour to Spain. It'd been raining so much lately she succumbed to the temptation.

She thoroughly enjoyed the warm climate and relaxed

lifestyle, but wasn't tempted into a holiday affair, even though there were two single guys on the trip who kept trying to chat her up. Her sketch book went with her everywhere and she enjoyed herself for months afterwards trying to re-capture the play of bright sunlight on water and frolicking bodies, in a series of paintings.

The experience gave her something else, a longing to live in a warmer climate. The sun was never that bright in England and the heat in Spain hadn't bothered her as it had some people on the tour. For all her skin was fair she hadn't even got sunburned, just developed a light golden tan that looked great with her blond hair.

She came back with the knowledge that there was a whole world out there just waiting to be explored. But she couldn't do it yet, not while Grandpop needed her.

Two years later Ben and Sandy again postponed starting a family because they'd bought a run-down old house and were renovating it, splitting it into two halves for rental purposes.

'I feel guilty making you work so hard,' he said.

'You don't make me do anything. It's my choice. I was the one who found the house and I want to have the security of rental properties behind us before I start having children. These houses will pay for themselves, you'll see. Two more years and we'll have our twins.'

A few months later they went to a fancy dinner at her uncle Rod's invitation. He said they'd meet some useful people there who might like to use their landscaping services.

Ben was running late, so Sandy drove to the hotel on her own and he caught up with her there.

'You look gorgeous tonight. I can't wait to get you home,' he whispered as they made their way out to their cars.

She smiled a promise as only Sandy could.

On the way home a four-wheel drive ran a set of red lights and smashed into Sandy's car. Ben braked violently, flung the door open and ran towards the wreck, but she was unconscious and trapped.

'I've already phoned for an ambulance,' a stranger said.

'Thanks. This is my wife.'

'Tough.'

There was little Ben could do to help her and he stood in helpless agony, holding her hand through the broken window as he listened to a man groaning and cursing in the other vehicle.

It seemed a long time till the ambulance and police arrived, even longer before they managed to free Sandy from the wreckage.

Ben followed the ambulance to hospital, leaving his car in the first vacant parking bay and running headlong across to the casualty department. 'My wife? She was just brought in after an accident.'

'The doctors are examining her now. If I could just take some particulars?'

Impatiently he gave her the information, keeping an eye on the area behind big semi-transparent doors. 'Can I go in to see her now?'

'Better to wait till the doctor comes out.'

It seemed a long time until a man in a white coat came out of the rear area. The receptionist pointed Ben out to the doctor who beckoned him forward and led the way into a side room.

'How is she?' Ben asked.

There was silence then the doctor sighed and shook his head. 'I'm afraid she didn't make it, Mr Elless. She had massive chest injuries from the impact.'

His words didn't make sense for a few moments and Ben frowned as he tried to sort through the information. Then it suddenly clicked and he felt anguish welling up in his chest. *Sandy was dead!* He'd lost her.

How could that be possible? It hurt so much he could only wrap his arms round himself and rock.

'Is there someone we can call?'

The doctor had to ask him twice before he remembered his mother's phone number.

'Can I see my wife?'

'In a little while. We're just tidying things up.'

'Did the man who crashed into her survive?'

'Yes.'

'Was he drunk?'

'The police are dealing with that.'

'He was drunk, wasn't he?'

'I can't tell you that, Mr Elless.'

When his mother came into the room, she held out her arms and Ben let himself sob. She understood how he was feeling as no one else ever would.

It was only her strength that got him through the next few days, and the funeral passed in a distant blur.

'It will get better, Ben darling,' she said to him several times. 'I promise you it will.'

'Not for Sandy, it won't.'

Grandpop had a two-year remission. He and Meriel had some wonderful outings together now she had a car. Then the cancer came back and he started to go rapidly downhill.

When he eventually died, her biggest comfort was that he had been more than ready to go.

He'd whispered to her from the hospital bed, 'Don't you grieve for me, lass. I've been selfish, I know, but I'm glad you stayed nearby till now. Afterwards, though, you go out and make something of your life. Get right away from here and follow that dream of yours. Keep it in focus and you'll get there one day, I know you will.'

He didn't say get away from your mother, but they both knew what he meant.

Meriel's grief wasn't as loud as her mother's, but it was a loss so agonizing she couldn't see her way past it for a while.

She applied to emigrate to Australia a few days after the funeral and was one of the lucky ones to be selected. It helped that she'd found herself a job in advance, because the senior partner of her firm knew someone in Western Australia and was prepared to give her a very warm recommendation.

'You've an eye for anomalies in business accounts,' he said. 'That's why I spoke up for you, though really you should do more studying and qualify as a forensic accountant.'

'I don't want to go down that path.'

He cocked his head on one side. 'Still doing your painting?'

'Yes, I am.'

'Well, don't let me down in Australia, now.'

'I won't, Mr Grimes.'

She waited until everything was arranged before announcing her plans to her mother. 'I'm going to live in Australia, Mum. I've got a job there.'

'I don't think much of that for a joke.'

'It isn't a joke.'

'Mmm?'

'Mum, listen to me, will you! I'm going to work in Australia.'

Denise stared at her open-mouthed. 'You can't mean it!'

'I do. I've always wanted to travel. You know that.'

'But that's not travelling; that's emigrating!'

'Yes. I like a sunny climate. You know how much I enjoyed Spain last year. I applied to emigrate after Grandpop died.'

Denise burst into loud, noisy tears. 'You can't do it! I won't let you! I'll never see you again.'

Meriel sighed and tried not to get angry at the accusations that were soon flying across the table about ingratitude and selfishness.

Not long, she told herself. Just a couple more weeks.

The plane landed in Western Australia on a hot day in November after a twenty-hour flight, by which time Meriel was heartily sick of being shut up in a big tin box.

She queued her way through Customs, smiling at the sniffer dog which checked everyone's hand luggage. One woman was pulled out of the line and scolded for having an apple in her bag.

At the airport entrance there was a queue for taxis. As Meriel waited in the line of tired people, she lifted her face to the warmth, entranced by the clear blue sky and the brilliance of the light.

She was just as thrilled by the ride into the centre of Perth. For the last part of the journey they travelled along by the river and although she'd looked up the city online when she applied to migrate and studied photos of it, the reality was far more impressive. A typical city cluster of multi-storey buildings was set back from the river behind a wide strip of grass which softened the whole scene. The river widened at this point and the water sparkled in the sunlight as a ferry chugged across and yachts tacked to and fro. To one side of the city was a small hill which she knew from her research to be King's Park. Buildings clung precariously to one side of the hill and a motorway – no, people called them freeways here – hummed with traffic below it.

The company which had offered her a job had booked her into a hotel, a modestly adequate place. Since she'd slept quite well on the journey, she only stayed there long enough to have a quick shower and put on a summer skirt and short-sleeved top. Then she spent two hours wandering round the city centre, feeling like a tourist, following the street map she'd picked up from reception.

At one stage she found herself in the street where she'd be working, so went to stare up at the tall building where Lee-Line International was situated. She disliked multi-storey office towers with their stale, canned air, but you couldn't have everything. At least accepting this job had allowed her to move to a warmer country.

Now she was going to focus on her most important ambition of all, becoming an artist. Whatever it took, she'd do it.

Four

Ben Elless went to work in Brisbane reluctantly. He preferred the days when he had to go out of the city to visit suppliers or to inspect gardens or developments for new clients.

It was two years today since he'd buried his wife and he still found it hard to settle back into business mode. Sometimes he fantasized about buying a piece of land and becoming a recluse – he'd been very tempted to do that after Sandy died – but the sheer satisfaction of creating beautiful gardens helped him cope.

He'd almost lost his small company after losing Sandy. Only the intervention of his wife's uncle Rod had saved him from bankruptcy, but he still wasn't sure he'd done the right thing in accepting that help, because one condition of the loan had been to find a job for Rod's son Phil. Ben had never liked Sandy's cousin – but he hated the idea of losing his business because it was one of the main things he had left of his wife.

Phil proved to be a good salesman, but he had no feel for landscaping or plants. He made Ben wince when he talked about 'product'.

The business was going really well now, because Ben's designs were proving popular. Well, he had long, quiet evenings to work on them and perfect them. But Phil said they could be making more money and that had led to several arguments. He wasn't going to let Phil persuade him to cut corners, whatever difference that might make to the bottom line. There was no way Ben would short-change the clients by putting in inferior plants and materials. He and Phil had argued about that only yesterday.

He switched on the computer and began to work on a new garden design, soon losing himself in it, so that his secretary had to shake him to make him realize someone wanted him on the phone.

Linda gave him one of those motherly smiles that reminded him of his real mother and patted his shoulder.

When he'd finished the call, she came back into his office. 'I need to know what you agreed with this new client. Just concentrate for a few minutes then I'll let you play again.'

'Yes, Mama!'

She pretended to slap his arm and left him to it. Thank goodness for her accounting skills, he thought. He wasn't the world's best with figures. Unfortunately she was retiring soon and he was wondering how he'd manage without her to keep him on track about the business side of affairs.

Garden design he could talk about; keeping accounts in order was definitely not his best skill. Sandy had done all that.

Phil gradually took over from Linda, promising to show her replacement what to do and keep an eye on that side of things.

That was such a relief. Ben loved the design and gardening side of things and knew he did them well. You couldn't be good at everything.

On the Monday following her arrival, Meriel started work. Her boss, John Repping, welcomed her formally into the West Australian branch of Lee-Line International, then handed her over to a young woman of her own age. 'Rosanna will show you round the office and she'll be able to tell you about − er − shopping and such.'

As soon as they were away from his office, Rosanna grinned. 'John's so stiff sometimes you wonder if he's going to crack down the middle next time he tries to smile! He's all right, though. Looks after his staff. How was the flight?'

'I slept most of the time. There wasn't much else to do. It's a long time to sit still in a small seat.'

'I've never been to Europe, but I'm going there on my honeymoon.'

'Oh? Are you getting married soon?'

Rosanna grinned. 'Not for a while. I haven't met the lucky fellow yet. But a girl has to plan. Are you single − or did you come out here with a guy?'

'I came here on my own.'

'Don't you like guys?'

'In moderation.'

Rosanna rolled her eyes. 'Moderation is for after you're married, not before.'

It was Rosanna who helped Meriel to find a small villa to rent. She also went shopping with her after work to assemble the essentials for survival. To her, this meant cooking utensils, sheets and towels, while Meriel's thoughts ran more in the direction of art supplies and a good easel.

On the Saturday, Rosanna turned up at the hotel with one of her many relatives and an open-backed van called a Ute, to help Meriel move her suitcases and parcels into the new flat. The relative also produced a bottle of champagne and the three of them solemnly christened the flat, drinking it out of three coffee mugs, because Meriel hadn't got round to buying wine glasses yet.

Gino would have stayed longer if Meriel had given him any encouragement. He kept giving her admiring glances. But she wanted to be alone to settle in, so Rosanna winked and took her cousin away with a cheery, 'See you on Monday!'

Meriel took a chair out into the tiny shaded courtyard at the rear and sipped the last of her champagne. A parrot flew on to a branch of the one tree and stared down at her solemnly. There wasn't a single cloud in the blue sky. Then another parrot landed with a shriek and shortly afterwards the two of them flew off together.

'I made it!' She raised her glass in a toast to her new country.

'Do you fancy going out for lunch today, for a change?' Rosanna asked two weeks later.

'Sorry. I have to register and buy some stuff.'

'For what?'

'For my art classes. I've enrolled at the Technical and Further Education College for a certificate course.' She explained about her obsession.

Rosanna shrugged. 'I hope being artistic won't stop you coming out for a drink sometimes.'

'Of course not.'

'And who knows, you may meet a guy at the classes.'

'I keep telling you, I don't want to meet anyone. I want to become an artist.'

'You've sure chosen a roundabout path. Me, I did enough studying when I was training to become an accountant. That's it, now. No more courses, unless they're short and sweet. But I'm not letting you turn into a nun.'

Meriel chuckled and gave her a hug, already feeling she'd made a good friend in Rosanna. 'OK. I promise not to turn into a nun. I'm so glad I met you.'

'Me too. They're a stuffy bunch here, aren't they? I was glad when you joined us.'

'Shh! Someone might hear you.'

Rosanna shrugged.

Within the month, Meriel was absorbed in her studies and was happier than she'd been for years.

She was even finding her new job more interesting than her old one. It still amazed her sometimes what a flair she had for analysing figures. But they were only a means to an end. They were not, definitely not, her whole life. And even less were they her future.

Mr Repping took her into his office after she'd been there a couple of months, and after much clearing of the throat, managed to say that he was pleased with her work.

That felt good, too. If she did something, she wanted to do it well, whatever it was. She was like Grandpop in that.

Ben smiled at the owner of the block of flats, who had just approved his design. 'I'm going to enjoy this job. And I think you're going to find it lifts the tone of the whole place.'

The man nodded, not nearly as enthusiastic as Ben. 'As long as you deliver the goods, that's all I care about. The rental industry is very competitive and your cousin has persuaded us that we'll get a better occupancy percentage if we can offer what other blocks of flats don't. Just keep that area easy-care and don't go over budget.'

'Can do.'

When the customer had left, Ben wandered across to Phil's office. 'What did he mean, you *persuaded* him?'

Phil rolled his eyes. 'Just what he said. I went out and looked for a target property and when I found it, I homed in on the owners.'

'I thought they approached us, because of those adverts.'

'Look, what's this all leading to? Was I wrong to get us that contract? No? Right then, I have an appointment at five, another useful lead, so I have to go.'

'It's just – I don't like the thought of over-persuading someone to use our services. And how do you know making a garden will raise the letting percentage?'

'I don't, but it's quite likely if it makes the place more attractive, surely?'

'Phil, I thought we'd agreed to—'

'Don't start on that again. I'm here to sell our services and manage the staff and finances. You're here to design gardens and install them. Each to his own.'

Five

At the end of Meriel's second year in Perth, Gary Stuart came as a client, lingered to chat and asked Meriel to go out for a drink after work.

She'd just finished her studies for the year and was feeling very relaxed, besides which he was an attractive guy. For once she accepted.

'You cannot possibly be an accountant,' he said as they strolled by the river that evening after a casual meal in a café.

'Why can't I?'

'Because you're far too pretty.'

'That's sexist.'

'So sue me.'

'I'll sue you tomorrow. I'm too tired today. I have to go home and get some sleep.'

'Tomorrow we're going for a picnic, Ms Ingram.'

'It's usual to ask first.'

He shook his head. 'No way. I'm not risking a refusal. My spies tell me you're a workaholic, so I'm doing you a service here, helping you relax. Give me your address and I'll pick you up at ten. Come prepared to walk through the bush. Trousers and stout shoes.'

Rosanna, who'd been telling her all year to go out more, didn't seem very enthusiastic about Gary.

'Don't you like him?' Meriel demanded, puzzled. 'You're the one who keeps telling me to find a date.'

'He's just too . . .' Rosanna sought for a word and managed only 'charming. You be careful. He's probably after one thing.'

Meriel laughed. 'I can't win. You've been nagging me to find a guy and when I do, you pull faces at him. Besides, I think I'm old enough to know when a man's sincere or not.'

A month later she was beginning to wonder whether she was in love at last. Gary had said he loved her. In fact, he joked that he'd fallen head over heels in love with his new accountant at first sight.

'Don't you feel anything for me?' he asked one evening in that warm sexy voice.

She stared up into the handsome face, with its deep, permanent tan and something turned over inside her. 'I – suppose I do.'

'Then show it, woman. You've been acting like my maiden aunt for long enough.' He gave her a slow smile and ran one fingertip down her cheek. 'You know very well that one day you're going to wind up in bed with me.' He held up one hand to stop her speaking. 'I'm not pushing it. In your own time. But it's as inevitable as the sun rising tomorrow, given the way we react to one another.'

He was right. A week later they made love, and although it was pleasant, she was disappointed for a second time in her life. Shouldn't she feel – well – closer to him now? What was wrong with her? She hid her disappointment. It was probably her fault. After all, she wasn't all that experienced.

'It'll be better for you next time, darling. You're out of practice.'

'Mmm.' She was relieved when he left.

She didn't see him for a couple of days, because her classes were starting again soon and she wanted to think about her options for the coming year. He protested but she was firm.

'Very well.' He kissed her and held her at arm's length. 'But only for a few days. See you at the weekend?'

She nodded and stood waving him goodbye.

Two days later Rosanna came into her office. 'We're going out for lunch today, remember?'

'I need to do some work on this project.'

'Have you forgotten it's my birthday? We arranged last Monday to go out together.'

'I thought that was tomorrow.'

Rosanna shook her head and waited, arms folded.

'Oh, no! I'm so sorry! I do have a present for you, but it's at home.'

'Never mind. I'm happy to have another birthday tomorrow. Anyway, I've arranged with Mr Repping to let us have a long lunch break and we're going to a nice Italian restaurant south of the river. Their pesto is to die for.'

As they drove out of town, Rosanna asked, 'Have you been to enrol for next year yet?'

'No.' Meriel was actually wondering about taking a year off from the art course, or doing only one unit instead of two. After all, it wasn't every year you met a man like Gary. And surely, it was more important to build a good relationship with the man you loved than to study art?

'Don't let him stop you doing your art,' Rosanna said. 'You've waited long enough.'

The restaurant was crowded and it wasn't until Meriel got up to visit the cloakroom that she noticed two people in the little side room. It was the man's honey blond hair she saw first. So like Gary's, she thought fondly. Then she frowned at the way the man ran his fingers through his hair to push it back out of his eyes. Surely there couldn't be two men who did that in exactly the same way?

She paused to see who he was with and her heart began to thump as she saw him lean over and kiss the hand of the woman next to him. He ran one finger down his companion's cheek in the way he always did to *her*. It couldn't be – it just couldn't . . . he wouldn't!

A waiter paused beside her. 'Are you all right, madam?'

'What? Oh, yes. I think I've just seen a friend.' She tried to smile, but wasn't sure it was successful. 'I'll move on in a minute.'

But she didn't move. She stayed and watched grimly as Gary played off all the tricks in his repertoire. Touches, gestures, searing looks, soft words. And the woman fell for them all – just as Meriel had. The silly fool was looking at him with a besotted expression on her face, as if he were the sun in the sky. It was quite obvious that the two of them were lovers.

Meriel wondered if she was going to be sick on the spot as humiliation seared through her, then anger took over.

How dared he treat her like that?

A waiter passed with a carafe of red wine. It was the work of a moment to snatch the carafe. Ignoring the guy's, 'Hey!' she marched across the room.

'Hi, Gary darling!'

As he turned to her, surprise making his mouth drop open, she poured the wine over his head.

All noise stilled around them, except for Gary's spluttering and exclamations as he snatched up his napkin and began to dab at his face.

Before he could say anything Meriel smiled at the woman with him. 'Don't believe a word this scumbag says. And unless you have him fitted with a male chastity belt, don't let him out of your sight for more than a minute. He's been romancing me for the past few weeks and I thought we were in love.'

She turned to Gary and stared at him, daring him to protest. Red wine trickled slowly down his face as he watched her warily.

The other woman looked from one to the other. 'Is she right, Gary?'

'I used to know her. I had to drop her. She's the jealous sort.'

'We were together only two days ago,' Meriel said. 'But if you don't believe me, I shan't lose any sleep.'

A waiter was hovering nearby. Smiling at him, she set the carafe down on a nearby table. 'Sorry to make such a mess. Put the wine on my bill.'

She walked back to Rosanna and said in a voice which sounded tight and unlike her. 'We're leaving. Now. I'll explain outside.'

Meriel saw her reflection in one of the wall mirrors and paused to stare at herself. White face except for two spots of colour in her cheeks and an expression that would have terrified the Gorgon.

She got as far as the next street then had to pause for a moment in the bright, mocking sunlight to pull herself together. She was only vaguely aware of her friend, standing patiently beside her. Taking a long shuddering breath, she said, 'Thanks for not arguing.'

'When someone gets that look on her face, you don't argue. Look, there's another café over there. Let's go and sit down for a minute at one of the pavement tables. You look like death warmed up.'

'I feel like it, too.' She tried to take a step and stumbled. When Rosanna caught her arm, she mumbled a thank you, at least she thought she did.

When things came into focus again, she was sitting at a table with a cup of black coffee in front of her. She saw how worried Rosanna was and managed a short huff of sound that might have been taken for a laugh. 'I saw Gary in there. Drooling all over another woman.'

'Ah.'

'What do you mean by "Ah"?'

'I wondered how long he'd manage to be faithful to one woman.'

'You knew about him?'

'I mentioned him to my family and it turns out my cousin Francesca does. They were at school together. Gary enjoys the chase much more than going steady. He never stays around for long – afterwards.'

'Couldn't you have told me that *before*?' Before she'd given in to that louse. Before she'd made such a fool of herself.

'And break up a good friendship?'

'I wouldn't have—'

'You might. People who don't like the message often try to shoot the messenger. And anyway, you'd not have believed me. He seemed pretty convincing about loving you.' Rosanna was fiddling with the sugar tubes, rearranging them in the bowl in the centre of the table. 'I figured all I could do was be there for you – if you needed me.' She reached across to pat Meriel's hand. 'It just happened more quickly than I'd expected.'

'Yeah.'

'You need to cry. And smash a few plates.'

'I poured a carafe of wine over him. That helped.'

'You didn't!'

'I did.'

'Oh, wow! I wish I could have seen that. I'd have had my mobile phone out and taken a photo of him.'

Meriel nearly managed a smile at the thought of that.

'Look, you're still white and shaken. I think you should go home. I'll tell Repping you're not well.' She grinned. 'I've only to hint that it's women's stuff and he'll be too embarrassed to pursue the matter.'

Meriel started to pick up the coffee cup, noticed that her hand was shaking and put it down again. 'I feel such a fool. No, worse than that. Totally humiliated.'

'Hey, everyone stuffs up from time to time.'

'But I got taken in by him. I *slept* with him. I thought I was in love with him.'

'You haven't had a lot of experience with men. It was inevitable that someone took advantage – if you don't mind me saying so.'

Tears spilled from Meriel's eyes. 'Yeah. I suppose so. Thanks for being around today. Sorry I spoiled your birthday.'

'We'll go out and celebrate properly next week. Now, go on home.'

Meriel dropped Rosanna at the office then drove home, where she destroyed every photo and memento of Gary.

The next day she enrolled for another year's art and design classes at the technical college.

The following day Meriel received another of her mother's handwritten letters. She'd tried to get her mother to use emails, but Denise had refused. She might have to use a computer at work but she wasn't having one of those things in her home.

Like the previous letters it was very repetitive. Denise complained of the cold weather and boasted of the pleasures of being a grandmother to dearest Helen's children.

Then she announced that she and Ralph were engaged. They'd been together a while, but neither of them had wanted to rush into anything. Oh, and she'd got another job, one that paid more money, but she'd had to attend another of those boring computer courses to get it.

Her mother's happiness seemed to emphasize Meriel's own unhappiness. What was wrong with her that she couldn't find a guy to love? She'd always had plenty of friends, of both sexes, but whenever she thought she'd met someone special, it always went wrong – though never as spectacularly as recently.

Well, at least the art classes were going well.

Six

Ben was working late and because her mother had had a fall, Linda's replacement, Nareen, had gone home early, leaving her desk in an unaccustomed mess. He glanced at the bank statement she'd left lying next to a pile of receipts and frowned. Surely they should have more money than that in the business account? He wasn't the world's best with figures, but he'd never have let it run so low.

He got out the previous statements and stared in shock at a series of withdrawals, quite major sums. He hadn't authorized these!

Phil came through the door, whistling and stopped to look at him questioningly. 'You look grim. Lost your wallet or something?'

Ben tapped the piece of paper. 'I think someone's hacked into our bank account. I'm going to call the police and—' He reached out for the phone.

Phil snatched it out of his hand. 'Don't!'

The two men stared at one another, then Phil scowled. 'I borrowed the money. I had some big expenses.'

'For the business?'

Silence, then, 'No. Personal.'

You took money out of the business for your own expenses?

Phil shrugged. 'Borrowed. Don't worry, I'll pay it back.'

'Too right you will. Tomorrow.'

'I can't manage it by tomorrow.'

'When can you manage it?'

'End of the month. Most of it, anyway.'

More than anything else, Ben wanted to sack him. Or call in the police. He'd been uneasy for a while about Phil's business practices, even though the business was doing well, getting more contracts than ever. But the man was Sandy's cousin, and because of that, Ben had given him more leeway than he normally would.

'If you don't manage to repay it by the end of the month,

I'm going to your father.' He trusted Sandy's uncle Rod absolutely.

'No need to do that! I'll find the money somehow. I don't want my father saying "Told you so".'

'Very well. But tomorrow we're going to make this a two-signature bank account. Plus, I'm taking your company credit card away.'

'The hell you are! How do you expect me to entertain clients?'

'You can pay your own way then claim the money back. I won't refuse to sign for anything reasonable. And while we're discussing finances, you're doing altogether too much entertaining of clients. Cut it back by about fifty per cent. We're not a big company. We can't afford to treat people so lavishly.'

'I've brought in some big accounts and I've got even bigger ones lined up. We *have* to treat them well. There are a lot of companies who'd be paying me fat bonuses for doing that sort of thing.'

'You can always quit and go to one of them. Anyway, I already told you: we can't cope with any more big contracts at the moment.'

'We can always hire more staff.'

'There aren't a lot of experienced staff around.'

'How experienced do you need to be to dig holes in the dirt?'

'More than you realize, clearly. Maybe you should come and work on a few projects, dig a few holes yourself, find out what goes on.'

Phil glared at him, seemed to be struggling to calm down. 'OK. I'll pay my own expenses and claim them back from now on. But I'm not into gardening.'

'Then why the hell are you working in a landscaping company?'

'I'm a salesman. I sell whatever the job needs.'

'Well, see that you pay back the money by the end of the month.'

'I said I would!' Phil picked up his briefcase and left, slamming the door behind him.

Ben went to sit at his desk, resting his aching head on

his hands for a moment. He was working all the hours he could while Phil was swanning around restaurants.

He almost hoped the money didn't get paid back. He'd had more than enough of working with Sandy's cousin.

A few weeks later Meriel's mother wrote to give her the marriage date.

> *So you'll need to book a flight home soon. I can't possibly get married without both my daughters in attendance, can I? In fact, why don't you come home for good while you're at it? Surely you've had enough travelling around now?*
>
> *You could live with your grandmother till you find some-where of your own. She gets lonely.*

The wedding date coincided exactly with the final exams for the year. Meriel wrote to explain that she was taking some art courses and asked if the wedding could be post-poned for two weeks.

The reply from her mother was full of exclamation marks and underlining. Everything was booked. They couldn't possibly change it, had had enough trouble finding some-where free around that time. Surely a mother's wedding was more important than an exam in a hobby subject?

But Meriel didn't give in to the emotional blackmail. She sent a nice present, a piece of antique silver she knew her mother would treasure, and apologized for not being there.

The letters stopped for a few weeks, then resumed again, little changed. The wedding photographs showed that her mother had lost weight and looked happy. Her sister had put on weight and looked – Meriel frowned as she stared at the pictures – Helen looked resigned, as if she wasn't particularly happy with life.

'Well, I'm never going to look like that,' Meriel muttered. Since the episode with Gary, she knew she'd been sharper with people. She hadn't given men up or anything neurotic like that, but she now kept things light. She wasn't looking for a permanent relationship at this stage in her life.

From then on, the letters from England hardly varied from one month to the next, always beginning with, *Well, dear . . .* and ending with the wish that Meriel would come to her senses and return home.

A few months later the envelope was addressed in thick black ink and carried the news that Meriel's grandmother had died in her sleep. She felt sad about that, but not nearly as sad as she had when Grandpop had passed away.

She phoned her mother, finding her uncharacteristically subdued.

'I'm going to miss Mum,' Denise said with a sigh. 'I enjoyed popping round to her house for a chat. There'll be no one to pop round and chat to me when I'm old.'

'Of course there will. Helen lives just down the road.'

Silence, then. 'She may be moving. Peter's been offered a job in Yorkshire.'

'Oh. I'm sorry.'

'Perhaps Ralph and I will come out and visit you one year.'

'That'd be lovely.' But she didn't think her mother was likely to undertake such a long journey.

'Ralph and I will be moving soon, too.'

'Oh?'

'I inherited everything from Mum. We're going to sell her house and both ours and buy a detached house with a garden.'

'That'll be wonderful. Are you into gardening now?'

'Ralph's teaching me. I do like a pretty garden. It sets a house off so nicely. I'll send you a memento before I dispose of Mum's things.'

Meriel had a sudden thought. 'Are Grandpop's tools still there?'

'Yes. Mum would never let me get rid of them.'

'Then that's what I want. I'll pay the freight.'

Denise roused instantly out of her lethargy. 'I can't believe you want those rusty old things.'

'I do. Very much. Just pack them up and send me a bill.'

The family wedding and funeral made Meriel realize she had no intention of ever going back to live in England. She'd fallen in love with Western Australia on the very first day and that love had only grown stronger as time passed.

The art course was the main focus of her life now. It was well structured and she was learning all manner of fascinating techniques. Straight A student, too. If only she could do it full-time. She got very tired sometimes of trying to fit everything in.

But what was the use of wishing for the moon? As Grandpop had said, you sometimes had to go the long way round to get to your chosen goal. At least she was well on the way now and there would be no more diversions en route.

Seven

By the time Meriel had parked her car and walked through Perth's central business district to her office, the wind had blown her hair into a tangle. She sighed as the lift stopped at several other floors on the way up to the eleventh. It seemed to get slower every day.

Outside the glass doors that led into her firm's new office suite she hesitated, then turned aside into the ladies' room to fix her hair, wishing yet again that it wasn't so fine. She combed the shoulder-length strands slowly, finding the action relaxing. She was feeling rather tense today because it was the final examination of the whole course.

She grimaced at her image. 'Aren't you the perfect little executive, Meriel Ingram? Pity your mother can't see you now.' Navy suit and cream blouse, just the sort of thing a rising young accountant was expected to wear.

When she went into her office, the feeling of irritation intensified. She couldn't understand what had got into her today. She knew she'd pass the exam, for heaven's sake. Before she even had time to sit down at the desk, she looked up to see Rosanna.

'Hi, Meriel!' Her friend's smile faded. 'Hey, you look angry. Is something wrong?'

'What? Oh, sorry, Rosanna. No, nothing's wrong. I'm just feeling a bit – oh, I don't know, disorientated. It's my final examination this afternoon and I can't think what I'll do with myself next year. I'm going to miss going to classes.'

'Most people are glad to get their studies over with.'

'Well I am too, in a way. But I've enjoyed meeting people and encountering new ideas, even being forced to try new media and methods.'

'I came to wish you luck.'

'It's not luck that passes examinations, but hard work.'

'Hey, don't bite my nose off.'

'Sorry.' Oh dear, she'd sounded just like her mother then.

Rosanna came forward to perch on a corner of the desk and leant over confidentially. 'You've seemed a bit down for a week or two now. Anything I can do to help?'

'Thanks but no. I'm sure I'll feel better once this exam's over.'

But would she? The more Meriel studied, the more boring she found her work as an accountant. The high-rise block seemed like a prison with its stale air, artificial lighting and pinging lifts.

In the evenings she would try to paint or draw, but was often too tired to produce anything worthwhile. Only, you had to earn a living, didn't you? Stand on your own feet and all that. So what other choice did she have?

And at least the people she worked with were great. That helped a lot. She forced a smile. 'I'm all right, really I am.'

Rosanna patted her shoulder. 'When this exam is over you should get out more, meet a few new people. I could fix you up with a date. I have this cousin – he's been working over in the eastern states, but he's back in Perth now. I think you'd like him and—'

'No, thanks! I've got a full and interesting life. It isn't obligatory to have a man, you know.'

'It's nice, though,' Rosanna's voice became more gentle and a tender smile crept over her face.

'Things still going well with Karl?'

'Mm-hmm. Are they ever! He's great, the kindest guy I've ever met.' She grinned. 'Even if he isn't a nice Italian boy!'

'Is your mother still complaining?'

Rosanna shrugged. 'She's getting used to him, especially since he started bringing her flowers. I told him that'd help.'

'I'm really glad for you.'

When her friend left Meriel told herself to focus on the bright side. She had just received another commission to do a book cover illustration because the publisher had been very pleased with the first one she'd created for them.

She loved that sort of work. It was a challenge to get the right message across on the cover of a book so as to catch a potential buyer's eye, showing at a glance what genre the story was and yet looking fresh and attractive. The money she earned by her art had been added to her savings, which were on target to give her a whole year off work in another three years' time. *If* she persevered. *If* she could get a year's leave without pay and still keep her job, that was. So many ifs!

She turned with a sigh to the papers on her desk. She had better check the figures and documentation for the coming meeting. Goodness, this Ben Elless had inherited a sackful of trouble! His uncle hadn't kept proper accounts for years and everything was in a real tangle, with pieces of property scattered over several country towns, not to mention a few bundles of shares and several bank accounts with very little in them. Sorting things out had nearly driven her insane at times, but at least this sort of thing was more interesting than straightforward number crunching.

The appointment was for half-past ten. By eleven o'clock the man had still not fronted up. Meriel walked through into reception. 'I think I'll get a bit of fresh air, Penny. My client hasn't turned up and—'

'Elless?'

'That's the one.'

'He's just phoned to say he's been delayed and is on his way here. He wouldn't wait to be put through to you.'

'Kind of him to let us know!'

Penny grinned at her. 'Having a bad hair day?'

'Sort of. I've got my final examination this afternoon.'

'Oh, sorry. I'd forgotten. Good luck!'

Meriel went back to her office and got out the Elless file again, sitting waiting, unable to settle to anything else.

Ten minutes later Penny rang through. 'Your client has arrived.'

'Tell him I can give him exactly half an hour.' Meriel gathered up her papers and marched out to reception.

Penny beckoned her over and said in a low voice, 'I've put him in the interview room. He's as mad as fire about something, so watch your step.' She went to throw open a door at the side, winking at Meriel. 'Ms Ingram is here now, Mr Elless.'

He was standing by the office window looking out at the traffic several stories below in St George's Terrace. His head was framed against the sunlight, which meant Meriel could only see him as a silhouette, and he was flexing his shoulders as if he was very tired indeed. When Meriel entered, he swung round and stared across at her, eyes narrowing in assessment. 'Ms Ingram?'

She nodded and walked quickly across to the table, putting her papers down and gesturing to a chair. 'I'm afraid I can only give you half an hour, Mr Elless. I have another appointment.'

'Damn!'

She deliberately didn't look up from the papers, but continued arranging them in front of her.

'Well, it's my own fault, so I suppose I can't complain. My last meeting ran on for too long. I'll have to schedule another appointment with you next time I'm in the west. But we can make a start now, surely?' He came over to the table.

'Yes, of course.' For the first time she could see his face clearly and what she saw took her breath away. He was quite simply the most handsome man she had ever met in her whole life, so handsome he seemed unreal. She wanted to reach for a pencil and start sketching. He'd make a wonderful hero on a book cover.

Closer scrutiny revealed no obvious physical flaws. Dark brown wavy hair and bright blue eyes fringed in thick sooty lashes topped more than six feet of lean, muscular manhood. In a small room like this he was overwhelming both to the artist and the woman in her.

Taking a slow, careful breath she picked up her pen and looked at him questioningly, forcing her mind back to his finances. His frown had disappeared and he was staring at her with an approving smile, as if he liked what he saw. She was used to that reaction from male clients and had learned to ignore it. 'If you're ready now, Mr Elless, perhaps you'd sit down? This is quite complicated.'

The frown returned as he took his place opposite her. 'You look too young.'

'I beg your pardon?' She put down the pen and prepared to do battle. This had happened before as well and she understood the exact implications of his statement without needing to ask for an explanation.

'No offence meant, Ms Ingram, but I requested an experienced accountant to handle my uncle's business affairs, not someone just out of university.'

She sat perfectly still for a moment. One did not throw folders of papers at the heads of one's clients, however much they deserved such treatment. 'I think you'll find that I know my job, Mr Elless.' She felt quite proud of the calm way she had spoken. 'Would you like me to summarize the situation with regard to your uncle's estate?'

'How old are you? You don't look nearly old enough to be a qualified accountant.'

She stopped trying to hide her annoyance. 'I'm thirty years old, *if* that's any of your business, and I think you'll find that I'm both well qualified and experienced. Mr Repping, the Senior Partner, has complete confidence in my ability to handle your account, or he wouldn't have put me in charge of it.' She shoved a summary sheet across the table at him with such force that he only just managed to catch it before it slid off the edge. 'Now, let me show you—'

'You look about seventeen.'

'I don't happen to have my birth certificate handy, but if it means so much to you, I'm sure Mr Repping will be happy to confirm my age in writing.'

He opened his mouth, looked at her face and shut his mouth again. Picking up the summary sheet, he began to study the figures on it.

His expression became serious as she took him through the muddles of his late uncle's business affairs. Total chaos was a more accurate description. She had to explain some things more than once and could tell he wasn't comfortable with complex figures, so went through them very slowly, stopping to check that he'd understood.

'So,' she wound up, glancing surreptitiously at her watch, 'I think it'll take several weeks to work everything out, and even then, we'll still have your late uncle's tax situation to deal with. As far as I can make out, he's not lodged a tax return for several years. I can't imagine how he got away with that.'

'So you don't know yet, then, whether I've been left anything worthwhile or simply a collection of liabilities?'

'I think you'll find it quite a substantial inheritance, though not in cash terms. He was land rich and cash poor, from what I can make out. Of course we only have a rough idea of how much the properties he's left you are worth at this stage and the council rates haven't been paid on them for a while. Still, you should realize a decent sum of money if you sell them, a few million dollars if you do it carefully.'

'That's Uncle Johnny for you! He had a ridiculous faith in putting money into land.' Ben Elless sighed as he leaned back. 'Quite frankly, this couldn't have come at a more inconvenient time administratively. I have heavy commitments in Queensland just now.' He yawned then stretched like a sleepy lion. 'I'm sorry. I had to fly over on last night's red-eye special and it was full of happy teenagers. I've had meetings from eight o'clock this morning straight through and the lack of sleep is beginning to catch up with me.'

She glanced at her watch again, her lips tightening in dismay when she realized they'd been here for well over the allotted half hour already. Today of all days she couldn't afford to be late.

His voice brought her back to attention. 'Can you carry on with this – sort out the taxes, then leave things until I have more time?'

'Yes, of course.' She tried to hurry things along. 'Well, if everything is to your satisfaction, Mr Elless . . .'

He didn't take the hint but leaned back in his chair and smiled at her again, a warm uncomplicated smile this time. 'I think I've been a little – er – brusque with you today.'

A little brusque! He'd been as tactful as a charging rhinoceros. If he were not her client, she would have enjoyed telling him exactly what she thought of arrogant men who traded on their good looks and left their manners at home. 'Just a little.'

'I apologize for that. Mind you, I still think that you look too young to be a senior accountant,' again his eyes raked her from head to toe, 'but if you say you're thirty, I believe you. You obviously know your stuff. So you'll continue to work on my uncle's estate?'

'Yes, of course.' She waited impatiently for him to get up and leave. To her annoyance, her stomach gurgled loudly.

He grinned. 'Not eaten yet, Ms Ingram? By the way, what is your first name?'

She ignored that question. Unlike her Australian colleagues she preferred not to get on first-name terms with clients. 'I haven't had lunch yet, so if you'll excuse me, I—'

'How about I buy you lunch to apologize?'

The last thing she wanted was to have lunch with a client, even if she was free to do so, which she wasn't. And this guy might be all sweetness and light now, but he had been extremely rude to her before, with no justification whatsoever. In fact, he'd behaved in an utterly chauvinistic way, doubting her capability as an accountant.

She leaned back and gave Mr Elless a cool stare. 'I'm sorry. I've made other arrangements for lunch.'

'Dinner, then?'

'No way!' The words burst out before she could stop herself. She could see his surprise, the way his eyes narrowed.

'I was that rude to you, was I?'

Time was passing. She was due to take that final examination in just over an hour, and she still had to eat and get across town to the college. 'I'm not free.'

'Pity.'

When he continued to sit there, she took the initiative by standing up and walking round the desk, ready to move towards the door.

He stood up, too, but instead of shaking her outstretched hand, he took it in both his and kept hold of it. 'Couldn't you take pity on a stranger to Perth and break your engagement tonight?'

He was so large and vibrantly male that her breath caught in her throat. She looked up at him and for a moment forgot everything. She had to take several slow deep breaths before she could get her thoughts in order. How could this be happening to her? She had never before reacted to a stranger on such an instinctive physical level and it shocked her. He was clasping her hand so tightly she didn't like to make an issue of pulling it away.

Then common sense took over. This was just a passing physical attraction, she told herself, straightening her shoulders and stepping backwards. It happened to people all the time. You met a stranger and something sparked between you. It was no big deal. If she ignored it, it would go away.

And so would he. After all, he lived in Queensland. She tried to remove her hand and his fingers tightened on hers.

'Sure you won't change your mind?'

'No, thank you. I'm – um – in a long-term relationship.' He didn't try to hide his disappointment and let go. But although she had her hand free now, she could still feel the imprint of his fingers on hers.

'He's a lucky man.'

She led the way briskly along the corridor to the reception area and said a crisp goodbye, but it wasn't until she sat down at her desk in the quietness of the long examination hall that Meriel managed to get the image of Ben Elless out of her mind. She forgot everything then but the questions in front of her. She had learned the basics of her new trade now, and one day she would earn her living entirely as an artist.

She had vowed to do that when she started on this course, and she intended to make the dream come true, however long it took.

When he left the accountant's office, Ben Elless stopped for a moment to shake his head in bewilderment. What on earth had got into him, pressuring a stranger for a date like that? He'd been acting like a seventeen-year-old with raging testosterone fever. The last thing he needed at the moment, the very last, was to get involved with a woman.

Then sadness took over for a moment or two. Such an instant attraction hadn't happened to him for a long time, not since he'd met Sandy.

To his ongoing annoyance, over the next few days he had trouble getting the beautiful Ms Ingram out of his mind. It wasn't her good looks, though that didn't hurt, it was something much deeper than that. He grinned at the memory of how indignant she'd been when he asked her age. Well, that had been absolutely stupid of him. Only she did look young and untouched, somehow.

It was strange that he should feel so attracted to her, because he didn't normally go for blondes. Or small women. And why the hell was he thinking about her again?

He was relieved when he finished his business in Perth

and could go home to Brisbane. He phoned the office from the airport, hoping to pop in and see Phil before he left for the day, but got only the answer phone. He was beginning to think his partner was avoiding him and to wonder why. At this stage they should be liaising closely on the current project.

Should he drop in on Phil at home? No, not today. Phil's wife would insist on Ben staying for a meal and he didn't want to involve her in any arguments because she was a nice enough woman. Perhaps there was nothing wrong, but Ben felt uneasy. Phil had been behaving himself since their last confrontation, but recently he had been rather elusive. It wouldn't hurt, though, to do some careful checking that everything was in order. Well, Ben knew he ought to have done so before now, but he'd been too busy to catch his breath.

Needing a bit of peace and quiet after all the hassles of his Perth trip, he picked up his car and headed out of the city centre. As he sang along to the music he felt the tension drop away. He wasn't really interested in being a high-powered businessman but he absolutely loved designing gardens, and the bigger the better.

One day he'd find a piece of land and start work on the big project he'd been dreaming about for years. Perhaps he'd even do this on one of his uncle's blocks of land. He had very fond childhood memories of living in York and learning about the bush.

Unfortunately, although the recent legacy from Uncle Johnny was good news in one way, it was bad in another because it'd take time and effort he could ill afford to sort everything out. At this stage he needed to focus on the business and keeping Phil in order. No small task.

He couldn't help smiling at the thought of his inheritance, though, and he was looking forward to seeing the old house in York again. He'd such happy memories of living there as a boy.

He'd have to see Ms Ingram again, too, when he visited the accountant in Perth. He wouldn't mind that, either.

Eight

The art examination was so straightforward it was an anti-climax. When it was over, Meriel felt empty and drained. That was it. She'd finished her studies.

She didn't really want to go out for a celebratory drink with the others but did it anyway. They'd become good friends as they studied and you never knew when you'd meet someone again in a place like Western Australia, which had a small population, however big its physical size.

She excused herself after an hour or so, pleading a date. Everything seemed a little unreal as she walked back to her car.

On her way home she stopped at the shops and pulled up short at the sight of a display of birthday cards. Oops! She'd nearly forgotten to get a card for her mother. She'd better buy one now and put it in the post for England straight away. If it didn't arrive on time, her mother would be upset and huffy.

As she was paying for the card Meriel noticed the Lotto machine on the counter. She didn't normally buy lottery coupons because the odds against winning were astronomical and it was a complete waste of money. She had told Rosanna so dozens of times, but her friend just laughed and said she enjoyed her weekly licence to dream.

Today, however, was a special day and Meriel had an urge to do something different to mark that. She hadn't been lucky in love, so she might as well test the old saying and see if she was lucky in other ways. 'I'll have one of those things as well,' she said.

'Slikpik?'

'Yes, all right. Give me a Slikpik.' She waited impatiently as the machine churned out a coupon, choosing her numbers for her, then stuffed it into her purse and left, already regretting her impulsive purchase. That money could have been added to her savings. She'd wasted it, absolutely thrown it away.

Back at her flat she hurled her handbag on the couch, dumped her shopping in the kitchen and sank into her favourite chair. She'd found the wooden rocking chair in a junk shop. Some idiot had painted it a hideous shade of green. Thanks to Grandpop's training, she had recognized its potential, stripped off the gunk and waxed the chair until it gleamed. The wood was now a glossy honey colour, the carved back fitted the curves of her spine exactly and she usually found sitting in it soothing. But not today. Today, nothing seemed to soothe her.

She wasn't worried about the exam. She knew she'd passed and probably done quite well, too. But she felt empty, not elated. Was that because she'd reached one of her main goals in life and what she really wanted now was to use her new skills? Well, she couldn't, had to continue number crunching and that was that.

She wished . . . oh, she didn't know what she wished! That was the trouble.

Meriel spent Saturday working on a painting. She was designing a series of greeting cards based on Australian flora and fauna, and was rather pleased with the results so far. As usual she lost herself in her work and it was lunchtime before she knew it.

While she was eating she flipped through a magazine. One of the male models looked a bit like Ben Elless and . . . She got annoyed with herself for thinking about him again. Anyway, the man in the magazine wasn't nearly as good looking and . . . she tossed it on to the low coffee table.

On the Sunday she slipped out to get some fresh air and buy a newspaper, enjoying the spring sunshine. Only when she opened her handbag did she remember that she'd bought a Lotto coupon. She scowled at it. Might as well throw it away now. But of course, she didn't. She would have worried that she might have won ten dollars or whatever tiny amount you did occasionally win on these things.

When she got back home she dumped the newspaper on the kitchen surface, made herself a cup of coffee then settled down to read.

Only later as she was putting her bag away did she remember to take out the Lotto coupon and check the numbers in the newspaper. It was hardly worth bothering, but still . . . Shrugging, she picked up a pencil. She might just, if she were very lucky, recoup her money.

A minute later she stared in startled disbelief at the line of circled figures. Six numbers, all in one row. Her heart was thumping so loudly she had to press her hands against her chest to calm herself.

'I won!' she said aloud, her voice hoarse and scratchy with shock. It was impossible odds, but she'd won! She stood up and walked round the room, feeling jerky and uncoordinated, then flopped down on the couch and said, 'I won!' several times more. She thumped a cushion to emphasize her words, before picking it up and tossing it in the air.

Then she shook her head. 'I must have made a mistake.'

She checked the numbers again, not realizing she was holding her breath until she had to let it out in a whoosh. There was no mistake. Six numbers. All in one row.

She sat staring at the ticket till everything ran into a blur. How much had she won? It could be anything from a couple of hundred thousand dollars, if the prize was shared between several people, to over a million. According to Rosanna, who had once won fifty dollars, you didn't find out how much you'd won until late Monday afternoon. Meriel groaned aloud. Over a day to wait! How was she going to bear it? She might – she really might be rich.

The thought that followed seemed to etch itself into her brain in letters of fire – *rich enough to give up work and try to become a full-time commercial artist.* She caught her breath on a gasp, then told herself to get a grip. She shouldn't count on anything till her win was confirmed.

She made another cup of coffee then wondered whether to open a bottle of champagne, but it was no fun celebrating on your own. She rang Rosanna to share her news, but her friend's mobile was switched off. The coffee was stone cold by the time she took a sip, as she tried to come to terms with the thought that she might be rich.

After a while, feeling as if the walls were closing in on her, she grabbed her shoulder bag and went out, driving into Perth then going for a brisk walk along the river. The beauty of the day gradually seeped into her bones and she could feel herself relaxing. Blue water reflected even bluer sky, its movement chopping up the reflections of the buildings on the southern shore into a million fragments that nonetheless formed a pleasing whole. The ferry chugged slowly across the river like a prim spinster aunt then chugged back again.

She felt better out in the open air. She always did.

Hunger drove her home again and the evening crawled past at an agonizing snail's pace. She kept trying to phone Rosanna's mobile and getting no answer. She kept looking at the clock and finding that only a few minutes had passed. She kept staring into space, hoping, praying that she would win enough money to escape being an accountant – for a while at least.

When she went to work on the Monday morning she said nothing to anyone, not even her friend, because Rosanna would be bound to shriek for joy and Meriel didn't want anyone else there knowing about her win yet.

'You don't look well,' Rosanna said. 'You should have stayed at home.'

'It's just a – a touch of the collywobbles.'

Rosanna chuckled. 'You don't have much of a pommy accent but you do use some funny words sometimes. Collywobbles! What does that mean?'

'Australian translation: I've picked up a stomach wog.'

Meriel spent most of the day locked in her office, pushing papers to and fro, but getting nowhere. Thank goodness she had no client appointments today. She couldn't concentrate properly on anything.

In the afternoon, heart pounding, she rang the Lotteries Commission hotline to see what this week's prizes were worth. A mechanical voice told her that the first prize was shared between two people and would amount to $956,321.40 each. She stood there, frozen in shock, with the recording still droning away in her ear.

What you gonna do when you win Lotto? The silly jingle from some TV adverts she'd seen a while ago began to pound through her brain again and she had to take several deep breaths before she could move. Setting the receiver down with extreme care, she left her office. She had to share the news with someone, just had to.

She made it along the corridor, then the world started tilting and she had to clutch the doorframe. 'Rosanna, I—' Everything started to whirl around her and the next thing she knew, she was staggering across the room.

When she collapsed into a chair, her friend stared down at her, plump arms akimbo. 'Did you eat any lunch today?'

'Er – no. I wasn't hungry. Rosanna, I—'

'What did you have for breakfast?'

'I don't remember.'

'Meriel Ingram, I don't know what's got into you lately. You aren't looking after yourself. If you get any thinner, you'll fade away. Are you turning anorexic on me?'

'No. It's not that.' Meriel clutched the desk and told herself to calm down.

Rosanna stopped scolding and perched beside her, asking in a gentler voice, 'You feeling better now?'

'Mmm.' But she didn't tell her friend the real reason for her faintness. She didn't want the rest of the office to know anything yet. The Lotto coupon was tucked away in her handbag and she wouldn't feel certain about the money until she had presented it to the Lotteries Commission and had her win confirmed.

Rosanna's voice was still blaring in her ears. 'I'm going to take you home, feed you and put you to bed. This can't go on.' And from that decision she refused to be moved.

Meriel trailed back to her office, worrying about how badly she was handling this.

Her boss, John Repping, came into her office to stare at her and insist she go home. 'And let someone else drive you. You're white as a sheet.'

'All right. Thanks.'

A few minutes later, Meriel buckled herself into the passenger seat of her own car and directed Rosanna to drive her north to Osborne Park. 'I have some things to pick up. It's urgent.'

When they got near the Lotteries Commission, she told her friend to stop for a moment, then got out of the car. 'We need to go into the Lotteries Commission. The reason

I nearly fainted this morning, Rosanna, is that I think I've won Lotto.'

'Yeah? Which Division?'

'Division One. All six numbers.'

Rosanna's shriek stopped two passers-by dead in their tracks, but the sight of her beaming face reassured them and they went on their way, smiling. She grabbed Meriel and gave her a big hug. 'Hey, that's marvellous! Congratulations! Oh, wow!' Then she held her at arm's length. 'Look, I'm coming inside with you. You might faint again when they confirm it! Are you sure you double-checked all the numbers?'

'I must have checked them fifty times, at least.'

Inside, Rosanna took the Lotto ticket from Meriel's shaking fingers and brandished it in the receptionist's face. 'My friend just won the First Division.'

The woman beamed at them and pressed a button. 'That's wonderful. Let me show you to the Winners' Room.'

The ticket was validated, then Meriel was asked whether she wanted a cheque or the money paying into her bank.

'Paying in directly, please.' She didn't want to risk anything happening to a cheque.

Once she'd given them her details, a woman came up to her. 'I'm a member of the Corporate Communications Team. Would you mind having a chat? We like to find out about our winners. And we need to know whether you want to remain anonymous.'

'Definitely.'

'Do you have any idea what you'll do with the money?'

'Yes. Give up work and become an artist. I've been training part-time and saving to take some time off.'

They chatted for a while and Meriel was given a pack with guidelines on making the most of her good fortune.

Rosanna chuckled when they did that. 'She's an accountant. I think she'll know how to look after her money.'

The woman smiled sympathetically. 'That's good. Take the pack anyway. Some of our past winners helped us put it together. The main advice we offer is not to rush into anything.'

'I won't.' Meriel closed her eyes for a moment. Coming here, being fêted, made it all real and she felt overwhelmed. She stood up. 'You've all been very kind, but what I need now is some peace and quiet to get used to it all.' She'd won nine hundred and fifty-six thousand three hundred and twenty-one dollars and forty cents. That meant freedom to do what she wanted with her life, at least for the next few years.

As she and Rosanna walked outside, she stopped to say firmly, 'You're not to tell anyone about this when you get back to the office.'

'But—'

'I mean that!' She spoke fiercely. 'I don't want anyone at work to know about my win until I've decided what to do with the money.'

'They're bound to find out sooner or later.'

'Let them.' She had to swallow hard before she added, 'I'll be gone by then.'

'Gone?'

'Yes, gone. I'm going to do what I've always wanted.' She spoke in hushed tones, feeling like someone standing at the gates of paradise, scared to tiptoe through them. 'Rosanna, I'm going to buy myself a little house somewhere in the country and paint.'

'You can't mean that!'

'Oh, I do. I'll phone John Repping tomorrow and give in my notice.'

She let Rosanna drive her home, where she ate a sandwich to appease her friend then pleaded weariness. After the door had closed behind Rosanna, the quietness seemed to fold itself around Meriel and the rocking chair beckoned to her like a dear friend.

'So,' she said to it, stroking the silky wood of the armrest, 'I really did win Lotto.' She wished this had happened while Grandpop was still alive. She'd have taken him on a world trip. He'd always wanted to travel.

And why she should suddenly remember Ben Elless again, she couldn't imagine, except that he had walked in and out of her thoughts all weekend. Sure, he was a good-looking guy, but he wasn't the first attractive man she'd ever met. Only, none of the others had haunted her like this. Perhaps she should have accepted his dinner invitation. That might have got him out of her system. He probably had a million faults which would have put her off him if she got to know him better.

She remembered how he had questioned her capabilities as an accountant. It was a long time since anyone had made her so angry. Then she grinned as she suddenly realized that someone else would now have to work on the Elless account. Someone else would have to put up with that man's rudeness.

Her grin became a beam of delight and she forgot Ben Elless and accounting completely, as she bounced to her feet and began to dance around the room. Her childhood dreams were about to come true. Well, she amended mentally, her dreams were going to come true if she had enough talent. That remained to be seen, but her tutors had praised her and the publisher had already talked of giving her other book cover commissions.

And now – now she would have all the time she needed to develop her skills. She smiled wryly. She'd thought she wanted to paint, but the course had taught her that she wanted to be a commercial artist and work on a whole range of different things that stretched her imagination.

Nine

Meriel went in to see her boss the next day to tell him what had happened.

'Goodness me! Well, er, congratulations.'

'I want to give notice, to leave as soon as possible.'

'Oh. We'd be sorry to lose you. Are you quite sure?' Then he snapped his fingers. 'Of course! Your art. Well, why don't we go through your client portfolio and see where you stand, then you can start passing your client list on to others here. I'll take one or two of them as well until we can find a replacement for you.'

'Thank you. I really appreciate your being so understanding about this.'

He began to fiddle with his pen. 'Did you ask to remain anonymous about your win?'

'Yes.'

'That's good. We don't want the firm linked to gambling and games of chance.'

She finished work two weeks later, endured a going-away party and then went back with relief to the quiet of her villa. The only work she had now was designing the book covers and she enjoyed that enormously, but it wouldn't bring in enough to live on and she didn't want to fritter away her winnings.

She tried to remember when last she'd had so much time to herself but couldn't. She seemed to have been rushing to get things done ever since her father left her mother, first at school, then at university and then looking after Grandpop.

Now she could do exactly what she wanted – or do nothing at all.

The main decision she'd already taken was to live in the country. The idea of owning a few acres of land appealed strongly to her. Maybe that was a reaction to her childhood in the crowded terraces of a Lancashire mill town. She'd always loved going for walks on the moors with Grandpop.

The problem of finding somewhere to live had her making lists as methodically as she had once done at work.

First of all she bought a newer car, a small four-wheel drive suitable for country roads, but not a brand new one, which would lose too much value the minute she drove it out of the sales yard. It was only a couple of years old, silver with grey upholstery, a huge improvement on her elderly runabout.

Next she spent some time exploring the country districts near Perth, because she didn't want to live too far away from the capital. She enjoyed these outings enormously, setting off at dawn with a flask of coffee and a map, going wherever the fancy took her, staying the night if she wanted to.

She invited Rosanna to come with her one weekend, but her friend declined to be parted from Karl for a whole day. For a fleeting moment as she put the phone down, Meriel wished she had someone to share things with. No, with her track record with men, she was better off on her own. Much better.

The more she searched, the more she enjoyed the open spaces, with only wind and rustling leaves, the humming of insects and sudden bird calls to break the silence. But she wanted to live somewhere with a strong sense of community, as well. The isolated five-acre blocks of land in the outer suburbs didn't appeal to her at all. She concentrated on various country towns, though 'town' was a grandiose word for some of the places she visited, which would not even have merited village status in England.

Then one weekend she drove out to York, which she hadn't visited before. It lay about a hundred kilometres east of Perth and had been one of the earliest inland parts of the State to be settled by Europeans in the 1830s.

After leaving Perth, she drove up the long slope of the Darling Scarp, finding the busy city traffic giving way to fewer vehicles and the open stretches of a wide country road.

She took a right turn to York, and found very little traffic at all. The road wound its way through gentle, hilly countryside with forests on either side. The white lines on the edges of the road were bordered by red gravel in various shades from pale dusty orange to a richer red, and these accented the dull greens and light trunks of the trees. This was regrowth, with none of the huge trees of untouched bushland. In places the ground and trunks were blackened where a small bushfire had gone through.

Then the road came out into farm land, the cleared pastures a beige-green in the dryness of summer, dotted with small clumps of trees. Every now and then there were smooth rocky outcrops that made her itch to get out her sketching pad.

She'd read enough history to know that the place names reflected the early days of settlement when people were limited to horsepower and marked the road by watering points: 13 Mile Spring, St Ronan's Well, 6 Mile Brook. When she stopped at the latter she found only a dry watercourse that had cut a v-shaped twisting path through the land, a mere couple of metres wide. It'd be a winter creek, she decided, only flowing during the winter rains and drying out in summer.

It made for an interesting visual mix and she would paint it one day.

Reluctantly she got back into the car and drove on into town.

This was another delight. The facades of the buildings that lined the main street were in a mixture of styles but looked like the originals to Meriel. She was entranced and strolled up and down Avon Terrace, shaded from the hot sun by the awnings in front of most shops and businesses. She'd take time later, she promised herself, to visit the motor and residency museums and find out more.

Was this . . . could it be the right place for her to settle?

After yet another row with Phil, Ben said quietly, 'We'll never work comfortably together. I think you should look for another job.'

'I already have a job that I like and my father has put a lot of money into this firm, so I'm not going anywhere.'

'Then I will.'

Phil laughed. 'I don't think so. It'd mean abandoning everything you've worked for.'

'If you go on trying to cut corners and treat customers

shoddily, you'll destroy the business anyway. It cost us twice as much to fix things with Sheverson as it would have cost to use good quality plants from one of my approved suppliers in the first place.'

'Sheverson had no legal claim on us, so I don't know why you put in new plants. He'd neglected that garden.'

'Even so, he still shouldn't have lost that many plants, so I consider he had a moral claim. If I'd been working on that project myself I'd have sent those plants back. You were banking on my being away when you arranged that. I'll go and see Uncle Rod, tell him I'm leaving.'

'Don't you dare. He's just been diagnosed with cancer and is going in for treatment.'

Ben stopped short. 'He's got cancer? Oh, no. I'm so sorry. What's the prognosis?'

'Not good.'

'That's terrible.' As Phil scowled and turned to go back into his own office, Ben added. 'But I'm still leaving and in the meantime, don't try any more cheapskate tricks.'

Meriel delayed telling her family about her Lotto win because she knew her plans would upset them, but in the end she rang her mother.

Once she had stopped exclaiming in delight at her daughter's windfall, Denise's first question was, 'So when will you be returning to England?'

Here it came. She took a deep breath. 'I won't be coming back, Mum. I really like living in Australia. I don't think I could face life in a cold climate again.'

'But Meriel, your family are all *here*! Surely you're missing us now that the novelty has worn off? I mean, I can understand your need to fly the nest for a while. I only wish I'd had the same opportunity, but I made a martyr of myself for my husband and family. A martyr. And—'

'Mum, I've made a new life for myself here. I've got friends and business contacts and—'

'Well, you can easily make business contacts in England. And some of your old friends are still around. Why, with the money you've won, you'll be able to buy your own accounting business, meet some nice men, maybe settle down at last.'

Here it came, the second revelation, the one Meriel had been dreading the most. 'I'm not working as an accountant now.'

'*What?*'

'You know I've always wanted to be an artist. Well, the money I've won will help me do that. It's like a dream come true for me.'

'But you're not trained as an artist. All you've ever done is a few part-time classes.'

'I've been studying seriously for the past few years and I have a Diploma in Art and Graphic Design. It's strange, but I took my final exam on the day I bought the Lotto ticket. It's as if fate was on my side. It's the only Lotto ticket I've ever bought in my whole life.' She stopped. She was gabbling, nervous about the long silence at the other end of the line. 'Mum? Are you still there?'

'*Well!*' It was more a whoosh of air than a word. 'I can't believe what I'm hearing! I simply cannot believe it. Absolutely wasting all that university training!' Denise's voice was rising. 'You've run mad, Meriel Ingram! Quite mad. I don't know what's got into you, I really don't!'

Meriel gritted her teeth. She had promised herself she wouldn't lose her temper. 'Nothing that wasn't in me already, Mum. I always wanted to be an artist. You know I did. It was you who forced me to become an accountant.'

'*Forced you?* Of all the ingratitude! Accountancy's given you a living all these years, hasn't it? And a good living it is, too. More than I'll ever earn. No one gave *me* any training.'

Meriel tried to divert her mother by asking about her stepfather. 'How's Ralph?'

'Well. He's always well. And don't try to change the subject.'

Stay calm, Meriel told herself, *stay absolutely calm.*

Her mother changed tactics, her voice growing softer and more coaxing. 'Darling, aren't you being just a little bit stubborn about all this? You could buy a nice house in England and work part-time if you're really determined to fiddle around with art. You could live near your family.'

Meriel shuddered at the thought. She'd never be able to call her life her own again if she lived near her mother and sister. They'd be forever popping in to see her. And why, in this day and age, did her mother think marriage was the only real future for a woman? 'I've told you, Mum: I like living in Australia and I don't particularly want to get married. And besides, I've already made contacts here and done some book covers.'

'You never told me. You never said a word about it, not a single word.' Her mother's voice sharpened into viciousness. 'You're as bad as your father! Secretive and selfish.'

'Everyone has to find their own way in life, Mum.'

'What's so special about this York-down-under place, anyway?'

'It's a delightful little country town, pretty and out of the rat race. In the spring there are stunning wildflowers in that region. Whole fields of purply-blue flowers called Patterson's Curse, and other fields full of yellow flowers. I don't even know their name yet, but I'm itching to paint them. It's fantastic. You've never seen anything like it. It's exactly the sort of place for an artist to settle.'

'You aren't an artist yet.'

Meriel had had enough. 'Look, I have to go now, Mum. There's someone at the door and I'm expecting a delivery. I'll give you a ring in a couple of weeks.' She put the phone down before her mother could protest. She'd write to her father, she decided. She couldn't face another harangue like this – or worse, indifference about what she was doing with her life.

Ironically, her father was much more supportive and wrote back to say how happy he was that she had won the money and to wish her luck in her new life.

Ben's last trip to Perth had been a flying visit to discuss future projects with the head office of one of his major clients. After all the arguments recently, he decided it'd be good to put a little distance between himself and Phil, so made plans to go across to the west and stay there for a week or two in his uncle's old house. He left his current projects in the hands of men he trusted with strict instructions to let him know if any of the materials or plants were sub-standard.

His uncle's lawyer had sent him a list of the properties he'd inherited and suggested he contact Bill Lansome, the real estate agent his uncle had always dealt with. 'He'll know more about them than anyone else. I gather the two of them were friends, so Johnny only dealt with Bill when he wanted to buy a property.'

Making allowances for the three-hour time differences between Western Australia and Queensland, Ben phoned Bill. The man talked very enthusiastically about the properties and was able to describe them in detail.

That left Ben with a lot to think about. He'd been surprised at how much land his uncle had owned, though no single property was big enough for what he needed for his own pet project. Maybe there would be land for sale near one of them, though.

It might be good to base his project in the west and get right away from Phil. Besides, any land suitable for what he wanted in the southern part of Queensland had been snapped up by property developers and would be way too expensive for him now.

As the plane took off from Brisbane Airport, he felt as if he was shedding a heavy load and leaned back, sipping a glass of red wine with pleasure. It was a long time since he'd taken any holidays and his mother had been nagging him for a while to get away and unwind. He grinned at the thought. No, not nagging. She never nagged in that sense, but trying to persuade him. She was a red-hot persuader when she thought something was right.

Meriel visited York several more times and in December she found her dream home. It was a hot windy day, with summer dust and dried gum leaves whipping around her car in a strong easterly wind that promised soaring temperatures for the next few days. She followed the directions the real estate agent had given her, driving out from York and losing her way only once on an unmarked side road. In the end, it was the FOR SALE sign which alerted her to the fact that she had arrived, and the fact that it was at a minor crossroads.

She unhooked the gate and drove along a dirt track.

The house stood on a small rise a couple of hundred metres inside the boundary. Somerlee, it was called.

She stopped the car and listened before she got out. Not a man-made sound to be heard. Wonderful! The house was new, but built in the old colonial styling with red bricks, creamy limestone quoins and window frames. There was a corrugated iron roof, gleaming silver in the sunshine. Best of all, there was a huge veranda all round it. She had always loved houses with verandas.

To the rear and down a gentle slope stood a row of European willow trees, probably planted long ago by some homesick migrant. Near them the land looked greener. That must be the creek the agent had told her about, a winter creek which only ran properly in the rainy season. There was a nearly full dam at the bottom of the slope, an ugly shed stood behind the house and a smaller ramshackle one was half-hidden behind it.

She stood stock still, staring, then smiled ruefully. She really liked the look of Somerlee, for some reason she couldn't define. She even liked its name, which made her think of the summer sunshine which gilded everything today. A warm breeze ruffled her hair and parrots were shrieking somewhere nearby. It felt . . . it really did feel as if she'd come home.

Her artist's eye noted immediately that the house was well sited, standing at an angle to the road just before the land began to slope downwards. Another garish FOR SALE sign marred the greenish-beige patch in front of it, which would have been lawn if anyone had given it the slightest encouragement.

She already knew the house was on a combination of bore water and dam water, not a tank filled by rain or a delivery man, so doubted they'd be short of water. Before she went inside, she dragged out the hose pipe and lawn sprinkler, which were lying in a tangled heap at the side, and turned on the tap, standing near it for a moment to let the droplets it flung outwards cool her face. She loved standing under garden sprinklers on hot summer days.

The front door was already unlocked. It seemed like an omen, somehow. Holding her breath she pushed it open.

The house was larger than it had appeared from the outside, but as the agent had told her, it wasn't completely fitted out. There was a big farm-style kitchen, open plan and running into a family room. She could just imagine how that would look in winter, with a log fire in the big combustion stove. She would probably be able to find the wood for it on her own property. It would be fun gathering it and sawing it up.

The other living area consisted of a long room stretching from the front to the rear of the house, probably meant to be both lounge and formal dining room. It would make a wonderful studio. It had the right sort of light, and if she added a skylight, it would be perfect for her needs.

She wandered along to the master bedroom, which had its own en suite bathroom, then into the unfinished wing, which contained three more bedrooms and the bare concrete shell of another bathroom, without tiles or fittings. 'I shan't need two bathrooms, so you can just stay unfinished,' she told it, then corrected herself. 'If I buy the house, that is. Oh, damn, I'm doing it again!'

She was getting a bit worried about her new habit of talking to herself. Then she smiled. You could afford to be a bit eccentric if you were self-employed. No need to wear business suits or spend your days in city canyons. And as for arrogant customers, they could go and jump in the Swan River as far as she was concerned. She had never felt so free and happy in her life.

When she went back to the kitchen she stepped right inside the walk-in pantry, one of the largest she had ever seen. Perhaps the previous owners had meant to grow and preserve their own food. She might grow a few things, too, easy things, but she wasn't going to try to be self-sufficient. That would take up too much of her time and energy.

She jumped in shock when a man's voice right behind her said sharply, 'Excuse me—'

She swung round, saw who it was and gasped.

'You!' Ben Elless seemed as dumbstruck as she was.

Meriel tried to speak but nothing came out. After swallowing hard she managed to say in a shaky voice, 'I thought you lived in Queensland!' Only then did she realize how close they were standing and took a step backwards, pressing herself against the coolness of the wall.

'What are you doing here?'

'That's none of your business! Come to that, you're the last person I'd have expected to meet today. What are *you* doing over here in the west?'

Unfortunately, he was looking more attractive than ever, with his summer tan making his eyes seem a brighter blue. His body looked to be in balance and sure of itself, the body of a man who used his muscles. She would really like to sketch that body.

He gave a short scornful laugh. 'If you remember anything from the short time you were handling my uncle's affairs – and by the way, I consider it highly unprofessional to quit in the middle of a job like that – he owned several country properties near Perth. I came here to look them over.'

'Is this house one of yours?' she demanded. If it was, she would leave at once.

'Well, no. I was just—'

'Then why are *you* here? If you've inherited several places, why would you want another? Or perhaps you're just sticky-beaking?' She fumbled in her skirt pocket and jingled a tagged key so close to his nose he jerked his head back. 'Bill Lansome, the estate agent, gave me a key so that I could look round, so I'm here officially.'

He dragged out a similar key and brandished it at her, saying, 'Snap!' but as he stuffed it back into his jeans pocket, he continued to frown. 'Why would a woman like you be looking at properties out here? Repping told me you'd left the firm, but he didn't say you'd gone into hobby farming.'

'I haven't. I'm merely looking for a place of my own, one with a bit of land.' She hated telling people she'd won Lotto and hated just as much exposing her dreams to strangers.

'A huge place like this?' He raised his eyebrows in such a supercilious manner that she was glad she hadn't told him anything else.

'I didn't know it was so big until I got here and then I couldn't resist exploring.'

'And watering the garden?'

She could feel her colour rising. She knew it was ridiculous to water a stranger's garden. 'I don't like to see plants dying for lack of care. What's wrong with that?'

'Nothing.' His eyes flickered to her ringless fingers. 'Isn't it a bit risky, coming to places like this alone? I'd have thought you'd have brought your boyfriend along to keep you company.'

'Boy friend? I haven't got a—'

'Ah!' he said softly.

She remembered suddenly that she'd pretended to have a steady guy in her life when she'd refused his invitation to dinner. 'Oh. I mean – we've split up.'

His eyes gleamed down at her. 'I'm glad to hear that.'

'I don't know why you should be.'

'Because we could maybe have that dinner together now. Are you staying in York?'

'I'm still too busy to accept!' she said hastily. He was having exactly the same effect on her as before and she didn't like feeling so vulnerable. 'I don't have dinner with everyone who pesters me for a date! I can manage without men, thank you very much!'

'You'll need a man if you're going to live in a place like this?'

'Why? I can change a fuse or hammer in a nail as well as you.'

'There are other jobs that need doing on a place this size. It doesn't take strength to change a fuse, but it does to put in fences and dig up trees.'

'It's the twenty-first century, for heaven's sake! There are power tools to give women the strength you big boys have. And if I can't do something myself,' she jutted her chin out at him, 'I can always hire a set of muscles to do it for me, can't I?'

He grinned. 'Ouch! That was a cruel blow.' Then his smile faded and he looked at her thoughtfully. 'I wouldn't have thought there was much scope for another accountant in a small town like York.'

'I'm not setting up as an accountant, here or anywhere else. I've come into a little money, if you must know. Now, if you've finished here, perhaps I can get on with my inspection. Otherwise, I'll wait outside until you've done.'

He didn't move but stood staring at her. 'I hadn't got you picked for a back-to-the-earth type, somehow.'

'Hadn't you?' She didn't intend to argue that point with him.

'So you're not really interested in buying a place as large as this?'

'I was given a list of properties to inspect so that I could find out what's available. I've got several others to see after this one. *If* that's any concern of yours.'

'Whoops! Sorry!' He opened his arms wide in a gesture of mock contrition. 'I've done it again, haven't I? Made you angry. Why do you always bring out the caveman in me, Ms Ingram?'

'It doesn't take much bringing out.'

'*Are* you staying in York? You didn't say.'

'Because,' she said through gritted teeth, 'that's none of your business.'

'Can't I persuade you to have dinner with me tonight?'

'No.'

'Are you sure?'

'Certain.' Why would he never take no for an answer?

'Is it me or men in general that you dislike?'

She sucked in oxygen. 'I'm just − not looking for any entanglements at the moment.'

'I've only asked you to have dinner with me. I wouldn't exactly call that an entanglement.'

It might turn out to be, the way he affected her. 'The answer is still no. Thank you, but no.'

He shrugged. 'Pity. Another time, perhaps. I'm not giving up hope. Who knows when Fate may bring us together again? It's certainly lent a hand today.'

As far as she was concerned, Fate could just butt out again and leave her to manage her own life.

He moved towards the door, pausing to raise one hand in a farewell salute, smiling that pirate's grin that made her toes curl. 'I'll leave you to do your research, then, Ms Ingram. And to finish watering the lawn. Happy house hunting!'

As he walked away, Ben's smile faded and he growled under his breath, furious with himself. Why did that woman always affect him like this? Fancy pressuring her for a date again!

He didn't allow himself to turn round for a final glimpse of her. Dammit, he should have better control over himself than this! He was thirty-four, not fourteen!

He didn't stop to look back until he was hidden by some trees. To his surprise she was still standing on the veranda, hands on hips, staring in his direction.

She was just as attractive when angry. He grinned again. And she had a way with words! 'Hire a set of muscles' indeed! Was that what she thought he was?

He was sure a single woman wouldn't be interested in a property with that much land, most of it undeveloped bush. If she was house hunting, she'd be looking for an acre or two of land at most. He'd come back later to look round properly, though the land was more important to his plans than the house.

He walked off through the bush to his four-wheel drive, trying to turn his thoughts to other matters.

But they refused to turn.

She was not only gorgeous, but feisty. He didn't think he'd ever had such a prompt and decisive turn-down, though. He must be getting old, losing his touch – if he'd ever had a touch with women. He'd not been interested in another woman since Sandy.

Until now.

Meriel stood on the veranda and watched him stride off up the grassy slope as if he owned it. If he'd parked somewhere else on the block, he must have a four-wheel drive.

But though she listened for a car engine starting, she heard nothing. In the end she decided she'd spent far too much time on Ben Elless and turned round to continue her exploration of the house and grounds.

She couldn't have left the garden plants to die in the hot spell that was coming, whether she was interested in the house or not, but she was interested, very. By the time she'd found a bucket and carried water to the semi-circle of wilting young trees on the other side of the big shed, the sprinkler needed moving again. 'The place is far too big for one person,' she told herself as she watched the arcs of water droplets sparkle in the sunlight.

She shook her head ruefully. She was a fool. She'd fallen in love with it! There was something attractive and special about the green hollow behind the house, with the dam below it and the cluttered bush and scrub on the slope which rose beyond that.

While the rest of the lawn was receiving a good soaking, she cleared an old plastic garden chair of spider webs and went to sit on it in the dappled green shade beneath one of the willow trees, thinking hard. Insects buzzed a counterpoint to her thoughts and the graceful fronds around her made a faint swishing noise as the hot breeze rippled through them. She felt as if she were sitting in the middle of an impressionist painting, all light and shade, and some of the shadows really did look purple.

This would need careful planning, though. The asking price was higher than she'd planned for and the house still needed finishing.

After a while she locked up and got into her car, starting up the engine reluctantly, not wanting to disturb the peace and quiet. She'd better go and have a quick look at the rest of the properties on the estate agent's list. If he found out how much she liked this one, that she hadn't gone to inspect the others, she would lose all her bargaining power.

When she got back to Bill Lansome's office that afternoon, she sat and discussed the properties she'd seen.

'You know, Meriel,' he said after a while, 'from what you're telling me, Somerlee fits your criteria best. I don't have a lot of properties that size. We have some huge farms for sale sometimes, but they'd not be what you want. Why don't you go and have another look at it?'

'We-ell, it's quite nice, but I'm not into do-it-yourself.' This was an outright lie, which gave her a brief twinge of conscience.

'The main living areas need nothing doing to them.'

'They're unpainted and I don't have the money to finish off the rest of the house properly.' Another whopping falsehood.

'But you do like it?'

'I think so. Only the asking price is way too high. No,'

she picked up her handbag as if making ready to leave, 'I'd better look for something that wouldn't entail so much expense, something smaller. Perhaps the estate agent across the road has something. Or I could try another town.'

Bill leaned forward in his chair. 'Don't go yet! Before you dismiss Somerlee entirely, let's look at the whole situation. I will admit to you – in the strictest confidence, mind – that the vendors are being rather optimistic in setting such a high price on it. I told them so, but they insisted and it's been on the market for a while. You couldn't have chosen a better time to buy, Miss – er – *Ms* Ingram. You could get yourself a real bargain here.'

She hummed and hawed, but allowed him to continue for a while, then left his office without committing herself. She did, however, agree to let Bill show her round some more properties the next day and to look over Somerlee again with him, so that he could point out its advantages.

She wondered as she walked away if Ben Elless really was interested in the place. No, he couldn't be. He was based in Queensland. He was probably just looking round it because it was near one of his uncle's properties. She couldn't remember where exactly they were, but there had been several in this area.

Ria's mobile phone rang and when she saw it was Bill Lansome she answered it. They knew each other from way back and he'd helped her a lot since her ex-husband ran off with most of their money.

'Don't move to that empty block I told you about yet, Ria. I've got a buyer interested. She's playing it cool, but I can spot genuine interest a mile off.'

With a sigh, Ria switched off her phone and turned to Pete. 'We can't move to that place after all. Bill thinks he's about to sell it.'

'We still have to be away from here by the end of the week, though, and you know how Big Jim hates living in caravan parks.'

'So do I.' She sat down to think. People thought they were crazy, living like a group of hippies in the twenty-first century, but she'd never been as happy. Nor had her kids.

Pete was right. Jim couldn't cope with people for long. Who'd have thought that service in the Vietnam War would mark a strong man like him for life?

Pete came to sit beside her. 'There's a block of land over the hill that might suit us temporarily. As far as I can see, the owners haven't been near it for years, except for having the fire breaks put in. Want to come and look at it?'

She beamed at him. 'We'll all go. Even if we can just stay there for a month or two, it'll be a help.'

Ten

Meriel had come prepared to stay overnight in York so went to look for a hotel. The old sign painted on the gable of one place: 'Rooms for Respectable Married Couples' made her chuckle as she passed it in the street, so she went inside.

It was a modernized two-storey colonial building, with verandas and balconies, typical early Australian architecture. Her upstairs room was cool and shaded, furnished with old-fashioned wooden pieces instead of shiny plastic furniture. It looked out over brick-paved courtyards filled with tubs of plants and flowers.

She wished she had someone to spend the evening with. Perhaps she should have accepted Ben Elless's invitation? No, better not. She'd checked the hotel register before she booked a room, to make sure he wasn't staying there. If he had been, she'd have found somewhere else.

When she went down that evening Meriel found the restaurant as quietly elegant as the rest of the hotel. As she was choosing her meal, a shadow fell across the table and she looked up into Ben Elless' smiling, sun-tanned face. Her heart started to thud and the worst of it was that she didn't know whether she was glad or sorry to see him.

'I'd really welcome some company tonight. May I join you?'

She hesitated, trying to resist the temptation to say yes, and failing.

'Please?' he begged, clasping his hands together at his chest in a gesture of mock supplication.

'Well . . .' she began, then fell silent. He really did have the most delightful smile. And perhaps if she got to know him better, it might cure her of this ridiculous reaction every time she saw him. 'You must be in the mood for an argument, Elless,' she said, smiling back at him in spite of herself.

'Couldn't we cry truce tonight? I'll promise to be on my

very best behaviour, if you'll just smile kindly at me from time to time.'

'Oh – why not? Sit down.'

It was his turn to hesitate. 'Be honest. Would you rather I took another table? I won't impose myself on you if I'm making you feel uncomfortable. After all, you've already refused to have dinner with me four times.'

'I'd welcome a bit of company tonight, actually.' What harm could there possibly be in sharing a table with him for one meal? As he sat down, she took the initiative firmly into her own hands. 'Tell me about yourself.'

'Thirty-four, in excellent health, only child. And you?'

'That's a thumbnail sketch if ever I heard one.' He was probably married. He must be married, a good-looking man like him. It was out before she could stop herself. 'Are you married?'

He stiffened. 'That's a very personal question.'

She raised her brows. 'I like to know where I stand with people.'

He tossed the question back at her. 'Why? Are *you* married?'

'No.'

'Divorced?'

'Certainly not! When I marry – if I ever do – it'll be for ever, as far as I'm concerned. I don't believe in on-off relationships. And you didn't answer my question. *Are* you married?'

'Not now.'

Why did she feel so disappointed. 'Divorced?'

'No.' He took a deep breath, then said in a quiet level voice that didn't match the pain on his face, 'My wife died in a car accident.'

'Oh, I'm so sorry. I didn't mean to . . .' Meriel couldn't think what to say, so laid her hand on his for a moment.

Before she could pull away, he had taken hold of her hand, as if he needed the comfort she was offering. He was looking down at it as he added, 'It happened four years ago. I should be used to it by now, but the memory still sinks its claws in sometimes.'

From the expression on his face, he must have loved his

wife very much. That was hard to reconcile with the image she'd built up in her mind. She looked away, giving him time to recover, but didn't like to pull her hand away.

When she raised her eyes to his, the mood changed again and he gave her a wry smile. 'Sexual attraction can spring up between the unlikeliest people, can't it?' He chuckled at her discomfiture. 'You did say you like to know where you stand, didn't you?'

She could feel the flush creeping across her face and couldn't think of a smart response.

He let go of her hand and picked up the menu. 'What shall we eat, then, Ms Ingram?'

'Why do you keep addressing me so formally?' She was rather puzzled by that after such a frank exchange.

'Because I don't actually know your first name, except that it begins with an M.' He put his head on one side. 'Mary doesn't suit you, nor does Margaret. Miranda, perhaps? Or Matilda?'

She couldn't help laughing. 'Not quite. My name's Meriel.'

'Meriel. Unusual, but it suits you. What on earth is a woman like you doing looking at properties in a small country town like York?'

'What do you mean by "a woman like me"?'

'Someone so attractive. You should be on the front cover of magazines, not hidden away on the back blocks.'

She could feel herself blushing furiously.

His voice was honey-warm as he murmured, for her ears only, 'You must be aware that you're good looking. I'm surprised you didn't go into modelling with that face and hair.'

She had never been good at accepting compliments, especially about her looks. 'I'm not tall enough. Models are usually six foot tall. I'm a shortie, only five foot two.'

'*Five foot two, eyes of blue,*' he sang in a rich baritone voice. '*Has anybody seen my girl?* Do you always blush like that when someone pays you a compliment?'

She scowled at him. 'Yes. So don't do it again. And my eyes are green, not blue.'

He smiled and patted her hand. 'I'll stick to insults and witty repartee from now on, then. So what *are* you doing here, Meriel?'

'I'm looking for a place I can call my own, a small house with a few acres and a view – as I already told you. And now that I don't need to work for my living any more – or at least, not full-time, I can please myself.'

'It must have been a considerable legacy.'

'Enough to manage on for a while, if I'm careful.'

'And have you found your Shangri-La yet?'

Innate caution made her say, 'Not yet.'

'What will you do with yourself when you do find your country retreat? Won't you get bored all on your own?'

'Perhaps. I don't think so, though. I have my – er – hobbies.'

'Dare one ask what they are?'

'If *one* is prepared to talk about one's own life and pastimes,' she retorted. 'What were *you* doing out at Somerlee?'

'Looking round my uncle's properties – especially the one where I used to spend the summers when I was a lad. I need to get some idea of their value and look at what borders them.'

There. She'd known he wasn't seriously looking for a home. 'And what do *you* do for a living?'

'Landscape gardening. Though it's more of an obsession, really.'

'*Gardening!* I can't imagine *you* gardening.'

'Now why do I feel you're not being complimentary when you say that? I'll have you know that I'm besotted with begonias, rabid about roses and quite delirious about delphiniums.'

She had to laugh and when he joined in, she realized yet again how attractive he was. Seeking a safer, less personal topic, she steered the discussion round to native plants and the correct way to develop a native garden in Australia. York wasn't in the outback, where you measured your property in square miles. It reminded her in some ways of England, a cosy little town, surrounded by rolling hills with occasional outcrops of smooth, rounded rock. But the colours were different. The grass in the fields had now turned to its summer shade of dusty beige, the soil was reddish and the gum trees were dull green in tone, not the fresh green of English foliage.

Even the houses were very different – one storey mostly, with colonial styling and verandas. Some of them were old and shabby, with corrugated tin roofs and walls formed by strips of wood on a rickety frame. They looked as if they'd blow down in a strong breeze.

Ben was very well informed about the techniques of landscaping with native plants, and she found what he said both interesting and useful. When he recommended a couple of books for beginners, she took out her notebook and jotted the titles down.

He chuckled. 'I might have known you'd carry a notebook.'

'What do you mean by that?'

'You even look as if you're well organized.'

'Not all blondes are dumb, Elless.'

'Indeed, they're not, Ingram. My mother's a blonde and no one would ever call her stupid.'

That remark disarmed her completely. He was, she decided, looking at him sideways, quite lethally attractive. She shouldn't have risked this encounter. She was sure he had set out to charm her this evening and he had succeeded, too, damn him!

When the meal was over, she excused herself and he made no attempt to detain her or follow her to her room, just walked with her to the door of the restaurant and left her there with a casual wave of the hand.

She had to admit to a touch of disappointment about that. Maybe he was only passing a pleasant hour in her company and would forget her as soon as he walked away. No! That wasn't true. He'd talked about the attraction between them and they'd both experienced it. Anyway, his eyes spoke for him. They showed exactly how he felt, lingering on her face, smiling at her, ignoring everything else that was happening in the room.

She hoped her eyes hadn't betrayed too much of what she was feeling.

Loneliness hit her as she locked the door of her room behind her and since she wanted someone to give her an unbiased opinion of Somerlee, she rang Rosanna before she went to bed.

'Would you like to drive out to York for lunch tomorrow and look over a place I'm thinking of buying?'

'York? Why do you want to live so far out of the city?'

'For the peace and quiet. Will you come?'

'Of course I will, but I'll have to bring Karl. Where are you? OK. Got that. We'll meet you at ten, then. Good thing I'm an early riser.'

'Thanks. I'll buy lunch.'

'No need. It'll make a pleasant day out. Look, I'll bring my cousin Paolo as well. He's in the building industry and knows all about property.'

She rang off before Meriel could protest that she did not want a date with Paolo. How many cousins did her friend have?

Meriel asked Rosanna not to appear enthusiastic in front of Bill when he showed them Somerlee. No pretence was needed. Rosanna teetered around the property in high-heeled sandals, shrieking at the sight of a big racehorse goanna running along the ground near the damp creek bed. She shuddered at the numerous skinks running in and out of crevices on the back veranda, though the tiny lizards were a common sight in the city as well, and she complained loudly about the isolation.

As the four of them stood in the kitchen, Paolo turned to Meriel and whispered earnestly, 'Not good, this place. Lousy location. Poor resale value.'

Watching her friend cuddle up to Karl, Meriel thought how nice it must be to be so much in love. Since the fiasco with Gary she seemed to have lost the ability to trust anyone wholeheartedly.

Get real, Ingram! she told herself. *The last thing you need at the moment is a guy in your life.*

She went to stand by the family room window, watching the estate agent stroll up and down the lawn to give them time to talk privately about Somerlee. 'I love it here,' she said softly. 'I think I'm going to make an offer. No, don't try to change my mind, because you won't. But don't tell Bill when he comes inside again. I'll leave it for a while, then I'll let him persuade me to try a low offer. Shh! He's coming . . . Hi, Bill. We're just leaving. I'll have to think things over.'

'But you do like Somerlee?'

'I like it but I don't like the price. I told you: I'm not made of money. And there's too much land.'

'It's not a good place for a woman on her own,' said Paolo severely.

Rosanna moved forward. 'Haven't you got something nearer town to show us, Mr Lansome? Something with neighbours?'

'This place has neighbours, well, one neighbour, anyway.'

'I can't see any other houses,' Rosanna objected. 'Neighbours should be within screaming distance, if you want my opinion.'

His scowl said he didn't.

'Who's the neighbour?' Meriel nudged her friend to be quiet.

'Johnny Elless's nephew.'

'What?' Meriel's heart did a big somersault. Right next door? Why did Fate keep throwing her and Ben together?

'He's living in Johnny's old shack, just over the rise there. Nice young fellow, he is. Single, too.' He winked at Meriel as he said that.

She kept her expression calm only with an effort. 'I've already met him. He told me he lived in Queensland.'

'He does. He's not here permanently, just visiting for a week or two. Used to come here as a lad, I remember. He's inherited a few other properties in the district as well. Great believer in the future of our region, old Johnny was. Sad loss that he died so young. Only seventy-one, you know.'

Meriel decided they'd been discussing Ben Elless and his concerns for too long. 'Yes, well, I wish Mr Elless luck. Are you open on Sundays, Bill? Right, then, I'll come into your office tomorrow. You said you might have some other places to show me. We'll talk it all over then. Perhaps something nearer town would suit me better, as Rosanna said.'

After that the four of them went for lunch and a stroll round town, but Meriel was glad when the others returned to Perth. There was absolutely no spark between her and Paolo, though he was a pleasant enough guy, as you would expect of Rosanna's cousin.

She sat on the balcony of her hotel room for a while, going over her calculations and mentally reviewing the situation. Perhaps she would stay on for another night or two so that she could get to know the area better. No need to make any final decisions today.

In the evening, she again put on the one smart dress she'd brought with her, midnight blue with a soft, floaty skirt that could travel without crushing. As she went down to the restaurant, she couldn't help wondering whether she'd see Ben again, hoping she would. He was an interesting companion, a good talker and an equally good listener.

She was disappointed to see no sign of him in the restaurant. How pitiful was that!

He appeared in the dining room only minutes after she'd sat down, however, and she wasn't surprised when he strolled across to join her. 'Another day's house-hunting?' He smiled and sat down opposite her, this time without asking if she minded.

She found herself smiling back at him. 'Some friends came out to have lunch with me and we inspected one or two more places, but I haven't offered for anything.' She wasn't going to tell him about revisiting Somerlee. Her Grandpop had taught her always to play her cards close to her chest.

'There's a lot to see here. The old jail and courthouse are particularly interesting. You won't believe how tiny the cells are, not much bigger than a single bed.' This led them into a lively discussion about the preservation of old buildings.

When the meal was over Ben looked at her with the devastating smile that made his eyes glint wickedly and his whole face shift into softer lines. 'Do you intend to flee to your bedroom immediately, or can I persuade you to take a stroll with me along the main street and have a nightcap in one of the hotels? It's a lovely warm evening.'

'I'd really enjoy a stroll, but I've had enough to drink, thank you.'

'A coffee, then?'

Afterwards, he escorted her right to the door of her room, but she made no move to invite him in. When he took her into his arms, she held herself away from him, looked up at him and said bluntly, 'I'm not into casual sex, Ben.'

'Not even a goodnight kiss?'

'Well – I—' Before she could move away, he bent his head towards her and then she forgot everything as he kissed her. When he drew away she clung to him with both hands or she'd have fallen.

'Are you sure you want it to stop there?' he murmured.

No, she didn't want it to stop there. She wanted – What was she thinking of? He lived in Queensland, for heaven's sake, two thousand miles away from Western Australia. Nothing could come of a relationship between them.

She pushed at his shoulders in sudden panic, more worried she might give way and invite him in than that he might try to force his way in. 'Yes. Yes, I'm sure. Very sure!' She fumbled in her bag for her room key.

One hand covered hers. 'Hey, don't panic! I can take no for an answer. However, I have a feeling that things won't end here.'

She scrabbled in her bag. 'I won't change my mind. And anyway, you live two thousand miles away.' Her fingers found the room key and she pulled it out with such haste she dropped it.

'Here. Let me.' He picked up the keys, unlocked the door and dropped the jangling bunch into her hand with a flourishing bow, stepping back and making no attempt to touch her again.

'Thank you.' Her voice was a mere gasp of air.

'Goodnight,' he said softly, as he turned away. 'Pleasant dreams.'

She didn't wait to see him walk away, but went quickly into the room, shutting the door and leaning against it.

Why had she panicked like that? She couldn't explain it. She certainly wasn't afraid of him.

On the other side of town Ben Elless slept badly, annoyed about the effect Meriel Ingram was having on him, the way he couldn't stop thinking about her. She was not only invading his thoughts but also sauntering through his dreams. He was juggling his various business interests to keep up a steady cash flow, working out how to buy Phil out and doing some serious planning for his next project. There wasn't *time* for romance on his busy agenda.

His thoughts stopped dead on that word. Romance! This wasn't anything to do with romance or love. It was simply a healthy man's attraction to a lovely woman.

He must focus on the long-term picture. He and Sandy had planned to develop their own business in a place where they could enjoy family life. He was good at making things grow and the rarest of plants responded to his touch, but he had bigger ideas than that, ideas that would lead to a small but upmarket tourist and garden centre, with accommodation – the sort of place families might come to for an outing or a pleasant night away.

This inheritance from Uncle Johnny had been a godsend, even though it was going to take him a while to sort out the financial side of things. It would give him a great start.

He would be glad to get out of the business. Phil seemed to be going off the rails again. Uncle Rod was the only person who could rein his son in, but when Ben had visited the old man in hospital he'd been shocked by how much Rod had aged lately.

He pushed the thought of business to the back of his brain, telling himself to relax and go to sleep. To his annoyance, Meriel's face instantly replaced it. It wasn't just her looks that attracted him, it was her gutsiness, the way she marched through life with a firm step.

A grin slid across his face. Well, until he kissed her, that was. That had flustered her big time. It was some consolation that he seemed to be having the same effect on her as she was having on him.

And if he didn't get some decent sleep he'd be good for nothing. He had to get things settled here before Christmas because there was a big project that needed finishing in Brisbane before he could think of selling the business there.

The next morning Meriel went back to Somerlee on her own and walked around the property for a while, going right over to the side fence in the direction Bill Lansome had pointed when he talked about her neighbour. She stood

there by the thread of rusty barbed wire that separated the
two properties only nominally, staring at the ramshackle tin
and weatherboard house next door. From here she could
see how badly the roof and veranda sagged. It looked as if
it would fall down in a strong wind. Surely Ben Elless wasn't
living in that? She couldn't see any sign of a car or of *him*,
but she didn't tempt providence by going any closer.

When she returned to town she strolled into Bill Lansome's
office and let him sound her out about her intentions. After
a while, she said cautiously, 'Well, I might make an offer on
Somerlee – it has some potential and I do like the view –
but I definitely can't afford the asking price.' She frowned
and added for good measure, 'And I don't know what I'm
going to do with all that land.'

'The land will take care of itself. You can always subdivide
and sell it later. It's not as if it's an orchard property, after
all, where you'd have to tend hundreds of trees. The Australian
bush has existed for millions of years without mankind's
help and it will still be there when we're all gone. Why
don't you just put in an offer?'

His voice had taken on that coaxing tone salesmen always
used when they felt they were about to clinch a sale. She
kept her expression worried. 'I don't know. I really don't.'

'I'll make sure the owners give your offer very serious
consideration.'

'Well – all right, then.' She named a price that made his
hand hesitate over the page, but she knew a low bid would
be a better starting point. 'Subject to the usual termite checks
and so on.'

'Very well. But don't hold your breath. That's rather a low
offer. Maybe there's a bit of room to manoeuvre?'

She sucked in her breath and pretended to reconsider,
then shook her head. 'I don't think so. But it *is* cash. I came
into some money recently.'

'Ah.'

After she'd signed the offer to buy, she decided to return
to Perth. She didn't want to risk another encounter with
Ben Elless.

If that was running away, she didn't care. There was no use
starting a relationship with a man who lived in Queensland.

You had to be sensible about such things – unfortunately. Look what had happened the last time she'd let an attractive man overwhelm her. Never again.

Her villa in Perth seemed smaller and more claustrophobic than ever, with the noise of other tenants' television programmes wafting in through the open windows so that she had to switch on her own set in sheer self-defence. She got out her sketch pad, but couldn't settle to anything. Even the television programmes were absolutely puerile, she thought, flipping from one channel to another.

She could have been having dinner with Ben tonight!

No, she wasn't that stupid.

Should she ring Rosanna and tell her about putting in an offer on Somerlee? No, not yet. She would feel she'd be tempting providence if she said anything before her offer was accepted.

At eight o'clock, the phone rang. 'Bill Lansome here.'

Meriel stiffened and excitement pulsed through her, but she kept her voice cool. 'Yes?'

'About your offer – could you raise it by a couple of thousand?'

'I told you: I'm on a limited budget.'

'Well, the problem is they've had another offer, a thousand more than yours. Amazing, isn't it? Two offers in one day, just like that. Only the other offer isn't cash, and it depends on the sale of a couple of other places, so if you can go just a little higher, cash, you'll get the place, for sure.'

'Hmm.' She chewed on her thumb nail, wondering if this was just a story designed to pump up the price. Then she remembered Bill's open face and blunt country ways and sighed. No, he wasn't the sort to tell lies. She was pretty sure of that. There really must have been another offer. And she couldn't bear to lose Somerlee. She was already living there in her imagination. 'All right. Another two thousand – but not a cent more!'

He rang back within the hour. 'Good news. Your offer's been accepted. The fact that it was a cash offer turned the scales, as I thought it would.'

'Good.'

'They want to get everything settled quickly. It's one of those acrimonious divorces. They quarrel every time they visit my office.' He chuckled. 'Look, how about I nip down to Perth tomorrow morning to get your signature on the amendments?'

'Fine by me.'

When she put the phone down, Meriel sat there beside it staring blindly into space, astonished that things could be settled so easily. She remembered the fuss when her sister was buying a house, the worries about being gazumped, the nail biting as they waited two months for the English solicitor to settle everything. Here in Australia an offer to buy a house was binding once it was accepted and it was settled much more quickly too.

So that was it. She'd done it: given up her job, bought a house and made possible the sort of life she had dreamed of for so long, a peaceful life as an artist.

Pity Ben Elless didn't live in Western Australia. Sometimes this country felt like two different countries, the West and the rest.

Bill was pleased with himself. You couldn't beat a juicy cash sale. He'd had a local guy inspect that block a couple of months previously and Terry had talked of putting in a development, but nothing had come of it. Some places were like that, hung around for months or even years. He'd been going to arrange for Ria and her friends to stay there, paying the owners a minimal rent and keeping the garden tidy. He'd have to keep his eyes open for somewhere else for them. Pity Ria's husband had lost all her money. She and the kids didn't deserve that.

He was amazed when Terry came bursting into his office a couple of days later.

'What the hell are you doing to me, Bill? I thought we had an agreement.'

'Come again?'

'Selling that block from under me. You didn't even give me a chance to better their offer.'

Bill scowled at him. 'You never made an offer. How was I to know you were still seriously interested?'

'I *told* you I'm working with some developers from Perth looking for land round here.'

'But you never got back to me.'

'They're not going to be pleased about this. They thought it was in the bag. They've already started developing concept plans.'

'Too bad.'

'Well, I don't think they'll take this lying down. Don't say I didn't warn you.' He stormed out.

Bill shook his head sadly. He'd known Terry Powers for years and nothing had ever come of his money-making schemes.

This would have been just another flash in the pan, he was sure. Even if there were any Perth developers, which he doubted.

Eleven

Ben was called back to Brisbane to deal with an emergency. He was bitterly disappointed when he phoned Bill Lansome and found that someone had put in a better offer than his. 'Why didn't you *tell* me?' he asked.

'I did tell you and suggest you better it if you were still interested. I sent an email to your office in Brisbane.'

'It never arrived. Are you sure you got the address right?'

Bill repeated it correctly, adding, 'I tagged it for confirmation and got a response that said it'd gone through *and* been read.'

'I'd have raised the offer if I'd known. I *really* wanted that block.'

'Probably wouldn't have done much good, unless you raised the money considerably. This was a cash offer. Yours was subject to finance. My vendors wanted a quick sale.'

'Who bought it?'

'That lady friend of yours.'

'Meriel Ingram?' Fury coursed through Ben. She'd let him think she wasn't interested. And now he'd lost the block that was the pivot of his plans for the future. 'I see. Thank you for letting me know.'

He didn't slam the phone down, but it was a few minutes before he let go of the anger for long enough to start working out what to do.

He'd never been so mistaken about a woman in all his life! But he wasn't going to let her get away with this.

The next day Ben finished earlier than he'd expected at the current project and went back to the office to talk to his partner.

He found Phil just about to leave. 'I thought we'd arranged to discuss our partnership after work today.'

'No can do. Important function to attend. New clients to bring to the fold.'

Ben was determined to have this out. 'We don't need new clients. This is my last project. I told you that.'

Phil glanced at his watch. 'Let's discuss it in a week or two. I'm taking Cheryl and the kids away for a few days. Don't you ever relax?'

'I also told you that I'd be back in Western Australia by then.'

Phil gave him one assessing look, heaved an aggrieved sigh and went back inside. He didn't go far, but sat down on the edge of the reception desk, folding his arms with a long-suffering air. 'Well?'

'Before we start our discussion, what happened to the email from Bill Lansome?'

'Who's he?'

'Don't pretend. He sent an email here, using the office address.'

'Don't remember it. If it arrived it'll be on the computer.'

'I've checked and it isn't there. But the sender told me it not only arrived but someone clicked on the link to say it'd been read.'

'Well, it wasn't me. Are you doubting my word?'

'Yes I am. I'm very unhappy about that email going missing. It lost me something I wanted.'

Phil's expression remained bland and bored.

'It won't affect my decision, though. It's time for us to go our different ways and since you won't go, I will.'

'Now is *not* the time to bail out. The company's doing really well, we've got several potential clients lined up and you're hot stuff as a landscape designer. Why throw all that away?'

'Because I'm tired of the pressure. I want a quieter life and now that I've come into some money, I'm going to get it.'

'From what you've said, the money you inherited from your uncle is peanuts.' Phil waved one hand dismissively. 'Don't you realize we're on to a good thing here, a chance to make big money? With your skills and my contacts we're going to cream the market. You'll soon be able to employ a team of designers and—'

'I like to do my own designs and I've never wanted to

be rich, only to have enough money to buy my own piece
of land.'

'Don't be an idiot. You'll get as much money as you want
if you stick with me for a few years. Now, I really do have
to go.' Phil stood up and moved towards the door.

Ben barred the way. 'I heard you'd been seen at the casino
again.'

'Did you indeed?'

'Yes. And the information came from a reliable source.'
His mother.

'Well, I had a client who wanted to go there, couldn't say
no.'

'How much did you lose?'

'I didn't; I won.'

There was silence, then Phil flourished a mocking bow
and walked out.

After a moment's hesitation Ben followed, in time to see
Phil drive away in a brand new BMW. Where had he got the
money for that? If Phil was gambling again, it was definitely
good that they were going to dissolve the partnership, because
it was only a matter of time before his partner started losing
heavily. He always did.

Back in the office Ben picked up the phone, managing
to get an appointment with his lawyer the next day. Then
he rang a friend who sold real estate and told him he needed
to dispose of all the property he owned in Queensland,
making another appointment for the following day.

If he wanted a new life, he had to make a clean break with
all this and that wouldn't upset him. He stared round his elegant
office, hating the tortured clumps of fashionable indoor plants
that an office designer had brought in, the angular modern
furniture and the stark blinds. Phil's office was bigger and even
more showy than his.

If Ben couldn't get that land back that *she* had stolen from
under his nose, he'd sell his uncle's block and look else-
where. Trouble was, with the extra land, that place would
be perfect for his needs. It had exactly the right configura-
tion. No he'd *have to* get it back. Meriel Ingram would no
doubt hold him to ransom on the price, but it'd be worth
the extra money in the long run.

From his boyhood knowledge of the local bush, he had plenty of ideas for how to develop that block. And the place had sentimental value too, memories of carefree summers and an uncle who always had time for him.

In fact, he'd set his heart on settling there.

Ben had agreed to spend Christmas Day with Sandy's family. He found it awkward because some of them made it clear they were on Phil's side. Even his father-in-law took him aside and had a quiet word with him about sticking with the people who had helped set him up in business in the first place.

Ben kept his voice calm. 'I take it Phil's told you I'm leaving once this project is finished?'

'You can't mean that, lad! You're not even giving him time to find a new designer.'

'I told him last August. He's had plenty of time to find someone else.'

'Men with your skills and talent aren't easy to replace. Surely you can stay on until—'

Suddenly Ben had had enough. 'No, I can't and I won't. Did *you* know Phil's gambling again?'

'He knows better than to get into that again.'

Phil's wife also took time to scold Ben for trying to break things up. 'What will the children and I do if he doesn't have an income?' Cheryl demanded, tears in her eyes. 'And to do it so abruptly, too. I'd thought better of you, Ben.'

He'd seen before how easily she wept, how she used her tears as a weapon to manipulate people, so he wasn't going to be taken in by that. 'I told him last August,' he repeated wearily. 'That's not abrupt. And you and your children aren't *my* responsibility.'

Strangely enough, only Phil's father didn't harangue Ben, or even mention his son. Rod Hantley had grown very quiet these days and looked frail, but he sat and watched everything with his usual interest. Ben had a long chat with him about his plans. It was the only part of the evening he enjoyed.

He left early, feeling guilty even though he knew he had nothing to feel guilty about. But he *wouldn't* continue working with Phil.

He spent Boxing Day in Brisbane with his mother and the new guy she was seeing. He suspected it was turning into something serious and was glad for her. She'd coped bravely with losing two husbands. But Jim seemed a really nice guy – and was younger than her, a fitness fanatic, so maybe he wouldn't die on her. She was still an attractive woman, looking and acting younger than her age.

In the evening Ben went for a stroll with her. After a few minutes, she asked casually, 'Who is she?'

Ben stiffened. 'What do you mean?'

'I've seen you in love before, remember. You're wearing all the signs, staring into space, sighing.'

'I'm not in love, Mum. In lust, more likely.'

'That's important too.'

'Not with this woman. She's pulled a sneaky trick on me. Anyway, I haven't *time* to fall in love. I've too much to sort out.'

'Tell me to mind my own business if you'd rather not talk about it, but are you having business troubles with Phil?'

He nodded.

'If it's money you need, I could find a little.'

'I'd not take it.' He hesitated then said, 'Phil and I have different views of where we want to go. It's more than time to end the partnership, which I'll do after I've finished this project.'

'Thank heavens for that! I never did trust him.'

He looked quickly sideways. 'You didn't say anything.'

'How could I when he was Sandy's cousin? Anyway, I'd hoped it might have been the making of him. Everyone deserves a second chance.'

'That's what his family said at the time. Now, half of them are blaming me for not continuing to support him, so I suppose if he goes to the wall they'll blame me for that, too.'

'He's a big boy, should be able to support himself by now.' She hesitated. 'Is your investment money all right? You shouldn't have left everything to him to sort out after Sandy died.'

'No, that's OK.'

'And you're well over the deep grief now.' She hugged his arm close to her side.

'Yes . . . only I feel guilty about finding another woman attractive.'

'You shouldn't. Life has to go on. It's normal to grieve and equally normal to make new relationships.'

Ben's time with his mother was the brightest spot of the whole holiday.

For Meriel, Christmas came and went in a blur of packing, getting new business cards printed and buying art supplies. She had a meal with Rosanna and her family on Christmas Day, at which everyone drank to her happiness in her new home.

'I'm going to miss you, Rosanna,' she said as her friend walked her out to her car.

'Well, you'll still be able to phone and email, and you can always invite me to visit. As long as Karl can come too. He's asked me to marry him, but I'm not telling Mum yet. You know how she'll fuss.'

'Well, there's a permanent invitation for you both to visit. No warning needed. Just turn up. You know that.'

Rosanna gave her a smacking kiss on each cheek. 'I do. And we'll come. Take care.'

Meriel moved to York two weeks after Christmas. The day was a scorcher, over a hundred degrees by the old Fahrenheit scale, the sort of temperature still called a 'century'.

On the appointed day she saw her possessions loaded into a small removal truck then drove to York on her own. A flat tyre slowed her down a little, but she changed that quickly and still managed to arrive at her new home half an hour before her furniture. The two men sweated the meagre collection of items inside, dumped things where she pointed and hurried off as soon as they could. Like everyone else, they seemed to think her mad for wanting to live alone on such a big block.

As the truck throbbed away into the distance, she heaved a sigh of relief and went back inside to start sorting out the chaos of cardboard boxes. She looked round and grinned. She had one double bed, a rocking chair, a cheap plastic garden table and six matching chairs, a computer desk, another old, scarred desk, an easel, a big cabinet for her art supplies and a large old sofa. Not nearly enough to furnish this house.

When she had finished unpacking as far as she could until she bought some drawers, she went out on to the veranda and sat there with a glass of chilled white wine to celebrate her new home.

As darkness fell softly around her it was filled with quiet rustlings, the murmur of the breeze in the trees and dozens of small animal noises. She sighed happily. Her life seemed to have been filled with one trauma after another since the age of fifteen, ending in her migration to Australia. You never understood how life-changing and traumatic that was going to be until you did it.

But everything had altered on the day she'd won Lotto. They said money didn't bring you happiness, but it had given her peace of mind, which was pretty close to happiness. She'd needed the security of something behind her, she knew.

The next morning she went into York to do some shopping, dressing casually in a white skirt, aqua top and flat white sandals, the whole outfit crowned by a wide-brimmed straw hat around which she had twisted an aqua-toned scarf. Even at this early hour of the morning heat was beating up from the pavements but the wide awnings provided cooler shadows from which to study the contents of the shop windows. She walked along happily, catching herself humming at one stage and hoping no one had heard. She'd never minded the heat, though she had to be careful not to get too much sun on her fair skin.

She stopped first at the tourist office, which also sold souvenirs and local books. After buying a postcard with a picture of the main street on it to send to her mother, she moved on. She fell in love with a dried flower arrangement in another shop, a huge basket crammed with wildflowers in every shade of blue, pink and mauve. She simply had to buy it. It would cheer up her living area.

It was astounding the variety of wildflowers that grew in Western Australia. No wonder the tourists flocked in to see them every spring. She still had a glowing memory of the

living carpets of blue and gold that she'd seen in this area
the previous year. Next spring she would try to paint them.
No wonder Manet had laboured over his fields of poppies
and Monet had been obsessed by his water lilies.

She wondered suddenly what wildflowers grew on her
block. There were bound to be many varieties in the
untouched bush areas, maybe even some of the tiny native
orchids she thought so much prettier than their large
commercial counterparts. They would look wonderful as
designs for greetings cards. She enjoyed doing meticulous
flower paintings.

She carried the flower arrangement carefully back to her
car, and propped it on the rear seat, then bought a can of
ginger beer from the nearest shop and drank it with relish
as she continued her slow tour of the main street. *I've turned
into a real Aussie*, she thought with a smile, *doing my shopping on a hot day with a can of chilled drink in my hand.*

Half an hour later, she bought an outdoor setting made of
jarrah, another item she fell in love with on sight. The slatted
table and six chairs were made in wood of such a rich dark
red that she just had to stroke it and then, of course, she was
lost. Especially as the designer of the chairs seemed to really
understand human anatomy in a way that reminded her of
her rocking chair.

The table and chairs would be perfect on her back
veranda, far nicer than her current plastic ones. She'd be
able to take her sketching materials out there and do the
preliminary drafts for her projects with the faint scent of
gum trees in her nostrils and the dry rustling of their leaves
filling her ears.

Life didn't get much better.

When someone knocked on the front door that afternoon,
she thought it must be the men bringing her new outdoor
furniture. It was strange, though, that she hadn't heard them
drive up. She opened the door, surprised when she saw who
it was. 'Ben!' In spite of her vows, she could feel her expression softening in welcome. She stared behind him. There
was no sign of a car. 'How did you get here?'

'I walked over from next door.'

His face was so grim and unsmiling that her happiness at seeing him again melted like ice in the sun. Why was he radiating anger?

'May I come in? I need to talk to you.' His voice was as sharp as the crack of a whip.

She realized she'd been standing gaping at him. 'Yes, of course.' She held the door open and led the way into the kitchen-family area, the only place that was even half furnished. 'I – er – didn't realize we were neighbours again. I thought you were just visiting York before Christmas to see what your uncle's properties were like.'

'Oh, did you?' Sarcasm was thick in his voice.

She looked at him in puzzlement. What on earth had got into him? 'Won't you sit down? Can I get you something cold to drink?'

'No to both. This is *not* a social visit.'

Shock at his attitude seemed to have robbed her of her wits. She pulled herself together. 'Well, *I'd* prefer to sit down.' She sat on the rocking chair and after a moment's hesitation, he sat down on the edge of the sofa opposite her, a clenched fist resting on each denim clad knee.

'You said you weren't interested in buying this property.'

He glared at her so fiercely she suddenly realized what this was about. Uh-oh! His must have been the other offer. Well, she wasn't going to let him blame her for his loss. 'No, it was you who told me it was too big for a woman, if I remember correctly. I simply didn't bother to argue with you.'

'It *is* too big for a woman on her own. You've been badly advised about this purchase, believe me.'

'I suppose it didn't occur to you that I might actually be capable of making up my own mind about such things?'

His eyes narrowed. 'Or perhaps you've been rather clever.'

'I beg your pardon?'

'You heard me. *Very* clever. Sneaky, even.'

'Now listen here, Elless!' She bounced to her feet. She wasn't going to put up with that sort of sneering innuendo.

He stood up too, arms akimbo. 'No, you listen here, Ingram. You made a fast move and got in first with this property. All right. I won't labour the unethical aspects of your action, considering you were my accountant at one stage. How much do you want for the place?'

She could only goggle at him. *'Want for the place?* But I've only just moved in! And anyway, why should *you* want it? You live in Queensland.'

He didn't answer, but looked scornfully around the room. 'Just moved in? Who do you think you're kidding? You're not even pretending to furnish it, only camping out here to make your point.'

'I don't have any point to make to you, Elless, so I think you'd better leave.'

'I'm not leaving till we've got a few matters straightened out. I'll give you fifteen thousand dollars more than you paid for Somerlee and I'll take care of all the legal and other expenses for the re-sale. You'll never make a quicker profit on anything.'

She could feel the anger swelling her up like a bullfrog, so before she exploded at him, she turned and marched down the hallway to fling the front door open. 'The property is *not* for sale, Elless, and I don't have to listen to your insults in my own home. Please leave at once.'

He got up but remained standing in the kitchen doorway. 'You're not a very good actress, you know. The anger's a bit overdone, if you ask me. But all right, twenty thousand extra, plus costs, and that's absolutely my last offer.'

'Which word don't you understand? *Not – For –* or *– Sale.* Now, if you don't leave my house this very minute, I'll call the police and have you thrown out.'

He moved towards the door and she kept a good distance between herself and him as she herded him along.

Halfway down the hall he swung round so suddenly she flinched and took a step backwards.

'I'll leave you to think my offer over, but I'll be back. I'm not going to pay you any more than twenty thousand extra, whatever you say or do. I know exactly how much you paid for Somerlee. It's highway robbery for me to pay so much more, but I need the land. You were very clever snapping it up like that.'

In the doorway he paused again, to add more quietly, 'I didn't expect that sort of thing from you.'

Her rage overflowed. 'How do I get it into your – your thick arrogant skull that I've bought this place to live in and for nothing else. I've no intention whatsoever of selling it, not to you and not to anyone else!'

Before she had realized what he was doing, he had taken a swift step forward, put his fingers under her chin and forced it up, so that she had to stare up at him.

'Let go of me!' She tried to shove him away and failed to move him an inch. His body was hard and muscular against hers. Anger coursed through her and with it a strange sense of exhilaration. 'Let me go, you big bully!'

As she tried to twist away from him, he put his hands on her shoulders and pinned her against the wall. 'As I said before,' the hands tightened on her shoulders, 'you're a poor actress. *And,*' he thrust his face forward till it was only inches away from hers, 'you're showing even poorer judgement in trying to blackmail me.'

Blackmail him! Blackmail! White hot fury seared through her and as his hands slackened, she stamped on his foot, following that up with a hard kick to the shins that made him yelp in shock and pain. She pushed him over the doorstep before he had recovered from his surprise at her sudden attack, then slammed the door in his face and locked it. She had to lean against it for a moment because she was shaking with rage.

He rattled the door handle. 'I'll be back tomorrow for my answer, you hellcat!'

'Go and find someone else to bully! You won't change my mind.'

His parting words echoed in her head as she stormed back into the kitchen and poured herself some iced water with hands that were still shaking. How dare he assume she was trying to hold him to ransom over the house? She set the glass down untasted.

'He's the most conceited, evil-minded brute I've ever met!' she exclaimed, stalking up and down the room. 'Coming here and threatening me like that! I'll take out a restraining order against him if he doesn't leave me alone.'

She couldn't stop thinking of the many things she wished

she had said to Elless, and would say to him, too, if he came here again.

'Who does he think he is?' she asked the rocking chair when she went back inside. She sat in it briefly, then sprang to her feet and left it rocking violently to and fro on its own.

'I'll give him "not even pretending to furnish it". I'll go out tomorrow and buy a whole houseful of furniture,' she told the fridge as she got herself another cold drink to replace the one that had grown warm while it sat waiting for her.

She went outside and stormed up and down the back veranda for a few minutes, glass in hand, but more of the water splashed on to the wooden floor than went down her throat. If he came back, she wouldn't even let him through the door. She'd just tell him calmly to go away then refuse to speak to him.

When there was a knock on the door, she thought for a moment it was *him* coming back and raced to the door ready to do battle. But it was only the men delivering the outdoor furniture.

'Where do you want it, lady?' one of them asked when she didn't move.

'Oh, er, out on the back veranda. You'd be best taking it round that side.' She pointed.

After they'd gone she couldn't settle to anything creative, though she had set everything up earlier for painting one of the fluffy, cherry-red blossoms from a small tree at the side of the house. After wandering round for a while, still muttering to herself, she stopped in the bedroom and stared at herself in the long mirror on the wall. 'What's the matter with you today, Ingram?' she asked her reflection. 'You're letting that bully get to you. Snap out of it, woman!'

Her Grandpop had always said that when you were upset the best thing was to keep busy, so she got out the tins of pale cream paint she had bought in town and started undercoating the bare plaster walls of her bedroom.

Painting walls didn't take her mind off Ben Elless, but she felt cheered up by the thought that at least she was doing something productive with her anger, something that would show him whether she really intended to live here or not. The first coat was finished by evening.

'If he tries to force his way inside that door again, I will definitely phone the police,' she declared later, as she chopped up some vegetables for her evening meal. 'Threatening me like that. He's nothing but a bully and you have to stand up to bullies.'

'And what's more,' she thumped the pillow for the twentieth time as she tried to get to sleep, 'if he so much as *hints* at sharp business practices again, I'll really give him something to sue me for!'

Ria came back from shopping to find two men in suits, who looked incongruously out of place on a country block, shouting at Pete.

She got out of the car and hurried across to them. 'What's wrong?'

'You're trespassing, lady, that's what.'

'Sorry. We thought this block was unused.'

'It still belongs to someone. We don't want vagrants camping out here.'

She looked down her nose at him. 'I'm not a vagrant. I'm employed by the Education Department as a counsellor.'

'Then why aren't you living in a proper house?'

'We've been house sitting for someone, haven't found anywhere else to live yet. Perhaps you'd like us to look after this block for you? We can provide references and—'

'All the owners want is for you to get the hell out of here.'

She looked at them and could tell there was no chance of persuading them to change their minds. 'Fine. We'll leave first thing in the morning.'

'You'll be off within the hour.'

'It takes longer than that to pack up.'

'We'll help you.'

Just then Jim came out of the bush, saw that something was going on and ran across to join them.

'What's the matter, Ria?' he asked in the deep voice that matched his large muscular body perfectly.

'These . . . *gentlemen* want us to leave within the hour.'

'Can't be done.'

'Two hours then,' one man snapped.

She could see Jim starting to get angry and laid one hand on his arm.

'Well, get started! Pack up!' one of the strangers ordered.

Jim moved her hand and stepped forward, picking up both men and carrying them across to their car before they'd recovered from their surprise. He dumped them down so that they stumbled back against the vehicle. 'We can leave in the morning and the place will be immaculate. Or we can leave in four hours and the place will be a mess. Your choice.'

Ria hurried across, knowing that simply by standing there she'd calm Jim down a little.

For a moment there was silence, then one of the men straightened his clothing. 'It'd better be immaculate, then.'

When they'd gone, she linked her arm in Jim's. 'You all right?'

'Yes.' He patted her arm. 'Don't worry. I've got the anger under control now, thanks to your help over the past year or two.'

'I know.' She turned and gestured to her children to get out of the car. 'Better start packing up, kids. I'll phone the campsite and see if they've a place for us.'

Jim sighed. 'I hate those public camping grounds.'

'Me too. But we are saving money living this way. One day we'll have enough to buy a block of our own land.'

Since it was three o'clock in the morning before she got to sleep, Meriel didn't wake up until almost ten. She still felt tired and stumbled round the kitchen, muttering to herself as she made some toast.

She nearly jumped out of her skin when the phone rang and snatched up the receiver, ready to do battle. 'Oh, Rosanna. You startled me!' It was a relief not to have *him* haranguing her again and the only reason she felt disappointed was because she was longing to give him a piece of her mind. She realized her friend had stopped speaking. 'Sorry, I missed that. Must be a bad line.'

'I was just ringing to see if you were all right, Meriel.

How's the house? Did the move go OK? You should have let us come and help you.'

If Rosanna had come, she'd have brought another of her many male cousins. No, thank you! 'Everything went fine. Just fine.' Meriel's voice sounded hollow, even to her own ears. She sighed and ran her free hand through her hair.

'What's the matter? Are you all right? Are you still there? Meriel Ingram, answer me this minute! What's wrong?'

That was the trouble with friends. They knew you too well. 'Nothing's wrong. I didn't sleep very well last night. I've only this minute got up and I'm still dopey.'

'I wouldn't sleep well any night if I lived in the middle of a big bush block like that. Look, Karl and I were talking about it. If you're going to insist on living there, you really ought to get yourself a dog.'

'A dog?'

'Yeah, a dog. A big one, with a loud bark and sharp white teeth.'

Meriel enjoyed a brief fantasy of a dog biting deep into Ben Elless's leg. 'Well, actually I was thinking about getting one – not because I'm afraid,' she certainly was not afraid to be here on her own, just let anyone try to break in and she would smash them over the head with the baseball bat she kept next to her bed, 'but for the company.'

'In that case, what would you think about a Labrador?'

'Come again?'

'A golden Labrador. She's a real nice dog, but my cousin Maria is going overseas for a year and her mother won't look after the dog for her, and anyway, they never expected it to grow so big, and it digs the garden up – only because it's bored on its own all day, not because it's a bad dog or anything. What do you think?'

'I'd have to meet it first. Dogs are a very personal thing. They're like people. You either take to one or you don't.' And sometimes you could be quite mistaken about a person. It was a lot easier with dogs.

'All right, then. Maria and I will bring the dog out to meet you. You'll love it. It's called Tina. How about we come today?'

'I don't think I – Oh, why not?' If Rosanna and her cousin

were there, not to mention a big dog, *he* would find it very difficult to start bullying her again. She would enjoy frustrating him. 'When shall I expect you?'

'About lunchtime. Tell me again which road I take out of York. You know how bad my memory is.'

Rosanna and her cousin didn't arrive until one o'clock, by which time Meriel was ravenously hungry and on edge in case Ben turned up before her visitors did. When a strange car bumped its way along the dirt track, sending up clouds of beige dust, she jumped to her feet, ready for anything, but it was Rosanna who poked her head out of the passenger window, waving one arm wildly.

The car door opened and a large golden dog erupted from it, paused to empty its bladder, then came over to sniff Meriel. It gave her a quick lick, thumped its tail against her legs a few times and set off, nose down, to explore its new surroundings, as any self-respecting dog would. It galloped to and fro energetically, venturing nearer for occasional pats, grinning widely all the time.

'Stay still, you stupid mutt, and get acquainted properly,' said its owner. 'Hey! Come here, Tina!'

The dog came, head cocked questioningly, tail still wagging furiously.

'Sit!'

It promptly flopped down on its belly and began to pant as if it had just run a marathon.

Rosanna came across to hug Meriel. 'This is my cousin Maria.'

Meriel shook Maria's hand. 'Why don't you come inside? It's another hot one today.'

'You can say that again.' Rosanna fanned herself with one hand.

Maria paused. 'Is it all right if Tina comes inside too? She doesn't know she's a dog; she thinks she's a person and therefore entitled to all house privileges. If you're looking for an outdoors-only dog, she'll be no use to you. I hope Rosanna told you that.' She glanced at the dog and shook her head fondly. 'You're a real terror, aren't you?'

The dog promptly rolled over and presented a plump hairy stomach to be tickled. Meriel couldn't resist the invitation and by the time they had gone inside, she knew she was hooked.

She'd always wanted a dog. Her father had once brought a red setter home that someone in the office was giving away, but her mother hadn't allowed the poor creature inside her immaculately clean house and he'd been the cause of another series of arguments between her parents. In the end, her father had given the dog back and Meriel, then aged eight, had cried herself to sleep.

Two hours later, Rosanna and Maria left. Tina whimpered for a few minutes then took up residence on the bed. Meriel shooed her off it several times, but the dog kept creeping back into the bedroom, which had a faulty door catch, and lying on the bed looking blissfully comfortable. Each time Meriel tried to banish her from the bedroom, Tina assumed a piteous expression and whined sadly and softly in her throat as she was moved out, then sneaked back at the first opportunity. Meriel had to laugh and in the end, they both rolled around on the bed, cuddling and grinning at each other.

There was no sign of Ben Elless all day. As dusk started to creep across the landscape, Meriel went to sit on the veranda, with Tina lying at her feet, chasing dream rabbits. She sipped the single glass of cool white wine that was fast becoming an evening ritual and stared at the shadowy landscape, then looked down at the dog. It was nice not to be alone.

As for Elless, he'd probably thought better of his ridiculous threats and gone back to the Eastern States. She didn't care if she never saw him again. In fact, never would be far too soon.

She couldn't quite persuade herself that she meant that. She'd really enjoyed his company till he got this bee in his bonnet about her home.

Twelve

The day after Rosanna's visit, Meriel got up early and put on her usual working outfit of jeans and a tee shirt, protecting her feet from snakes and spiders by wearing work boots. She walked all over the nearest part of her block before the sun was hot, trying to learn the overall lie of the ground, where it sloped upwards, where it dipped. One day, she vowed, she'd be able to recognize every tree and plant on it, but for the moment, she didn't have the faintest idea what some of them were.

Tina bounded along beside her, rushing off every now and then to pursue some fascinating scent trail or other. She seemed to have settled in well, though every now and then she would stand looking towards the road as if expecting someone.

Her obnoxious neighbour was right about one thing, Meriel conceded ruefully, as she took an hour to explore the small cleared area of her property. This place was far too big for her needs. Five or ten acres would have been just right. Seventy was ridiculous. Perhaps, if he calmed down and began to act in a more reasonable way, she might offer Elless the sixty or so acres of uncleared bush she didn't need.

'Get real!' she told herself. 'That man's not going to calm down after what he said to you. And anyway, why should I offer him anything? I certainly don't want *him* as a neighbour.' She realized she was talking to herself yet again and clicked her tongue in exasperation. See what he was doing to her! Or did all people who lived on their own talk to themselves?

She sat down on a fallen tree trunk and stared at the low hill that marked the far boundary of her property. The bush could stay untouched as far as she was concerned. The kangaroos, lizards and cockatoos were welcome to it. All she needed to do for the moment was to arrange for the perimeter fire-breaks and fences to be maintained, which was her legal responsibility, though she didn't see how a fire-break a car's width would stop a raging bush fire.

She stared at a group of grass trees on the far side of the cleared patch of land. When the huge flower spikes were in bloom, the trees had looked to the early settlers like aboriginal hunters carrying spears, so had been called black-boys, but now you had to call them grass trees, which was more politically correct. They were a very strange sort of plant to her English eyes, a stubbly tree trunk blackened from bush fires, with a huge tuft of coarse strands coming out of the top. As each layer of the tough strands died, they formed the next ridge on the trunk.

It was getting warmer now so she started reluctantly back towards the house. She wasn't stupid enough to stay out in the hottest part of the day. She didn't want to damage her skin. She turned to look for Tina but there was no sign of the dog. After calling out several times she began to get annoyed. Then she thought she heard . . . yes, that was definitely a faint bark in the distance.

She listened carefully and realized in dismay that the sound was coming from the next block.

She walked to the fence line and stopped there, calling loudly and, she hoped, sounding firm and in control. This time there was a whole series of yips and barks in response to her calls but still the dog did not reappear.

Resigning herself to another confrontation, she stepped over the sagging wires. 'This is the last time you do this to me, Tina,' she said aloud. 'The very last time! I need another meeting with Ben Elless like I need a hole in the head. If you keep visiting in that direction, I'll have to walk you on a leash until he leaves and you wouldn't like that!'

Besides, if he saw her coming on to his property, looking as if she was seeking him out, he might think she had capit-ulated. In his dreams!

As she got closer, she stopped again but couldn't see the dog. She called as loudly as she could, but there was no sign of movement near the house. Perhaps she was lucky and he'd gone out. She hoped so.

She moved forward again and followed the barking right up to the old shack, dismayed to see his car there. Then she heard another sound, a faint noise which she couldn't quite place. Pausing to listen, she looked round, worried that he might come out of the house to ask what she was doing there.

The roof of the old weatherboard house caught her eye. It was sagging so markedly on one side she couldn't believe the place could possibly be safe. It looked as if it was about to fall down. Why on earth was Ben living in such a hovel?

As she rounded the corner she stopped dead in shock. The whole of the rear lean-to section had caved in and Tina was standing beside the resulting mound of twisted sheets of tin and broken pieces of wood and fibreboard, whining loudly. The dog kept looking towards Meriel and pawing at the pile of debris.

From underneath it came a groaning noise, the sound Meriel hadn't been able to identify before. It was definitely a groan. Someone was trapped there!

'Ben!' There was no answer and the pile of debris remained ominously still. 'Ben! Are you there?'

Tina whined again, pointing her nose at the mound with one paw half raised, as if indicating a piece of game they were hunting together.

Meriel spoke soothingly, not wanting the dog to start leaping around. Ben must be lying under the debris. There was no other explanation for Tina's behaviour. 'Yes, all right, girl. Stay there. *Stay!* Just give me a minute or two to check things over.'

Before she moved into the disaster area, she ran her eyes anxiously over the house. The part that had collapsed was an add-on at the back. The walls and roof of the main house looked sound enough and since most of the lean-to's roof had already come down, she should be fairly safe if she moved slowly and carefully.

When had this happened and how long had Elless been lying there under the debris? Was he badly injured? He might be bleeding to death, for all she knew.

She didn't let that panic her into doing something foolhardy, however. It'd do no one any good if she got hurt as well.

Very carefully, her heart pounding with anxiety, she began

to pick her way through the clutter, pulling bits and pieces out of the way until she came close to where Tina was standing on a sloping piece of corrugated roof tin. There had been no more signs of collapse from the house behind her – nor had there been any more sounds from underneath the pile of rubbish.

He couldn't be dead. Someone so large and exuberantly alive couldn't possibly be dead! The thought was unbearable.

Tina barked and moved, causing a few small pieces of wood to slide sideways. When she reached solid ground she stood still again, watching.

Meriel studied the area where she thought Ben was trapped. One by one, she began to pull away the bigger pieces of lumber and roofing tin, working slowly and cautiously, with her ear cocked for any untoward noise that might presage another cave-in. She already had an escape route picked out and a rough pathway through the debris cleared.

Splinters lodged in her hands, dust rose up to choke her and the sun beat down mercilessly on her unprotected head and arms, but she didn't dare go for help until she had found Ben in case he was bleeding.

Tina stayed near the edge of the pile, whining softly to herself and fretting to and fro.

What seemed like an eternity later, breathless and pouring with sweat from her exertions, Meriel uncovered Ben's head and shoulders. She bent over him, breathing a sigh of relief as she verified that he was still alive, if unconscious. He had a nasty bruise and swelling on his forehead, though.

By the time she got his upper body clear of the chunks of wood and plasterboard from the inside walls, he had started to regain consciousness and was blinking up at her. 'What are *you* doing here?'

He didn't seem to realize the state he was in or the danger that still threatened if the rest of the house collapsed around them.

'I'm trying to rescue you, Elless. Don't make any sudden moves.'

He stared at her groggily. 'What?'

'The back of your house caved in on top of you. I'm still not sure whether the rest of the building's safe, so lie still until I get this stuff off you.'

He took a ragged breath and looked round, his eyes slowly starting to focus better. 'Hell! How did that happen?'

'Don't you remember?' She brushed some fragments of plasterboard and splinters of wood off his face and neck. He was very pale and there was a trail of dried blood down his left cheek from a small gash. 'How are you feeling? Is there any pain? I don't want to try to move you if you've broken something.'

He sighed and closed his eyes for a minute. She thought he'd lost consciousness again until she saw that he was wiggling his fingers one by one, then his whole hands and arms. 'Top half of me seems to be working,' he said, his voice a husky thread.

'Good. Rest for a minute, then try your legs.'

'Mmm.' He took a few breaths, then moved his right foot and leg. 'That one's OK.' He tried to move his left foot. 'Ouch! That one hurts.' He moved it again, more cautiously. 'I don't think it's broken. I broke an arm once. That felt different. Much sharper pain.'

'Are you sure?'

'Well, it hurts, but I'm pretty sure it's not broken.'

'Right. Then we'll try to move you.'

She knelt down and very carefully unlaced the sneaker on his left foot. As she slipped it off and tossed it across the pile of rubbish towards the dog, Ben groaned and she winced for him. 'I'm sorry, but your foot's badly swollen. If we'd waited much longer, we'd have had to cut your sneaker off.'

'Right. Thanks.'

Was he going to lose consciousness again? She tried to keep his attention. 'Do you know how this accident happened? I mean, was there a gas explosion or something?'

'No.' His words were coming in bursts, as if it were an effort to speak. 'I was up on the roof – fixing a sheet of tin that was loose before it blew away.' He paused to lick his dry lips and frown at her then went on with his explanation.

'Suddenly everything gave way. I remember starting to fall, then . . . I don't remember anything else until you turned up.' He grunted as he moved his head unwarily. 'What brought you over here, anyway? Last place I'd have expected to see *you*.'

'My dog came exploring. I was chasing her. And if you're going to insult me, I can always go away again.' She didn't mean that, of course.

'Sorry. Don't go. Need your help.' His eyes closed again and his words came in short bursts. 'Head's throbbing. Can't think properly. Must have banged it.'

'There's a large bruise and grazing on your forehead. I should think you've got concussion.' She didn't like the way he kept drifting into semi-consciousness. She needed information from him. 'Elless!'

'Mmm? What?'

'Where was your telephone? I need to call for help. Or do you have a mobile somewhere? If it's in the front part of the house, I may be able to get to it. We need to call an ambulance for you.'

He blinked up at her, then turned his head to study the remains of the little house. 'Only got a mobile. Landline's not connected. I'd just been using the mobile. It was on the table over there!'

She followed his eyes and saw what looked like the corner of a table flattened on the ground, protruding from underneath a heap of jagged timber pieces and debris. 'Well, I'm not diving under any piles of rubbish to search for your phone. I'll run back to my house and call for an ambulance from there.'

'No!' He grabbed hold of her arm with a strength that surprised her. 'I'm not going off in some damned ambulance. Look, if you can just give me a few minutes to recover, then help me to my car, I'll be all right to go and see a doctor about the leg.'

'You won't be able to drive anywhere in that condition.'

'I'm not going in an ambulance.'

She heard him gulp. It was a soft, strangled sound and for some reason it made her feel sorry for him. 'Why not?'

He closed his eyes and swallowed hard. 'They took my wife away in one – after the accident. I was following her car in mine, so I saw it all happen. Then I followed the ambulance and – and I never saw Sandy alive again. Hate even to see an ambulance now.'

Meriel stared down at him, anger warring with pity. He was doing it again! Just as she'd settled down to disliking him, he'd said something that made her feel sorry for him. He wasn't thinking straight about the ambulance, but it wouldn't do him any good to get agitated. She fought against her own instincts, lost, and patted his hand to offer comfort. He turned his over and grasped hers, not saying anything, but holding her tightly.

As his hand slackened, she said, 'We'll see if we can manage without an ambulance, then. I'll drive you into town if we can get you to a car. I hope there's some sort of emergency service at the hospital.'

He looked at her. 'Mmm. They usually call in one of the local GPs.' Then his eyes closed and he drifted away again, so she waited. The sun was blazing down on them so brightly her eyes hurt, a cloud of bush flies was buzzing hungrily around nipping at her soft flesh, and her thoughts were buzzing just as loudly inside her head.

As soon as he opened his eyes again, she stood up. 'I'll go and open your car doors to let the hot air out. When you feel capable of moving, I'll help you over to it and then I'll drive you to the hospital. I know where it is. I saw a sign.'

'Mmm. Aw'right. Good idea.' He tried to sit up and knocked his shoulder against a chunk of roof beam, which slid sideways with a domino effect on the piles of debris around them. Small pieces slithered this way and that, larger pieces rocked and hesitated.

As clouds of choking dust rose to torment their dry throats, Meriel tensed, ready to leap out of the way, but after a minute it all settled down again. Her voice came out more sharply than she'd intended, because she'd seen the only remaining wall of the lean-to shaking, and with it the wall of the main building. The edge of a loose piece of tin roof flapped around gently, as if in sympathy.

'Don't try to move yet, Ben! *Please stay still!*'

His words came out in a hoarse whisper. 'Can't get out of this without moving.'

'If you knock something else the rest of the house could fall in on us. Let me shift things gradually, till you're clear.'

'All right.' He sighed and lay back again. 'Thirsty as all hell. Feels like I've swallowed a bucket of sand.'

His voice sounded so rusty that she felt her own throat tighten in sympathy. 'I'll see if I can find you something to drink.'

'A brandy would be nice.' He tried to smile, but the smile faded quickly. 'Got some in the front room.'

'And that's where it's staying! You're only having a sip of water, in case they have to operate on your foot.'

'Bully!' His voice was a mere thread of sound, but there was a hint of a grin on his face, which she took as a sign that he was feeling a little better.

She studied the house. The front part looked more solid than the remains of the lean-to. She went round to the front door, opened it and banged it shut a few times, poised to leap away. A few things rattled, but nothing else showed any signs of collapsing.

'Here goes nothing,' she muttered. Moving cautiously she walked into the central passageway. The door to the rear section was open at the far end. To the left was the bathroom. 'Thank goodness!' she muttered. Before she went inside it, she looked along towards the end and froze. Above her were the jagged edges of some broken roof timbers. But some of the edges weren't jagged – they were newly sawn off, just where the two parts of the house met.

Her breath caught in her throat and horror curled inside her belly. *Fresh saw marks?* Surely someone hadn't been trying to hurt Ben deliberately? Why would they do that?

'Meriel! Are you all right?'

His voice was faint, but it recalled her to her main task, which was to get some water for him. To her relief, the bathroom tap was still working, so she bent for a quick slurp, then filled the tooth mug and dampened the dusty facecloth that was lying among the debris in the sink. On the way out, she studied the edges of the roof beams again, sharp lines against the sunlight, shaking her head in disbelief. Definitely sawn through.

Ben was still lying in the sun with his eyes closed. She could see the tension on his face and the sweat on his forehead. His mouth was half open and he was breathing raggedly. Now wasn't the time to say anything about the roof.

She let him sip a little of the water and used the rest to bathe his face, leaving the wet cloth across his forehead while she tried to think how best to get him out of there.

After a few minutes, he grasped her hand and squinted up at her. 'Thanks. That feels a lot better.' Then he frowned. 'Where did you get that water from?'

'The bathroom.'

His fingers jerked on her wrist and tightened. *'What?'*

'I was very careful. It was the rear lean-to that fell down, not the main house. I just went into the bathroom.' She hesitated. Should she tell him now? But he looked so white she shook her head. No. Not yet.

'Don't take any more risks like that!' His voice was urgent. 'Please. Nothing's worth risking your life for. I'd never forgive myself if anything happened to you.'

She patted his hand. 'Believe me, I'm being extremely careful.'

Slowly his fingers relaxed and he let go of her arm. When she looked down, his eyes were closed again and his face had a dirty whitish tinge that made his suntan look like poorly applied make-up.

'Well, all right or not, just stay where you are while I check out your car.'

She reached his car and glared at it. Trust him to have a huge four-wheel drive! She was too small to drive cars like this comfortably.

Leaving the rear door of the vehicle open she went back to help Ben. Carefully she moved more of the debris then helped him stand up. He clung to her for a minute as he swayed to and fro on one leg.

'Still feel a bit dizzy,' he muttered.

'We'll go very slowly. There's no hurry.'

It took longer than she'd expected to get him to the car, because they had to keep stopping so that he could rest. His arm lay heavy and warm along her shoulders, a hot breeze wafted around them and beige dust rose from the dry earth at every step they took. They seemed to be alone in a sun-scorched universe, with the heat pulsing around and through them.

Tina circled them as they walked, giving the occasional yip, though whether that was for encouragement or in protest at the way she was being ignored, it was impossible to tell.

When they got to the car, Ben leaned against it, breathing hoarsely and still clutching Meriel. 'Wait. Just a minute.'

Tina crept forward and whined at them.

'That your dog?'

'Yes.'

'Didn't see a dog the other day.'

'I only got her yesterday. And you've got *her* to thank for me finding you. She ran away and came over here exploring, so I had to come after her. She was whining and standing near where you were lying, refusing to move. I couldn't see you because you were covered in debris, so I wouldn't have realized you were there but for her.'

'Owe her a big juicy bone for that.' He closed his eyes again and leaned his chin against the top of Meriel's head. 'Still feel a bit woozy,' he admitted, his breath hot in her ear. 'Nauseous too. Can't move just yet or I'll disgrace myself.'

'I told you, there's no hurry. Stand still until you feel better. I couldn't lift you up again if you fell.'

After a couple of minutes he stirred. 'I think I can move now.' His voice was tight, as if everything were a huge effort.

Carefully, Meriel eased him down, breathing a sigh of relief when he was sitting safely on the edge of the rear seat with the swollen foot sticking out. 'Just slide slowly backwards. That's right. Good, good.'

She left him there while she ran back for the piece of the sawn-off rafter she'd seen lying on the ground, wrenching it away from its chunk of roof tin. It was heavier than she'd expected but she dragged it across to the car and managed to heave it up into the rear. It seemed wise to keep some of the evidence safe.

When she went to check on Ben, he was slumped against the far corner of the seat and his eyes were closed. Then he opened them, flailed one hand round and tried to run the window down, but the ignition wasn't switched on. 'Too hot.'

'I'll have it open in a minute. Shall I fasten the seat belt round you? I don't want you rolling about and hurting that foot again.'

'No. Leave it. Rather sit sideways.' His voice was slightly slurred.

She suddenly realized she'd forgotten one rather important thing. How could she have been so stupid? 'Where are your car keys?' If they were under the debris, she'd have to run across the block and drive her own car round here, then help him move from one vehicle to the other.

He didn't seem to hear her. 'Sunglasses in the glove compartment,' he muttered, his forehead creased into a frown and one filthy hand shading his eyes.

She found the sunglasses and passed them to him, grimacing with him as he knocked the earpiece against the bruise on his forehead and sucked in a sharp breath.

'That's better.'

'Tell me where your car keys are,' she repeated patiently.

'In my pocket.' His fingers scrabbled at his jeans, but he couldn't seem to co-ordinate well enough to pull the keys out.

'Let me get them. You lie still.' She had to kneel on the edge of the seat and lean across him, slipping her fingers past the soft warmth of his bare midriff into the nearest pocket.

The keys weren't there, so she had to lean further and try the other pocket.

'You smell nice,' he murmured, nuzzling at her ear.

She jerked at his touch. 'Just lie still, you idiot!'

He put his arms round her, trapping her on top of him. 'Mmm, yes. Could lie here like this all day. Love your perfume.'

'It's flower soap, not perfume.' She breathed a sigh of relief as her fingers touched metal. 'I've got them.'

One of his arms was round her.

'Let me go, you fool. We have to get you to a doctor.'

Instead he pressed his lips against her cheek. 'I'll let you go in a minute. I need kissing better first.' He pressed his lips to her other cheek.

'You're the one kissing me, so how's that going to help you get better?' In spite of her worries about his injuries, she had to smile.

'I knew there was something wrong. You ought to be kissing me, of course. Go ahead! I probably won't have to see a doctor at all if you kiss me better.' He puckered up his lips.

'Look, Elless, we need to – to get you some help.' She tried to wriggle away from him and the arms tightened still further around her. She did not dare pull away too forcefully in case she banged his swollen ankle or his bruised forehead.

'Kiss me better first!' he insisted. 'Then I'll let you go.'

He wasn't thinking straight and it was no use arguing, so she kissed him quickly on the lips.

'Not good enough. You need a lot of practice at kissing, if that's the best you can do.'

'Elless—'

'Won't let you go till you kiss me properly.'

She leaned towards him. 'You're crazy.' This time her lips lingered on his and she drew a shaky breath as she moved away.

'That's better,' he stared into her eyes. 'Your lips are beautiful. Made for kissing.'

'Elless, we need to get you to a doctor.'

'Your hair gleams like silver silk in the sunlight.'

He ran his fingers through it and she shivered involuntarily at his touch.

'Not really an ice maiden, eh, Ingram?'

She closed her eyes and sighed. 'No.' No use denying the obvious.

'We'll try this again when my head stops thumping.' The fingers stilled and then the hand fell away to lie loosely across her shoulders. His eyes closed and he started frowning again.

She wriggled free of him. 'You're delirious,' she said. 'You shouldn't—'

His hand suddenly fastened on her shoulder. 'I'm recovering rapidly. Better by the minute. And I'm perfectly aware of what I'm doing and also of how you're responding to it.'

A fusillade of barks and whines broke the spell.

She seized the opportunity to slide off him and out of the car. She didn't dare move quickly because of his injured ankle and was relieved when he made no further effort to stop her.

Now he was grinning at her. Why?

'You've not only got nice legs, you have a delightful taste in underwear.'

She looked down and gasped, flushing scarlet and pulling her tee shirt down over the very minimal bra she was wearing. 'Let's get you to a doctor now, Elless. You're not – you don't realize what you're doing.'

He gave a rusty chuckle. 'Oh, I do. But unfortunately, I'm not in a condition to follow through on the opening shots. That'll have to wait until another time.'

'You must be more delirious than I'd thought! You don't even like me. You – you suspect me of—' She broke off. What was the use of arguing with a man suffering from concussion?

'You don't have to like someone to find them physically attractive.'

'Well, I do! I have to like them very much.'

She was furious that she'd responded to his touch. Where were all the smart answers with which she usually fended men off?

As she reached out to close the rear door, Tina pushed past her and leaped inside, just missing Ben's injured ankle. With a brief pause to lick the nearest hand, she installed herself beside him on the floor, with her head on his arm. She was panting heavily and dribbling on the leather upholstery.

Meriel tried to get hold of the dog's collar without touching Ben. 'I'll get her out again.'

'Leave her where she is. We can't leave her wandering about the block, can we? She could get lost.' His voice sounded clearer, his hand was caressing Tina's head and there was a half-smile on his lips, though his eyes were hidden once more behind the sunglasses.

Meriel strapped herself into the driver's seat. 'All right. Er – I'm sorry about the mess in your car.' She glanced back at the pale blue leather upholstery. It was amazing how much dirt one large dog and one dusty man could spread around in a few minutes.

'Doesn't matter. It'll wash off. And your dog's more than earned a ride today.'

Tina gave Ben's hand another quick lick then looked from one human to the other as if to say let's go.

Meriel started the car, stealing glances in the rear view mirror to see how Ben was standing up to the movement. The car jerked as she pulled away, because she underestimated the pulling power of the engine. She heard him grunt in pain as she braked. 'Sorry. I'm not used to a big car like this.'

'Even a guardian angel is entitled to one or two mistakes.'

In the mirror, she could see how tightly his right hand was clenched on the top of the seat back. The jolt must have banged the ankle quite hard. He didn't open his eyes for the rest of the journey and his mouth was a thin, bloodless line.

She went inside the hospital to get a wheelchair and an orderly brought it out. They were lucky and there was a doctor already working in the tiny A&E section, so they were seen by him a few minutes later.

He examined Ben, said, 'Concussion', and sent him to have his ankle X-rayed.

Meriel waited on a very hard wooden chair till they wheeled Ben back. He was looking a little more alert, she thought, but now that his face had been washed, the bruise and swelling stood out starkly.

The doctor was very hearty and she could see that his loud voice was doing nothing for Ben's aching head. 'Well, at least it isn't broken, Mr Elless, so we just have to deal with bruising, concussion and a sprained ankle. Your – er,' he shot a doubtful glance at Meriel, his eyes dropping to her ringless left hand, 'your friend can take you home again if she promises to make sure you rest for a day or so and keeps an eye on you.'

'Ms Ingram is just my neighbour – unfortunately.' Ben had recovered enough to grin at Meriel as he said that. 'I'd better book into a hotel. My uncle's shack is no longer habitable.'

The doctor shook his head decisively. 'I don't think that's advisable. If you haven't any friends or family who can help, we'll book you into hospital overnight.'

'No way!' snapped Ben, all traces of a grin vanishing from his face.

Meriel was reminded of his reaction to the suggestion that she call an ambulance.

'Mr Elless, you *must* have someone with you to keep an eye on things, someone who can call for help if there are any other problems. Booking into a hotel is not adequate.'

'Well, it'll just have to do. I don't have any family or close friends in Western Australia.'

He was looking so white and strained Meriel was afraid he'd collapse. She'd always been a sucker for someone in trouble so was only mildly surprised to hear herself saying, 'You can come home with me, if you like, Elless. I've got a spare bedroom.'

She regretted the words as soon as they'd left her mouth, but she saw the look of utter relief on his face as he turned towards her and she couldn't withdraw her offer.

Helping people wasn't always comfortable, but you had to do it. Even when a person thought you were a liar and a cheat.

'I'll get the nurse to give you instructions about keeping an eye on someone with concussion,' the doctor said. 'Bring Mr Elless back if you have any worries whatsoever about him.'

Thirteen

As they waited for the paperwork, Ben stared up at Meriel from the wheelchair. 'I've hardly endeared myself to you lately. I must be the last person you'd want as a house guest.'

'You are. And I doubt *you* want to be indebted to me. But if you've nowhere else to go, you can't afford to be picky, and I daresay I can put up with you for a few days. Think how virtuous I'll feel afterwards!'

'Do you have a spare bed? You didn't seem to have much furniture.'

'Oh!' How ridiculous that she hadn't even thought of that. 'No, I don't. But I'd intended to buy one for when friends come to stay. We can stop off at the furniture store and get one. They delivered my things the same day last time.'

'I'll buy the bed, then.'

'Look, there's no need to do that.'

'I'm buying it.'

'Well – all right.'

He was still staring at her, but his voice lost that hard edge as he asked, 'Are you sure about this, Meriel?'

'I'm sure I'm crazy to make the offer, but you don't have any other real options apart from the hospital, do you? Unless you like taking risks?'

'No. I definitely don't like taking risks with human lives, mine or anyone else's. They can be extinguished all too easily.' There was a pause, then, 'Thank you. I'm extremely grateful.'

She could sense him studying her while the nurse gave instructions about what danger signs to watch out for in the day or two after concussion and when she sneaked a glance at Ben, his brow was wrinkled, as if he was puzzled.

As they left the hospital he was wheeled to the car, then the orderly took the wheelchair away.

'You'll need a walking stick, at least,' she said. 'Look, I'll stop at a pharmacy. They're bound to have one.'

'Thanks.' He slid backwards into the car, receiving a bois-
terous greeting from Tina.

Meriel called the dog to order while he levered himself
carefully into position and leaned back with a tired sigh.

She drove into town and stopped at a pharmacy. 'I won't
be long.'

Ten minutes later she came back with a walking stick, a
couple of cans of lemonade and a bottle of cold water, which
she gave to Tina bit by bit, only spilling about half of it.

'All right to go now, Ben?'

He handed her the empty can. 'Thanks. You think of
everything.'

She drove slowly along the main street and stopped the
car outside a furniture shop. 'I'll just go in and buy the bed.'

'I'll pay.' He fumbled in his pocket pulling out his wallet,
but couldn't find his credit card. 'There's a cheque book
somewhere in this car. We'll find it when we get back. And
buy a queen size bed.'

She looked at him suspiciously.

'I'm a tall man.'

'But it's a waste of money. I mean, a queen size is nearly
twice the price of a single. And if it's only for a short
time—'

'I like my comfort. Single beds are designed only for children and anorexic dwarfs, as far as I'm concerned. Tell the
furniture people I'll pay when they deliver it.'

'Well, do what you want, but I'd like to make it plain
from the start that I'm not keeping the bed afterwards. I
don't need bribing to help a neighbour in distress.'

'Is this the right time to discuss that?'

He was looking at her as if she was his enemy, not his
benefactress, so she glared right back. 'Just so we get things
straight from the start, Elless.'

He closed his eyes. 'All right, Ingram. Whatever. I do
solemnly promise to take the bed away with me afterwards.
I'll need it in my next place anyway. I'll have to find somewhere to rent as soon as I can get about again. It's obvious
I won't be able to live in my uncle's shack. Pity it couldn't
have lasted a few months longer, though. It was perfect to
be able to live on site and use it as an office.'

She watched him move his head restlessly and grimace. His face had gone paler again. She went into the furniture shop without any more argument.

'All arranged,' she said cheerfully when she came out. 'Let's go home. The furniture will be sent over shortly.'

'One more thing—' his voice was tight and harsh.

She paused with her hand on the ignition key. 'What?'

'You're not the only one making conditions. This kindness of yours won't make me raise my offer for your property by one brass razoo.'

His eyes were hidden behind the sunglasses again, his lips set in that tight, thin line once more. If he hadn't been hurt, she would have pushed him out of the car there and then. 'Nor will your present piteous state make me accept your offer to buy my house, Elless. Somerlee is not for sale and never has been. The idea that I'm black-mailing you is just a figment of your – your lurid and over-heated imagination.'

Tina growled in her throat and they both fell silent.

Before Ben could say anything else hurtful, Meriel started up the engine. All she could see in the rear view mirror was a pair of sunglasses and a badly bruised forehead. She tried to blink the tears from her eyes but they overflowed and she had to reach up to brush them away. She hoped he hadn't noticed her moment of weakness.

'I need to buy some groceries.' She stopped the car and slid out before he could toss another insult at her. She found the idea that he considered her a mercenary opportunist very painful indeed. Not because it was him, she decided, taking a deep breath and holding her head higher. No, it was nothing to do with him personally. It would have been painful whoever it was who held such a low opinion of her, because she prided herself on her integrity.

When she came back to the car she found Tina graciously allowing him to scratch behind her ears. From the expression of blissful idiocy on the dog's face, the man was no stranger to canine weak spots.

What stupid weakness had made her offer him her spare bedroom?

Grandpop's training, that's what. He had been a firm

believer in people helping one another, at whatever cost to themselves.

At first it was a relief when Ben didn't speak, then she started worrying about what he was thinking or whether he was still drifting in and out of consciousness. He was probably thinking that she was crazy doing this, she thought as she turned off the road and bumped along the track to her house.

That would be the one thing they agreed on.

When she stopped, he insisted he could get out of the car without her help but took only a few halting steps towards the house using the walking stick. He was swaying and shaking his head as if to clear it. Dizzy still, obviously.

Meriel marched up to him and took his free arm in a firm grip. 'You'd better let me help you, Elless. I don't want you falling over. You've done yourself enough damage for one day.'

'Thanks.' His voice was no longer slurred but it still sounded as if it were an effort for him to frame the words. 'I thought I was OK when I was sitting down, but I'm still a bit dizzy when I try to move around.'

While she fumbled for her key, he sagged against the doorpost and pushed his sunglasses up on top of his head. 'Phew! It's a lot more comfortable in the shade, isn't it?'

She turned the key in the lock and tried to step aside to let him in, but somehow, he moved the wrong way and their bodies collided again.

He chuckled, a soft tired sound, but a chuckle nonetheless.

'What's so funny?' she demanded, trying to guide him towards the family room.

'You are. Trying not to touch me.'

'I – I –' Words stuck in her throat.

'I don't bite, you know, especially when my head is aching like this.'

She immediately felt guilty for thinking of her own feelings when he was in pain. 'I'll get you a glass of milk and some painkillers as soon as you're safe on the couch. Come and sit down until the bed arrives.'

As they reached the couch, he swung her round and planted a chaste kiss on her forehead. 'Thank you, Ingram. You really did save my life today.'

She realised with a fluttery feeling of shock that he was right. It hadn't struck her so forcefully before, because she'd been too busy rescuing him and getting to the hospital. She'd actually saved a life. 'Oh, I – it's – someone else would have found you. Or you'd have crawled out of the debris eventually.'

He eased himself down on the couch with a sigh of relief. 'I don't get any visitors and I wasn't expecting any deliveries, so I'm fairly certain no one else would have found me.'

'Oh. Well, it was Tina who found you, actually,' she said, trying to turn it into a joke. 'Don't forget to buy her that bone.'

'She didn't get me out from under the rubble. You did. At some risk to yourself. And for that I'm extremely grateful.' Again that tired whisper of a chuckle.

'What are you laughing at now?' she demanded.

'Well, in some societies, if you save another person's life, you're responsible for them from then onwards.'

She stiffened. 'That's merely a primitive superstition!'

'I wouldn't mind you being responsible for me, Ingram,' he said, turning the full force of his devastating smile on to her. 'Especially if you have anything to drink in that fridge of yours. I'm afraid I'm thirsty again.'

She became abruptly aware of her duty as hostess and temporary nurse. 'I'll get you a glass of milk right away, then you can take the painkillers safely. Or would you rather have a cup of tea?'

'I'm not a tea drinker. And I don't think this is quite the time for strong black coffee or even a beer. Do you?'

'Definitely not.' She busied herself in the kitchen, wondering how she was going to cope during the next few days.

He took the glass of milk from her, but shook his head at the offer of biscuits. 'I'm not hungry. In fact, as soon as that bed arrives, I'll fall into it, if that's all right with you. I have an overwhelming desire to sleep.'

The doctor and nurse had both warned her this would be likely, but she studied him through narrowed eyes, in case there were any other symptoms.

'It's all right. You won't find yourself with a corpse on your hands. I'm just tired. I didn't sleep well last night.'

Not after a phone call from Phil and a nasty argument. He held out the empty glass. 'Thanks.'

'I'll still keep an eye on you. As per instructions.'

His eyes raked her from head to toe. 'I'll be quite happy to return the compliment.'

'And I'd be grateful if you'd refrain from personal remarks like that while you're living here. As far as I'm concerned, I'm merely helping a neighbour out. We're not – I mean, you shouldn't—' She broke off, her face burning. 'You know what I mean.'

'I know exactly what you mean. We've talked before about this physical attraction between us. Why do you keep trying to deny it?'

'Because that's all it is. A temporary physical attraction and – and quite inexplicable, since your opinion of me is hardly flattering. And also,' she was nearly yelling by now, 'because I don't want any involvements, temporary or otherwise!'

'What *do* you want, then?'

'To be left in peace.'

Someone hammered at the door and she sighed with relief as she hurried to open it. The same men who had delivered her outdoor furniture were standing there with a mattress held between them.

'Where do you want it, lady?' She led the way towards the spare bedrooms, relieved that the men wouldn't have to pass through the family room and see Ben. It took only a few minutes for them to unload the bed and set it up, then they waited expectantly in the doorway.

'Payment on delivery,' one of them said laconically, holding out an invoice.

'My cheque book's in the car, darling,' Ben shouted, proving that he was listening to everything and was ready to take advantage of the situation. 'Will you go and get it for me?'

The delivery men grinned broadly and exchanged knowing glances.

Meriel stormed outside to get the cheque book, hunting through a mess in the rear of the vehicle and muttering about, 'Untidy slobs.'

When she came in, she found all three men in the family room, chatting about the hot spell and how long it might be expected to continue, or if there would be a cool southerly change.

She slapped the cheque book down in Ben's hand and went to get a pen, then waited, foot tapping, as he wrote out the cheque. But of course, he had to exchange a few further remarks with the men about how much more comfortable queen-sized beds were than ordinary double beds.

She could feel her cheeks flaming. After all her kindness to him, why was he trying to suggest that they were sharing a bed as well as a house? She had a good mind to throw him out this very minute. Only he could hardly walk, let alone drive, and he had nowhere else to go.

'You did that on purpose, Elless!' she yelled, as she stormed back inside after seeing the delivery men out.

'Guilty.'

'Why?'

'I couldn't resist it.'

'They think we're – we're—' She was nearly choking with rage.

'They'd think it anyway, whatever we said or did.' His eyes were dancing with laughter.

'They would not!' She paused, then realized that he was right. 'Oh, very well, I suppose they would. But I'm not sharing that bed with you, and I have no intention of doing so! Ever!' She could see his mouth opening and added savagely, 'Whatever the inexplicable and unwelcome physical attraction between us.'

'Are you challenging me?' He was lying back, still chuckling.

'No, I'm not!' She was almost dancing with fury and if there had been a vase within reach, she would have hurled it at his head.

'Because if you are, I'd like to bet that you'll lose, Ingram. The way we react to one another, it'll be a miracle if nothing happens between us.'

'Not a miracle, but my choice, Elless. And I refuse to allow you to provoke me. You're not thinking clearly because of the concussion.' She drew in a deep breath, then said more calmly, 'If you'll give me a few minutes, I'll make up your bed, then you can have a rest.'

'Thank you – darling.'

The calmness vanished. '*Don't* call me that!'

'Dearest? Beloved? Honey-babe? Cuddlepot? Snookums?'

Her lips twitched in spite of her annoyance.

'That's better,' he approved. 'Never lose your temper if you want to win a battle.'

'I'll remember that next time.'

When she came back, he was lying back, with his head on a cushion, and the bruise on his forehead was looking dark and nasty, surrounded as it was by raw grazed skin. He opened his eyes and she saw that they had completely lost the mischievous look. He was obviously fighting against sleep.

'Your bed's ready.'

'Thank you. Er – where is the bathroom.'

Only then did she realize that he would have to share her en suite bathroom. 'Oh no! I forgot. The bathroom at your end of the house is unfinished. You'll have to share mine.'

'If I weren't so damned tired, I could make something of that, but at this moment all I want is to get to the bathroom, then go to bed for a zillion years. And for that, I need your help. Cry truce?'

'Yes.'

This time when she helped him up, there were no mischievous glances, no casual brushings of one body against another. Instead, it was a grim endurance feat for him to hobble along to the master bedroom and a few times she heard air hiss suddenly into his mouth, as if his ankle was hurting badly.

When she got him into the en suite and sitting on the plastic stool she used in the bathroom, he looked longingly at the shower. 'Would you mind if I washed this grit off?'

'No, of course not. I'll get you a towel and a polythene bag to cover your bandage with.' When she brought them back she realized he had no clothes to change into.

He seemed able to read her mind. 'I can wrap the towel round myself afterwards. I promise not to flaunt my body at you. This will be the quickest shower on record.' He stood up and held on to the vanity unit, staring at himself in the mirror.

'I'll have a nice black eye by tomorrow, to match my other bruises.'

'Yes.'

'And there's sand in some very delicate parts of my anatomy.'

She ignored that remark. 'Just let me fix a plastic bag over your bandages. There. Can you manage on your own now?'

'Are you offering to scrub my back?' His voice was a mere whisper of sound.

'No!'

'I thought not. Pity.'

'You said we'd cry truce,' she reminded him.

'Sorry. So I did. The idea of you scrubbing my back was just too tempting.' He closed his eyes for a minute, then gave her a genuine smile, with no hint of mockery. 'I'll manage all right, Ingram, then call you when I've finished. I really do need your help to get around the house today.' He stood up and groaned. 'I seem to be hurting everywhere.'

When he called a few minutes later she knelt to unfasten the plastic bag. As she helped him along the corridor, she was too worried about how white and exhausted he was looking to bother about the damp naked body hobbling along underneath her best guest towel.

He lay back on the pillow and closed his eyes. 'This is probably the most comfortable bed on earth,' he murmured, speaking so quietly she had to lean forward to catch the words. He opened his blue, blue eyes and smiled up at her as angelically as any choir boy. 'I really am grateful. For my life and everything.'

'Mmm. So you said. You don't need to keep on saying it.'

'All right. I can see that it embarrasses you. And don't worry. We'll work things out somehow. Aahhh.' His yawn tailed away and his eyes flickered shut. She remained by the bed for a minute or two, to make sure he really was asleep.

His breathing deepened and his fingers uncurled. He had the longest eyelashes she had ever seen on a man, and one damp twist of hair had dropped over his forehead, probably the same one her fingers had itched to brush away before. Without thinking, she bent down to kiss his cheek, then gasped and jumped back in shock. What lunatic impulse had made her do that? Thank heavens he was asleep!

When she turned at the door for a final glance at him, his lips were curved upwards in a half-smile, as if he was enjoying a pleasant dream. She took yet another deep breath and strode out of the room. Get away from him, you fool, she thought, before you do anything else stupid! You've already won the dunce's prize today, that's for sure.

Then she remembered someone had tried to kill or hurt him. At least, that seemed a fairly likely explanation for the sawn-off beams. She shook her head. No, she must be wrong. Such things didn't happen in sleepy Australian country towns. Only – how else could you explain the beams? Not quite sawn through, either.

As she went to put away the shopping, she decided to bake a coffee gâteau. And some scones as well. And those flowerbeds were full of weeds. She went to look in every hour, to check that he was all right, but managed to keep herself very busy until it was time for bed.

Nothing she did would keep her unwanted guest out of her thoughts for more than a few minutes, though. Or get rid of her worries about his safety.

Bill received a phone call from Terry.

'My colleagues want you to make an offer to the Elless guy and that city woman who's bought the block I wanted.'

'Oh? Offers to both of them?'

'Yeah. Offer her fifty thousand more than she paid to sell it quickly. And what's the market price for Elless's block? Right. Top that by twenty thousand dollars.'

'You'd better come in and do the paperwork.'

'Go and sound them out first.'

Bill hesitated, then shrugged. He was puzzled by this, didn't think either party would sell, but it never hurt to offer people money.

What was Terry up to, though? Would this housing development actually come together? Even if it did, the other guys had chosen their local partner badly.

Bill decided to speak to one or two of his friends on the town council and see what they thought of the prospect of a development in that area. He'd understood the land was to be kept zoned rural.

Ria was driving back from visiting a client when she noticed there was something wrong with the house where old Johnny Elless used to live. She slowed down, wondering what it was, then realized that part of it had fallen down.

She'd seen Johnny's nephew out there once or twice, tinkering with the house, but didn't know him well enough to call in and ask if he needed help, though she'd had coffee with old Johnny regularly.

This time it wasn't the nephew, but two men with surveying equipment who were using it in the area beyond the house. She wondered who they were and why they were there. Perhaps Johnny's nephew had employed them to survey the block?

There was something familiar about them, though, which teased at her till she got back to the camping ground. Only then did she remember they were the men who'd chucked her and her friends off the disused block of land they'd been camping on. She'd not taken to them at all. And they didn't look like surveyors.

What were they up to? Was this legit? She was pretty sure they didn't come from the district. They had a city look to them.

She forgot all about the strangers, however, when she saw her kids facing a hostile semi-circle of older boys from the other caravans.

She sighed. That's what came of being different. But she wasn't going to change how she was raising her son and daughter. She didn't want Neil and Penny growing up like those yobs.

Home schooling was something she believed in passionately, and she was fortunate that the friends she lived with enjoyed sharing that task with her. Indeed, she suspected that Pete was learning nearly as much as the kids were about some things. He'd said once that he'd been a rebel at school – when he'd attended – and had since regretted his lack of an education.

Speaking quietly she defused the situation and got some

of the other kids interested in a game she knew. Soon they were laughing and playing.

Only then did her mind go back to what she'd seen. The trouble was, she wasn't sure what, if anything, to do about it.

She'd discuss it with Bill once she had a spare moment.

Fourteen

In the middle of the night Meriel awoke to the realization that someone was in her bedroom. She yelled and fumbled for the light switch and baseball bat at the same time, causing Tina to leap off the bed and start barking furiously.

Blinking against the sudden glare, she saw why the dog hadn't barked before. 'Oh! It's you.'

Ben tried to shrug while still holding the towel around his body and leaning on the walking stick. It was a failure and the towel dipped dangerously low. 'I needed to use your facilities. Sorry I woke you. I tried to be quiet, but I'm not very good at moving yet.' He grinned and leaned against the wall, waving his walking stick. 'Please don't hit me! I surrender absolutely and unconditionally.'

'Fool!' She put the baseball bat down and gestured to him to go into the bathroom. When she looked down, she gasped and pulled the covers up to her chin, in spite of the warmth of the summer night. Her nightdress was a flimsy thing, semi-transparent. Why on earth had she put this one on?

There was the sound of the toilet flushing and of water running, then the door of the bathroom opened and her guest reappeared. He stopped for a moment and leaned against the door frame, looking weary and in pain.

'Is it hurting?' She looked round for her dressing gown, but it was over at the far side of the room on a chair.

'A bit. I think I'll take some more of those painkillers, if you'll tell me where to find them.' As an incautious move-ment brought his swollen foot into contact with the door frame, he yelped and clung to it, breathing heavily.

She forgot her state of undress and swung out of the bed. 'Sit down for a minute.'

The only place within reach was the corner of her bed and he subsided on it with a groan. 'I'm really sorry about waking you up.'

'It doesn't matter. Just stay there while I get you the tablets. When you've had a rest, I'll help you back along the corridor to your room.'

'Thanks.' He smiled tiredly up at her. 'You're a real life-saver, Ingram.' Then his smile broadened. 'And you have a very sexy taste in nightwear.'

As she looked down she let out a yip of embarrassment and rushed across to the chair, dragging her dressing gown around her. If he said one more word, just one, she would definitely throw something at him. Several things!

Only when she felt respectable again did she turn to look at him. He had swung his injured leg up on the bed and was hunched over it, rocking slightly with pain. As if he felt her eyes upon him, he looked up. 'Sorry. I must have knocked a particularly tender bit on that door frame.'

She forgot her annoyance and hurried out to get what he needed.

When he had drunk the milk and taken the tablets, she took the glass from him. 'I'll just go and get myself a drink of water and I'll put one next to your bed, too. It's a thirsty sort of night. Stay there till I come back then I'll help you along to your room.'

When she returned, he had rolled over and was lying on the bed with his eyes closed. 'Elless . . . Ben?'

He didn't stir.

She stood hesitating. His face was wrinkled in a half-frown, as if the pain was still there, even in sleep. She didn't have the heart to wake him up again and force him to limp back along the corridor.

She hesitated. Should she go and use the other room? No, somehow she didn't want to spend the night in what she thought of as *his* bed. Besides, what if he woke up and didn't know where he was? He might hurt himself.

'Elless?'

His breathing was so deep and even, he couldn't possibly be feigning sleep. She tip-toed across to her walk-in robe and found a sheet to spread over him. No need for a covering in this heat, but that towel was slipping again.

She was exhausted. No way was she spending the night on the couch. This was a large bed, after all. Slipping off her dressing gown, she slid under the other sheet, yawning. It had been a very eventful day. Anyway, she'd probably wake up long before he did.

Ben woke at dawn and couldn't at first remember where he was. Then he turned in the bed and saw her lying there, sleeping soundly, looking tousled and altogether too gorgeous. He almost reached out to touch her beautiful hair then pulled his hand back.

How had he got into her bed? He had a vague memory of making his way along to the bathroom and . . . he frowned . . . she'd gone to get him some more painkillers. He watched her for a few moments, remembering with a pang what it had been like to wake up beside Sandy, to have someone to share with, to cuddle, to tease.

Meriel stirred and he heard a soft murmur of sound as she began to surface. When she saw him, she came instantly awake.

'Good morning. You sleep as soundly and easily as a child. No, don't jump out of bed. We're perfectly respectable, each in our own nest of covers.'

She yawned and stretched. 'How do you feel this morning? You look a bit better.'

'I feel all right – until I try to move. I'd prefer to take more of those painkillers before I get up, though.'

'And your headache?'

'The thumping seems to have dulled down to a background ache.'

'That's good. You'd better not have any tablets until you've had something proper to eat.'

He couldn't resist teasing her. 'I won't if you say not, nursie dear. I'll be the most docile, co-operative patient that ever was.'

She snorted her disbelief. 'For how long? Five seconds? Ten?'

He assumed an expression of virtuous indignation and was pleased when it made her smile. 'How can you accuse me of such things? I'm cut to the quick by your mistrust – distressed, forlorn, broken-hearted, inconsolable, mortified, chagrined. I shall probably go into a decline and pine right away.' He laid one hand on his chest and gazed at her soul-fully till she chuckled.

Then he couldn't resist it. He stretched out one fingertip to stroke a strand of her hair that had been tempting him for several minutes. He watched as her breath caught in her throat and when she didn't pull away, felt a sense of triumph.

'The colour's quite natural, isn't it?'

'Of course it's natural!' She grimaced. 'I wish it weren't quite so – blond. I'd rather have dark hair.'

'Never wish that. Your hair's glorious.'

'People assume you're dumb if you're a blonde and treat you accordingly.'

'I don't think you're dumb.'

'No, but you do think I've been trying to blackmail you.'

He could see tears well up and make her eyes over-bright. 'I don't think that now. I changed my mind yesterday after-noon.'

'Oh?' They stared at each other in silence for a minute or two, then she asked, 'Why?'

'When we were in the car coming back from town, I saw tears in your eyes after I'd accused you again – I don't know why I did it anyway – and I suddenly realized I was wrong about you, that you weren't the sort to blackmail anyone. I'm truly sorry now that I accused you of it. I meant to apologize yesterday, but the pain distracted me somewhat.'

He grimaced as he looked down at his foot, 'Perhaps I could have those damned painkillers now?'

She came back with them to find Ben lying with his eyes closed, a frown creasing his forehead, and hovered anxiously by his side as he swallowed the two tablets. 'Let me look at your pupils,' she demanded, as soon as she had taken the empty glass away from him.

He turned the full power of his bright blue eyes on to her. 'What's the verdict, nursie dear?'

'You'll probably live, Elless.' It helped to use his surname, kept him at bay – well, sort of. She managed to speak lightly but had trouble tearing her eyes away from his. 'Look – um – I'm going to get my shower now. You'd better stay here until you've had yours, then I'll help you along to the family room or back to your own bed, whichever you prefer.'

'All right.'

'And – um – you'll need some clothes.'

'I suppose so.'

She went into the walk-in wardrobe and came out with an oversized tee shirt and a sarong which she laid on the foot of the bed. 'I'm afraid these are the best I can do.'

When she'd grabbed some clean clothes for herself, she took a quick shower then went to prepare breakfast. The amount he ate eased her worries. He couldn't be that ill if he could eat a big plate of bacon, eggs and tomatoes.

Afterwards she settled him on her couch in the family room and offered him a choice of books to while away the time.

'Aren't you going to sit and hold my hand?'

'No, I'm going to paint some walls.'

He grinned. 'That'll keep you out of my way nicely. Which walls?'

'The ones in the next room to this.'

'What are you going to do with it? This is quite a big house for one person. I'd have thought you'd spend most of your time in this room. Why the rush to do the rest?'

'This is the room I'll be living in, certainly, but I'll need that one for – for—' She broke off as she worked out where this was leading.

'For what? What's your deadly secret, Ingram? I'm still trying to understand why a woman like you would want to hide herself away in the country.'

'Because I'm going to be – no, I *am* an artist.' She still felt self-conscious saying that to people. 'So I need a studio.'

'Aha! The mystery begins to unravel.'

She avoided his eyes. 'Not a mystery, just a chance to do my own thing. I haven't really started yet, commercially. I've been studying at night school for years, learning my trade, though I have been commissioned to do several book cover illustrations, and I've sold some greeting card designs.'

'So the money you inherited has allowed you to follow your dream?'

'Yes.' She grimaced. 'But this place cost more than I'd intended to spend and I still need to get the firebreaks done, so I'll have to be very careful how I go from now on. I'll need some money to live on for a year or two, at least, and it only makes sense to keep some in reserve.'

'What was the money? Legacy from an elderly aunt?'

She could feel another blush creeping up her neck. 'No. Actually,' she had to clear her throat, because the words wouldn't come out easily, 'I won Lotto.'

He stared at her incredulously, then threw back his head and roared with laughter. 'And you're embarrassed by it?'

'Well, it's the only time I've even bought a ticket. I couldn't believe it when I won. It seemed an enormous amount of money at first, but by the time I'd bought this place and a car, well – I don't like to run my savings down to nothing.'

'You shouldn't be ashamed of winning,' he said softly. 'Be glad, be joyful. It's not a sin to be lucky.'

She changed the subject. 'Yes, well, even lucky people have work to do.'

Mid-morning she got them both a cup of coffee and scones.

He raised his eyebrows at the sight of the plate. 'Home made?'

'Yes.'

He took a big bite and made mumbling sounds of pleasure. 'You have hidden talents, Ingram. Any chance of another? My appetite seems to be returning.'

Just as she was clearing up, the phone rang. 'Oh, hi Bill. What can I do for you?'

He explained about the offer.

'I can't believe this. But I'm definitely not selling. That's the second offer I've had to sell the place.'

'Who's the other?'

'Ben Elless.'

'Ah. I heard you'd taken him in. Is he still at your place?'

She didn't bother asking how he knew. York was a small town. 'Yes. Do you want to speak to him?' She passed the phone to Ben.

He listened carefully, then said, 'Not interested. No, not at any price.'

When he put the phone down he said, 'I've had an offer for my place. A good one. I gather you had one too.'

'Yes.'

'There's only one sort of person who'd want two blocks next to one another.'

She finished it for him. 'A developer. Well, they can just go and do their developing somewhere else. I'm not selling.'

'My sentiments exactly.'

'I'll get back to work.'

When she peeped in on him half an hour later, worried by the silence, he was fast asleep. She stared across the room at his bruised face, feeling her gaze softening, then shook her head and went back to work.

By lunchtime she was sick of the smell of paint and her arms were aching, but at least she'd finished the second coat. It was another warm day and the paint had dried almost as soon as she had put it on. That, she thought, looking up and nodding approval, was enough for anyone.

She cleaned and packed away her equipment then took a shower. Putting on a clean white top and blue knee-length shorts, she went back to face him.

He was awake again, holding one of the novels she'd given him but frowning into space. He put the book down immediately she entered the room and gave her a welcoming smile.

Tina, who had been lying by the side of the couch, heaved herself upright and came over to lick Meriel's hand and press against her for a cuddle. She was a most affectionate dog and didn't seem to be missing her former owner too much.

Ben's deep voice washed over Meriel. 'Painting over for the day?'

'Yes. I can't face any more of it.'

'It's a waste of time, an artist doing such a hack job.'

She shrugged. 'Needs must. It offends my artistic soul to have bare stained plaster around me while I work. But it'd offend me even more to pay someone else to do a simple job like that.' She changed the subject. 'Hungry?'

'Yes. Very. I'm afraid I have a rather healthy appetite. We must come to some arrangement about food. Just tell me how much I'm costing you.'

'All right.'

When he didn't reply, she looked up to see him grinning at her. 'What's so funny?'

'That must be the first time we've reached agreement about anything without quarrelling.'

'That's because you're being reasonable, for once, Elless.'

'I just *lurve* the way you call me Elless.' He let out an exaggerated sigh.

'Don't push your luck! You're being *reasonable* today, remember?'

'Ouch! That was a hit below the belt, Ingram! And me an injured man, too!'

She chuckled, pushed Tina away and walked into the kitchen area to start pulling food out of the fridge.

His voice followed her. 'After lunch, could we talk? My head seems clear enough now to do some planning. I need to sort out quite a few things, like how to get my surviving possessions out of that shack, not to mention finding somewhere to live and getting proper clothes to wear.' He gestured to the tee shirt she had lent him, a loose tent of a garment on her, but one which was tightly stretched across his shoulders.

Below it, he was wearing the sarong she had bought one day at a market on an impulse, after falling in love with its shimmering colours. Beneath the dark blue shot with silver and bands of lighter blue and pink, his sun-tanned legs were bare.

'I should have gone into town this morning and bought you some more clothes,' she said guiltily. 'Or I could have gone back to your place and tiptoed into the bedroom. Why didn't you remind me of your needs?'

'There was no hurry. And I don't want you going back into that shack, not under any circumstances. It's far too dangerous.'

He raised her hand in a halt signal as she would have protested that she'd have been careful.

'I'm not going inside it, either. The whole place needs to be demolished now.'

She shrugged.

'Anyway, how could I come between a woman and her paint roller?'

She blew a loud raspberry at him.

'Besides, I wanted time to think before we had our talk.'

'What about?'

'We'll discuss it after lunch, unless you want me to fade away from starvation.'

She produced a plateful of salami and salad sandwiches, accompanied by crunchy pieces of carrot and celery. Afterwards, she watched in satisfaction as he demolished some of her coffee gâteau while making noises of extreme appreciation.

'Ingram, you certainly know the way to a man's heart. That was delicious. Now, will you come and sit down for a while?'

For some weird reason she felt shy as she went to sit opposite him on her rocking chair. 'So, what do you want to talk about?'

'I want, no I *need*, to talk about,' he began ticking items off on his fingers, 'you, me, my needs, your needs, the future. I think there are a great many things we should discuss, actually.'

'That sounds like a pretty comprehensive list.'

'Yes. But it's hard to concentrate with you sitting there looking so luscious.' His smile broadened into a grin. 'And blushing so charmingly.'

'Will you just get on with it, Elless!'

'Very well then. Number One: I have a short-term need that can quite easily be filled – clothes. I'll give you my size and you can go into town and call in at a men's wear shop. They'll be delighted to help you pick out a few clothes for me and then they can ring me for my credit card number. I thought I'd lost it, but it was among that stuff you brought in from the car.'

'OK.'

'Number Two: my uncle's house. When we've finished our chat, I'll ring Bill and ask him to find someone to rescue any of my possessions which have survived and then demolish the place. It's too dangerous to leave as it is. Bill seems to be a Mr Fix-it round here and I bet he'll know someone who'll do a salvage job for me.'

She nodded again. No doubt Ben would then move

back to Queensland. That thought made her catch her breath, horrified to find that she didn't want him to move so far away.

'Now where did you just go to?' he asked softly. 'Your eyes glazed over and you looked quite upset for a moment or two. Surely I haven't said anything to offend you?'

'No. No, of course not. You know how it is. A stray thought. Nothing to do with you. Do go on. Number Three?'

'Number Three: I need somewhere to live. And quickly. That's more of a problem. There are always houses to rent, I know, but they want longer-term tenants than me and anyway, I shall be coming and going a lot. The trouble is, I don't want to move far away from my uncle's block.'

'Why not? Surely you've finished looking things over in York? I'm surprised you didn't take the offer to buy it so you can go back to Brisbane.' She hoped her voice sounded casually confident but doubted it. Hell, she was a stupid fool, hankering after a man who was only here temporarily! Swallowing hard, she jerked up out of her chair and went to stand over by the window. 'Go on!' she said, her voice thick with the unshed tears. 'I'm listening.'

'Come over here, Ingram, where I can keep my eye on you.'

'I need to stretch my back. You get a crick in it when you're painting walls. I wonder how Michelangelo coped with the whole of the Sistine Chapel. He must have—'

His deep velvet voice cut through her babble. 'If you don't come here this minute, I'll get up and limp after you.'

She turned round slowly. 'I—'

'Stop putting up a smokescreen of words and come over here.'

It seemed unfair to run away and make him struggle after her. She had no doubt he meant what he said. She started to move, putting one foot carefully in front of the other, each step slower than the one before.

She arrived at the couch and stood looking down at him. His eyes were clear now, the warmth in them unmistakable. His lips curved into a smile and suddenly she could fight the attraction no longer. When he reached out an arm to pull her down towards him, she went willingly, sitting on the edge of the couch within the warm circle of his embrace. A trap? Or a shelter? Or both of those?

'No struggles, Ingram?' His voice was husky in her ear.

'I've been struggling against you for days, Elless, no, for longer than that. Maybe familiarity will breed contempt.'

'And maybe it won't. You aren't the only one who's been side-swiped by this attraction.' He pulled her head gently round to face him and leaned forward to place a tender kiss on the tip of her nose. 'It isn't just sex that I've missed since Sandy died and it isn't just sex that I want from a woman; it's the touching and cuddling, the smiles, the sheer fun of being two, doing things together, coming home to one another.'

'I've never really had that sort of long-term relationship,' she admitted.

'It can be wonderful. I think we should see if our attraction builds into something like that. We'd be fools to ignore such a wonderful possibility.'

She couldn't think what to say to that. Only yesterday she'd been quite sure that her art was the most important thing in her life, but now . . . Well, she *was* attracted to him, no denying it, but she didn't want to give up her independence, either financial or emotional.

There was a pause, then he added very quietly, 'I hadn't thought I could ever feel this way again. I loved my wife very much and we were truly happy together, but Sandy's been dead for four years now and nothing will bring her back. I shall always love her, but I'm not hung up on the past, not trying to find another Sandy, I promise you. If things work out as I hope, you won't be second best. I've seen it with my mother, who's been married twice and is now with another guy. It's just – different with another person, not better not worse, but different.'

Meriel relaxed against him. 'I'm glad you loved your wife so much. It's wonderful to hear someone talk like that.' She picked up his hand and began to play with his fingers. 'I need to take things slowly, though, Ben.'

They sat quietly for a few moments and she marvelled at the feeling of warmth she got from their togetherness.

When he spoke again, aeons later, his voice sounded more normal, but what he said made her jerk upright in surprise. 'Wouldn't it make sense, on all counts, if you let me rent some rooms in your house?'

Fifteen

After one betraying jerk, Ben felt Meriel grow still. When she turned a rather suspicious glance in his direction, he wondered what had given her such a distrust of men. 'I don't mean I want to *buy* time with you. I mean I want to rent your two spare bedrooms for business purposes.' He cocked his head on one side, his eyes steady on hers. 'I can sleep in one till you know me better and the other will be my office. And we could have the second bathroom finished off, too, while we're at it, so I don't need to intrude on your privacy.'

Marvelling at how easy it suddenly was to say 'we' again, he put one fingertip under Meriel's chin, tilted her face up and stared into her eyes. 'Not that I don't want to sleep in your bed – I do – but I intend to do that only with your full consent and approval.'

She sat there with one of his arms lying round her shoulders. 'Why is it so important for you to stay near the block? I can't understand that. I thought you were going to sell it.'

'We-ell . . . Don't tell anyone else yet, especially here in York.'

'I promise.'

He wriggled to the back of the couch, giving her more room to lean against the warm angle of his body. 'I'm a landscape designer by trade, and I love shaping larger landscapes. They're much more interesting than fiddling with people's gardens. I've done pretty well, got myself a bit of a name for it in Brisbane. I also own a couple of places which provide self-catering holiday accommodation, though I've got those on the market now.

'The firm in which I'm a partner – Elless-Hantley Landscaping – has been working on a big project recently and it's nearly finished. Last August I gave notice to Phil, my partner, that I intend to dissolve the partnership and once that's all sorted out, I want to create something of my own, here if possible. A mixture of holiday accommodation, eco-tourism and plant nursery – supplying retailers as well as selling plants myself. I want to focus on rare plants and natives.

'I'd enjoy taking people on guided tours of the bush. I spent my childhood on the block next door and I know every inch of it, every little creature that creeps or flies or jumps. Tourists enjoy that sort of thing if it's done by someone who understands the small ecologies that can change from hilltop to valley. And if things go well, I want to make my home here, settle down, raise a family . . .'

She squeezed his hand in encouragement. 'Go on. How will you finance it?'

'That's what's been holding me back. It took a few years to set up the two places I own in Brisbane. Sandy and I worked our butts off doing things ourselves in the early days. Thanks to her life insurance they're fully paid off, so when I sell them I'll have some money to invest. The partnership may be worth something, or there again, it may not. Phil knows nothing about landscaping and plants, so he'd have to find someone to replace me or he'd have no business at all.

'I *am* good at landscaping large areas, Meriel, but I keep having to follow other people's ideas, even when they're not right.' He went a bit pink. 'I've even won a couple of awards for my designs. So . . . now I'd like to try to do a development all by myself from scratch and – and make it beautiful, yet keep it in harmony with nature and the local flora and fauna. I could sell people an afternoon, a weekend or a couple of weeks of peace and exploring our local ecology. Whatever.'

She frowned. 'But there's no grand scenery or sweeping coastlines or anything spectacular in York to attract people in the first place.'

'I was intending to sell them the smaller beauties of nature – kangaroos, emus, cockatoos and parrots, skinks running along their verandas – you know the sort of thing. And wildflowers, especially in the spring. Then there's the Avon Descent in the winter. People love white-water events. This inheritance was a godsend. Here I can give them the quintessential bush of Western Australia and nearby, the quaintness of a small colonial town.'

She was still puzzled. 'But the bush isn't all that beautiful here. It might be, if this were a permanent creek, but it's a winter creek only. And untouched bush looks – well, it can look downright scruffy. For most of the year, anyway. It might look better in spring with the wildflowers out, but that's only for a short time and – and—'

'You're forgetting my talent for landscaping. I can make a big difference without destroying the basic ecology. Trust me on that.'

'Enough to attract people?'

'I think so.' His eyes were alight and excitement was crackling through his body. 'I want to create a small lake, you see. I've checked and there's plenty of water under the ground, so I could sink a bore. I'd place a low waterfall at one side to help aerate it and perhaps a fountain in the middle. I'd make the edges of the lake beautiful. But I need to survey the whole area properly before I can get down to designing it.'

She found his enthusiasm very attractive. 'That could be lovely.'

'Yes. I really think it could. I'd do a little landscaping around each tourist unit, then I'd mark out a few well-defined bush trails of varying difficulties, at least one of them suitable for wheelchairs. I'd leave most of the bush untouched, though I'd add some of the prettier local native plants at strategic points. I'd positively encourage birds and I'd scatter wildflower seeds everywhere.' His expression became wry, 'Or I would have done all that, if I'd had your block as well as mine. Without your block, I'm sunk. I need the low-lying land intact, you see, for the lake.'

'That's why you were so very angry that I'd bought Somerlee. I just couldn't understand it.'

'I thought you'd nipped in on purpose to blackmail me.'

'And all I'd done was fall in love with it.'

'Which may perhaps turn out all right in the end,' he

looked at her challengingly, 'if I can persuade you to sell me some of the land, or come in as a partner.'

She frowned.

'Don't answer now – I'm not asking you to come to any hurried decisions. Just think about it for a while, ask me questions and so on. You don't exactly need seventy acres, after all.' He paused, watching her carefully until she nodded, at which time he judged he'd said enough. 'Right, then, if you'll help me make a list, then go and buy me some clothes, I'll be happy to continue the business discussions later. I'm getting a little tired of strutting around half-naked.'

'But your development—'

He pressed his fingertips against her lips. 'Don't say anything now, Ingram. Just think about the basic concept. Hmm? Details can be worked out to suit.'

She could feel his charm washing round her, but no amount of charm was going to make her take any rash steps or put her precious financial security in jeopardy. 'All right. I'll definitely do that. And of course I'll have to see the books, check the figures and so on.'

'Are you an accountant or an artist, Ingram?'

She stared at him, mouth open, then let out a little puff of surprise. 'I never realized . . . I'm both now, I think.'

It wasn't until she was on her way into town that she remembered the sawn-off ceiling beams. Why hadn't she mentioned them to him? What was that about? Was someone trying to drive him away? If so, whoever it was would have two people to deal with from now on, not one.

But they might attack his development too. It might be dangerous.

When she got back from the shops she found that Ben had eaten more of the coffee gâteau and was giving a very fair imitation of a lame, caged lion. She deposited some plastic carry-bags on the floor next to the couch and he pounced on them.

'Thanks. I hate to see you doing all the donkey work. I should be the one unloading the car.' He moved incautiously and winced.

'Women have always been quite capable of bringing the

shopping in. Oh, and by the way, I checked your oil and tyres, and they both needed attention. You've been neglecting that car of yours, leased or not.'

'You what?'

'I checked your oil and tyres.'

He stood gaping at her. 'You know, you're constantly surprising me. I suppose you couldn't give the car a service while you're at it?'

'I could, if you really want me to. But I'd charge you for it. My time is worth money.'

His grin was slow and reluctant. 'I'm sure you would. And yet, you look like the fairy on top of the Christmas tree. Where on earth did you learn to service cars?'

'From my Grandpop. He believed that everyone should know how to look after their own possessions – including cars. The first time he bought one, when he was a young man, he pulled it to pieces to see how it worked and then put it together again. He did most of his own maintenance and repairs right until the year before he died.'

'You sound to have been close to him.'

'Very close indeed. I was always Grandpop's little helper. I miss him very much.' Her smile wavered. She still found it hard to talk about him without tears coming into her eyes. 'I'll go and get the rest of the stuff in.'

Just as she was finishing Tina began barking and yelping at two men in a small truck who had just turned up.

When they knocked on the door Ben clicked his fingers and ordered the dog to sit. Tina looked disappointed, but did as he told her, easing down by his side and looking up at him adoringly.

'Are you trying to take over my dog, too?' Meriel asked.

'Dogs and small children always like me,' he said smugly. 'They say animals can tell what a person's like.'

'What about snakes and bats and cockroaches. Do they adore you too?' She went to open the door.

'We got a message to contact a Mr Ben Elless about a demolition job.'

'You'd better come inside. He's hurt his ankle.'

Within minutes a brisk business conference was under

way, a price had been agreed and the men had left to start the retrieval-demolition job on the remains of the shack.

It wasn't until they had gone that she remembered the sawn-off beams and went to fetch the one she'd kept. It seemed to get heavier each time she picked it up.

He didn't say a word as he took it from her and examined it.

She waited impatiently. 'I'll go and tell the men to stop work, shall I? We probably need to get the police in to investigate.'

'Drive me over. I want to see it for myself before we tell anyone.'

'Are you sure?'

'Of course I'm sure!' Grim-faced, he picked up his walking stick and limped out towards his car. She picked up the keys and followed.

At the block they found the men walking round the half-ruined house, talking and gesticulating.

'Something up, mate?'

'I thought I should inspect it for myself before you got started.' Ben used the walking stick to help him limp across to the edge of the pile of rubble.

Meriel stood beside him, staring in amazement at the roofline. 'More of the roof has fallen down since yesterday.'

Ben turned to her. 'You're quite sure of that? I was in no state to remember clearly what it was like.'

'I'm positive. The rest of the building seemed pretty solid, so I don't see why it should have fallen. I tested it out carefully before I went inside. Someone must have been here since then and pulled more of the roof down deliberately. The sawn-off beams were over there, where the new fall happened.'

One of the men came over. 'You should have left it all for us, y'know. Demolition's dangerous when you don't know what you're doing.'

Meriel saw Ben stiffen. 'What do you mean? We haven't been back here since the accident.'

'Well, someone has.' The man pointed to the part of the roof Meriel had just been talking about. 'And they didn't bloody know what they were doing, trying to pull it down like that.'

'Must have been vandals,' Ben said quickly as Meriel opened her mouth. 'You'd better get started, mate, before they come back.'

'Yeah, that old jarrah's very popular. Good strong wood, better than the pine they use these days.'

'I'd pay extra to have the place watched tonight. Know anyone who'd do it?'

One man grinned at him. 'Me, as long as it's cash in hand. I'll bring my dog over and we can sleep in the back of my ute in hot weather like this.'

'Done.'

They shook hands.

Ben turned to Meriel, his face expressionless. 'Would you drive me home now, please?'

When they got back to the car, she scowled at him. 'Why did you cut me off short? We should have investigated, seen if we could find the sawn-off beams.'

'Because I didn't want any rumours starting.'

'But you might have been killed!'

'I don't think that was intended. Not for the sake of a piece of land. No, I think someone just wants me to leave. If I don't have somewhere to live, they make it much harder for me to stay.'

She went to hold his arm for a moment and hug it close. 'They might not have intended to kill you, but they nearly did. I can't ignore that, even if you can. Come on, let's go home.'

For the rest of the afternoon and early evening the small truck groaned backwards and forwards between the shack and Meriel's house. A surprising amount of furniture had proved salvageable and was gradually unloaded into the spare rooms, including a brand-new computer which needed only a new monitor to replace the one that had been smashed. There was some new office furniture that had been in the front part of the house and had come through almost unscathed, except for a few scratches and dents from flying debris.

'That's not temporary equipment,' she commented.

'I was setting up for a long project. It's good that we haven't lost everything. Saves us some money.'

She looked at him sideways. *We* and *us* again. Was he including her already? Was it possible to slip so easily into being a pair? He'd done it easily – but then, he had more experience of that than she did.

'Your bed was crushed flat,' one of the men said cheerfully. 'Good thing you weren't lying in it, mate.'

By the end of the following day, all the contents of the shack had been retrieved or discarded, the fallen timbers had been sorted out into usable and rubbish, and thuds from the next block marked the demise of the rest of the house.

Meriel was taking in some washing when the two men brought a pile of the timber round and started dumping the pieces at the side of the house. She rushed across to them. 'Hey! What do you think you're doing?'

'Ben told us to bring the timber round here.'

'Well, you're not dumping it on my lawn!'

'Got to put it somewhere, lady,' one of them said, in the tones of an intelligent person reasoning with a moron.

'Not there you don't, *mate*. Just stop what you're doing while I find out what this is all about, then I'll tell you where to pile the stuff.'

The men shrugged. 'Better sort it out quickly, then. There are several more loads to come tomorrow.'

She stormed into the house and erupted into the family room. 'Just what do you mean by turning my front lawn into a salvage yard, Elless?'

'Oh, hell, I forgot to tell you. Don't blow a fuse. We can sort this out.'

'We certainly can – as soon as you get that wood off my lawn.'

He looked at her admiringly. 'Did anyone ever tell you how magnificently your eyes flash when you're angry.'

'I'm not angry, I'm furious, and if you don't get that wood moved, I'll make a bonfire of it.' She folded her arms and glared at him. 'I believe wood ash is good for the soil.'

He struggled to his feet. 'I'll have to come out and talk to the men. Look, I'm sorry. I'm so used to steaming ahead and getting the practical things done that I didn't think.'

'You certainly didn't. And what on earth do you want with a pile of second-hand timber, anyway?'

'Character.'

She stared at him. 'What?'

'The beams and posts in my uncle's shack are jarrah and so are the floors. That wood will still be good in another hundred years and it'll polish up beautifully once it's sanded down. It's very West Australian, jarrah is. And it's good to recycle scarce resources, don't you think?' He ran a hand through his hair. 'I'm not organizing all this well, am I? I get started on design ideas and forget where I am. Dammit, I could do with a site foreman and general factotum. I can't hobble very far and I was in the thick of some calculations and—'

She looked at him, head on one side. 'How much would you pay me to do it?'

His face lit up. 'Whatever you think reasonable. Hourly rates?'

She stuck out her hand and they shook. Smiling, she went to put on some sunscreen lotion and a shady hat. Fine businessman he was! He hadn't even asked how much she wanted. Then she frowned. He *should* have asked! Surely he couldn't be that impractical?

Later she looked out of the window at the piles of timber set neatly to one side of the house beyond the cultivated patch of ground and wondered if she was doing the right thing helping him out. Every step she took seemed to bind them more firmly together.

It scared her.

It delighted her, too.

At ten o'clock she stood up. 'I'm going to bed now.'

He'd looked at her questioningly.

'Could you use the bathroom before you go to your own room?'

He gave her a long steady scrutiny, then nodded as if accepting her decision before hauling himself to his feet.

She watched him go, chewing one corner of her lip. She wasn't ready yet to sleep with a fully-conscious Ben, even if he wasn't in a fit state to do much about their feelings. And she was still a bit worried that he was taking risks, wished he'd called in the police, wished . . . Oh, she didn't know what she wished.

When he'd finished she said goodnight, made sure she was wearing a nightdress that didn't reveal all and climbed into her bed. But when she looked at the space beside her she suddenly wished he was there.

How stupid could you get? She hardly knew the man.

In the middle of the night Tina leaped off the bed and started rushing to and fro, barking frenziedly. Meriel woke with a start and went to investigate, heart pounding. When she opened the bedroom door, Tina made straight for the kitchen door, still barking. Meriel put on the outside lights and peered out, hearing Ben come hobbling along the corridor to join her.

'Can you see anything?' he whispered, putting his arm round her. 'Ought we to let her out?'

She leaned against him, glad he was there. 'No way! If someone's there they might hurt her. It's enough that she barks, surely?'

'Normally I'd go out to investigate.'

'That'd be stupid. You don't know how many people are out there.' She turned back but could see no movement outside.

Tina stopped barking and lay down near the French window, head on paws.

Ben looked at Meriel. 'Whatever was upsetting her seems to have gone away.'

'Well, if I find footprints outside in the morning, I'm going into town tomorrow to see the police about intruders.'

'They won't be able to do much about it.'

'I'm still telling them.'

In the morning she got up early, went to investigate and found new tyre marks where someone had parked by the side of the main road near her gate. They must have walked on to the block from there. What had they wanted?

When she went to investigate the piles of lumber she smelled kerosene and one corner of the pile of wood stank of it.

She turned round to see Ben standing on one corner of

the veranda watching her, so went across to tell him what she'd found. His expression grew grim as he listened and for all her protests, he moved slowly and painfully across to look at the pile of wood himself.

'We'd better hose this down,' he said quietly.

'I'll do that after breakfast. I wonder why they didn't light it?'

'I must have been right: they just want to frighten us away.'

'Who are they?'

'Developers. Must be.'

'Well, that settles it. I'm definitely going to the police this morning.'

'Couldn't you wait?'

'No.'

The police listened to her story and promised to keep an eye on her place.

'I do have a friend living with me,' she added, feigning embarrassment, 'but he's hurt his foot. He couldn't do much to help me if – if anyone tried to break in.'

'It's a bit lonely for a woman out there,' the officer said. 'You may have taken on more than you can chew.'

'I'm sure this vandalism is only temporary. When they see you officers turning up a few times, they'll go away.'

She wasn't so sure about that but it seemed a sensible precaution to take!

The following day the weather changed suddenly and a southerly wind made the temperature plummet, which Ben said happened sometimes in summer. Meriel shivered and went to find something warmer to wear if she was going to be outside in that.

Once the demolition men had finished dumping reusable material from the old house, she went into the kitchen to start making the evening meal, Ben limped in to join her. 'Can I help you with anything?'

'You could peel the potatoes.'

He sat down on a stool near the kitchen bench and set to work. 'I could get very used to domesticity again.' He beamed at her.

That touched her deeply. In fact, she was coming to realize she had stereotyped Ben, no doubt because of his startling good looks. He wasn't a Romeo, he was a family man, and the more she got to know him, the more she liked him as well as being attracted to him physically. Very dangerous for an independent woman, that combination.

He looked across the table at her, his head slightly to one side, a question in his eyes if not on his lips.

'Will you be all right on your own tonight?' she asked at last.

He gave her a wry smile. 'Yes, of course. Will you?'

She nodded.

'I'm glad you've got Tina in the bedroom with you.'

'Why? Do you think they'll come back tonight?'

'I doubt it.' He levered himself to his feet. 'I'll just use the bathroom.'

She watched him limp out, nearly followed to ask him to stay with her, but lost courage at the last minute and cleared the table instead.

It was a good thing his injured ankle was giving them both a breathing space, she told herself firmly as she made her way to her own room. She'd be mad to rush into anything.

But as she put on her nightie she suddenly realized that if Ben limped back along that corridor, she'd welcome him into her bed without hesitation.

Why hadn't he even tried it?

She tried to settle to sleep and couldn't. She kept thinking of him and finally faced the fact that *she* was the one keeping them apart.

Why?

Because she was afraid, that was why. She wasn't usually a coward, didn't like to think of herself that way.

Along the corridor Ben was also finding it impossible to get to sleep. Meriel had made it plain she wasn't ready for intimacy yet and he'd not tried to persuade her because he didn't want their first time to be a fiasco with his ankle spoiling things. But it was hard on a man.

He punched the pillow into shape and tried once again

to sleep, but in vain. Images of Meriel wearing that sexy nightdress continued to taunt him.

When he heard a door open at the other end of the house, he was suddenly alert. As footsteps moved slowly towards his room, hope raced like lava through his veins and he reached for the bedside lamp, switching it on, looking towards the door . . .

She stood there for a moment, her expression a mixture of bravado and nervousness. His breath caught in his throat, she was so lovely and yet so vulnerable.

'We're consenting adults,' she declared, chin going up in that sassy way he loved so much. 'We want one another and neither of us can get to sleep because of that. So why not . . . ?' The words tailed away but her eyes said that she wanted him as much as he wanted her, that she'd come to terms with whatever had been stopping her.

She slid in beside him and he drew her gently into his arms but needed to make something clear first, so cradled her face in his hands and said, 'It's not just sex, Meriel darling. It's *you.*'

For a moment her eyes searched his then she smiled. 'I know. It's the same with me. I need *you*, Ben.'

As they lay there afterwards, he pulled her to nestle against him, not wanting them to move apart. His ankle was throbbing in pain and though he tried to hide that, of course she guessed.

She pushed herself up on one elbow and asked, 'Would a cold compress be any help to that foot, do you think?'

'If you don't mind.'

'We should use my room, so that I can keep the compress cool and wet.'

He swung himself into a sitting position and stared at her, trying to work out how she really felt about that. 'Am I staying there afterwards?'

'Do you want to?'

'Of course I do. But if you'd rather I didn't . . .'

'You're treading very carefully, aren't you?'

He nodded. 'It's important to me not to mess things up.'

She stared at him, but didn't say anything else, just gave a small nod then followed him along the corridor.

As sleep slid over him, he could feel happiness and hope murmuring through him as gently as a flowing stream. He loved her already, but it wasn't time yet to say the words because she wasn't ready for them.

But she would be, he was getting more and more hopeful about that.

Sixteen

Ria had to drive near the block where they'd lived for several months, so made a short detour to look at it again.

To her surprise, the two men who'd been on the old Elless property were surveying that one now. Never one to hang back, she parked the car and went across to them. 'Hi. I saw you working and wondered what's going to happen to this place.'

'None of your business. This is private property and I'd be grateful if you'd leave.'

She did as they'd asked, because it was no use banging her head against a brick wall. But after that, she couldn't resist driving past whenever she was in the area. They were surveying one side of it only, working their way along by the fence. Out of curiosity she drove round the twisting backroads to confirm her guess about which property that backed on to. Yes, it was the Elless block.

She discussed it with Pete who said he'd wander over that way on foot later.

Some time later she got back to the campsite from another appointment and found Big Jim sitting in the caravan with headphones on, looking depressed.

She signalled to him that she wanted to talk and he took them off. 'Where are the kids?'

'Pete's on late shift at the hotel. He took them out for a nature walk.'

'They love that.' She hesitated, then said, 'It's getting you down here, isn't it?'

'Yeah. Too much noise, too many people. Does my head in. How about giving your friend Bill another nudge? Maybe there's somewhere out of town that we can rent.'

'If we do pay rent, we'll have more trouble saving money.'

'That's my fault. I'm an old crock, not good for a young woman like you.'

She laid one hand on his arm. 'You can't help having that problem.'

'It makes me damned useless as a man, though. And I'm too old for you, nearly double your age.'

She smiled and reached across to hug him. 'I don't think you're too old. We're kindred spirits and that's what counts most. And actually, I've not been this happy for a good long while.' She judged she'd said enough and changed the subject by telling him about the men surveying their old block.

'They want to bring more good old suburbia out here, I suppose. But if the owner demolished that house, he can't be expecting to stay here, can he?'

'No. Not our business, though.' She started preparing tea. Pete and the kids were always hungry.

She'd hate to see the trees and vegetation on the Elless block razed. It was such a pretty place. They'd sneaked on it for walks a few times, with Pete making sure they did no damage. He was very careful about that sort of thing.

The following morning Meriel got up before Ben woke. For all their intimacy she still felt wary and uncertain how to treat him. She'd never lived with a guy before. He had better skills in that direction and seemed to have an instinctive understanding of when to push her and when not to push, for which she was grateful.

'I'll start on the accounts today,' he said, sighing.

'Do you need any help?'

'Not at this stage.'

Mid-morning, she made him a cup of coffee and took it down to his office, stopping in shock in the doorway. He was holding the edge of the desk and pulling a piece of paper towards him along the floor with a ruler. She bent to pick it up for him and saw it was an unpaid bill, then turned to stare at the things on the desk. 'What are you trying to do here, Elless?'

'I told you. Sort out the accounts. I emptied the files and brought the contents with me. I need to know where I stand before I go back to Brisbane next week.'

'I can do that for you.'

'I didn't want to take advantage.'

'I thought I was going to be your paid factotum?'

'Well, as long as you let me pay you for your help.'

She nodded. 'You're looking tired. You need a rest.' He nodded and she knew he must be very weary to admit it.

When she'd got him settled on the sofa, Meriel went back to the room he was using as an office and groaned under her breath as she looked at the mess there. How could any reputable business base its finances on chaos like this? Didn't they have a secretary, for goodness' sake?

By lunchtime she'd sorted through enough of the paper tangles to know that most of the documentation for the current project was missing. This was mainly small stuff, office expenses, car servicing costs, the occasional meal receipt. Where were the most recent bank statements, not to mention the taxation information?

Ben sat on the couch with his foot up, staring at the floor as she spoke crisply, listing the main items, things that should have been there. 'This goes beyond mere carelessness,' she ended. 'And the data should all have been entered on a computer. Did you check that?'

He nodded. 'Phil had said a while back that Nareen was doing it, but there was nothing on the office computer that I could find. I downloaded everything there was on to a thumb drive.'

'It's my guess that someone's kept the other receipts away from you – and perhaps some of the money, too. What about Phil's computer?'

'I'll check that next time.' He stared at her unhappily. 'I can't believe Phil would – no, no, he wouldn't *steal* from me on that scale, surely? He borrowed some money without asking before, but he paid it all back. He's Sandy's cousin, for heaven's sake!'

'You get rotten apples in the best of families.' She'd seen enough to guess that this Phil was rotten or at best highly incompetent, which was bad enough. But that other sense had kicked in, the one that made her a good investigative accountant in such situations. She was beginning to feel more than a bit suspicious about this Phil Hantley.

Ben surprised her by saying, 'I'd better fly back to Queensland on Friday then, instead of next week. I don't want to leave it any longer to sort out the accounts if they're as bad as you say. My ankle should be all right by then if I strap it up. And there's another reason: the clients we're just finishing a project for have emailed to say they want to see me about the final touches to their landscaping.' He stared at the floor again, as he added, 'There are quite a few discrepancies in the accounts, you say?'

'Yes.' It was her turn to hesitate. She waited a little longer to hear him say it, but he didn't, so she said it for him. 'If I'm to be your accountant, perhaps I should come with you?'

He shook his head immediately. 'No. Not this time.'

'Why not? You need someone who understands accounts. *You* certainly don't.' She was amazed at how much of the financial stuff he'd left to others.

'You'd distract me.' His attempt at a leer was unsuccessful then he fell silent again.

She had to shake his arm to get his attention. 'Don't try to fob me off, Elless. What's the real reason you don't want me to come?'

'This is something I should sort out on my own. It's Sandy's family, so I don't want to – well, hurt those who aren't guilty. My uncle, Phil's father, has cancer, you see. I'm very fond of him.' He stood up. 'I'll get on the Internet and book a flight. Good thing there's a phone line in my office here, eh?'

After that he changed the subject and didn't discuss his trip again.

She let that go and got him talking about his plans for landscaping his uncle's block, because she needed to know more about it if she was to invest in his project.

She was relieved by what he said. He might be inefficient when it came to business details – no, not *might be*, definitely *was* inefficient – but he was inspiring when he talked about the land and by the time he'd finished, she could almost see how it would look when finished.

On Thursday, Ben's foot was much better. 'I suppose I'd better go and pack. I won't take much and I'll bring some

more of my clothes and stuff back with me, if that's all right
with you.'

She followed him into the bedroom, feeling shut out and
annoyed.

He glanced at her, hesitated, then said, 'Meriel, you will
be careful, won't you? Perhaps you should go and stay in
town at night, just to be sure?'

'No way. Forewarned is forearmed. I'll take care, I promise
you, and I have my mobile set for instant dial to the police.'

She watched him pile some clothes into the suitcase any
old how and clicked her tongue in annoyance. 'Get out of
the way, Elless, and let me do that.' Scooping the clothes
out again, she began folding and rolling them neatly. 'Are
you taking any shoes with you? They'll need to go in first.
Something smarter, more businesslike, perhaps?'

He looked down at his sandals and the ankle that still
needed a support bandage. 'I don't think I could get into
my business shoes yet. I hate wearing the damned things,
anyway. I'm more the casual sort. Phil's the fancy dresser
because he's the front man.'

'What about your toiletries?'

'Hell, yes. I'd forgotten them.' He limped along to the
bathroom and returned clutching a bag.

She took it out of his hands, checking that he'd got everything. 'Toothpaste? You can borrow mine till you go. Sit down.
I'll fetch your toothpaste.'

'I'd better get the stuff from the office and put that in, too.'

She followed him, pushing his hands away as he made to
scrape up the papers into one pile. 'Don't you dare! I've just
spent hours sorting those out.' She got some manila folders
from her own office and a big marking pen, putting each
pile of papers into its own folder, neatly labelled.

He said so little while she was doing this that she peeped
at him sideways. He was staring into space again and whatever he was thinking about wasn't making him happy. 'There
you are.'

'Thanks.' He looked at his watch. 'Since the plane leaves at
six a.m., I think I'll drive down to Perth tonight and take a
room at one of those hotels near the airport. I'll get a better
night's sleep than if I leave here at three a.m.'

'You shouldn't be driving at all with that foot.'

'It's an automatic car. I can manage without using my bad foot.'

She stopped trying to persuade him to do anything. She felt cheated and left out after their closeness of the last few days. 'As you please.'

He pulled her into his arms. 'Look, I'm sorry. It's just—' Again he clamped his lips shut on a confidence, sighed and murmured, 'Trust me with this. It all started before we met, and I need to deal with it myself. What we do together will be truly shared, I promise you. OK?'

She hugged him. 'You I trust, though not your capacity to deal with accounts. But your partner, I don't trust at all and I'm worried he'll pull the wool over your eyes financially.'

'I won't let him do that, I promise.'

Later, as he was about to get into his car, he turned to say, 'You *will* be careful, won't you?'

The place felt empty without him. She wandered from one room to the other, amazed at how quickly Ben Elless had become a part of her life. It felt strange to keep all the outer doors locked, but she intended to be very careful, even during the day. And wherever she went in the house, the mobile phone did too, in a waist pouch. The police had promised to run patrols past her house at night and given her their emergency number.

You couldn't let fear of what might happen stop you living.

In the end, she went back to her painting and managed to lose herself in that. Well, most of the time.

Ben walked into the Brisbane office to find Phil kissing the secretary in a way that said they knew one another very well indeed. He hadn't realized they had a thing going. He wondered how many times Phil had been unfaithful. They jumped apart when he cleared his throat.

Phil ran a hand through his tousled hair and moved across, hand outstretched. 'Ben! Why didn't you tell me you were coming back?'

Ben shook the hand because to refuse would have looked

bad, but this time he didn't believe the handshake or the direct, smiling look that went with it. 'Sudden decision. I barely had time to jump on the plane.'

'Come into my office. Nareen, get us some coffee, will you? Hey, what's with the bandage and limp?'

'Twisted my ankle. It's nearly better.'

As Ben followed him into the big corner office he saw Phil sliding some papers under the blotter pad.

Ignoring his ankle, he strode across to the desk and yanked them out again.

'That stuff is private!' Phil protested.

'Then what's it doing here at the office?' He shuffled through them, realized they were calculations and the word 'casino' at the head of one set of figures leaped out at him. He turned to look accusingly at his partner. 'You're in debt, gambling again, aren't you? How could you possibly let yourself lose so much money?'

Phil shrugged. 'Nothing I can't handle.'

'You said that last time, but you had to borrow from the company to pay off your debts. Where is this money coming from?' He wished he understood figures at a glance, as Meriel would have done, wished now that he'd brought her with him.

'Look, I'm keeping on top of it. I've learned not to get in too deep.'

Ben looked at the totals again and let out a whistle. 'This looks deep enough to me.'

Phil snatched the papers out of his hands and crammed them into a drawer. 'I've taken out a second mortgage, if you must know. It's all sorted.'

'Have you found another landscaper to take my place yet?'

'No.'

'Have you looked?'

'No.'

'I meant what I said about leaving.'

'I don't believe you. If you need a break, why don't you just take a sabbatical and leave the partnership as it is for a month or two?'

'No chance. I'm going to get my lawyer to sort out the arrangements to dissolve our partnership.'

'I won't sign anything.'

'Then we'll work out how to split the assets without you and the business will lose all its value, instead of being a working, saleable commodity. We do have those ongoing maintenance contracts still on the books, you know, and other clients who've promised to use our services in future ventures.'

'I'm *not* signing you off.'

Ben watched in amazement as Phil stormed out of the office.

Nareen poked her head through the door a short time later. 'Do you know where Mr Hantley's gone? He has a meeting at five.'

'Sorry. I don't.' Ben looked at his watch. 'Look, it's half-past four now. Why don't you pack up for the day? I'll wait for Phil and if he doesn't come back, I'll close the office.'

'I'm not in a hurry. We were going to work late tonight.'

'I bet you were.'

She flushed but went back to sit at her desk, looking stubborn.

Ben thought about it for a minute, then decided to do the thing openly. He rang a transport company he knew, then began opening his drawers and files, piling the contents up on the desk. He went into Phil's office and did the same.

She followed him. 'Are you looking for something? I'm sure I can find it for you without all this mess.'

'Oh, I'm finding what I want.'

'What are you doing?'

'Taking the account books home to study them.'

A short time afterwards he heard the outer door of the office suite close. She was probably going out to ring Phil on her mobile. Well, by the time his partner got back, it'd be a fait accompli.

A knock on the office door heralded the arrival of a driver from the transport company, complete with a few folded packing boxes. 'Ah, come in. I'm nearly finished. If you'll unfold those magic boxes of yours and start piling the stuff on that desk into one, I'll pack the stuff from next door. It's really urgent that this gets away quickly.'

Phil arrived back just as he was locking up.

'Meeting go on for a long time?' Ben asked.

Phil shrugged. 'You know how it is.' He went into his office, opened a filing cabinet drawer, cursed and began opening the other drawers. He came marching into Ben's office. 'Have you been going through my things?'

'Yes. I need to go through the paperwork, since you can't seem to find us another accountant.'

'Where have you put it? I need to keep referring to it.'

'It's already on its way to the west.'

'But – how can I run the business without it?'

'Oh, I'm sure you'll manage. After all, we're not taking on any new projects, are we?'

Phil glared at him. 'Are you trying to destroy everything we've built up?'

'I'm the person who built it up, with Sandy. You came in when it was already established. I've every right to keep an eye on things.'

'I want that stuff back. Otherwise—'

'You'll sue me? I think not.' Ben slammed the door behind him as he left.

Phil didn't come running after him.

Which was a good thing because he wasn't quite ready to let the lid off how he really felt about Phil. He was still hoping to get out of this without hurting Uncle Rod. A man struggling against cancer didn't deserve to have bad news about his son dumped on him as well.

And anyway, this was Sandy's family. For her sake, he wanted to keep everything quiet and not stir up trouble.

The following evening Ben phoned Meriel and said without any preliminaries, 'I've taken all the paperwork from the office and it's being freighted across to you. There are receipts, plus the cheque book stubs, bank and credit card statements, plus all the office files and account books. I downloaded everything from Phil's computer as well as the secretary's this time. The thumb drives are in there too. I'd be grateful if you could go through everything as soon as the stuff arrives. Make it a priority.'

'Why? What have you found out?'

'Phil's gambling again. As for the rest, I don't know,

I just . . . suspect. I think that secretary has been getting me to sign cheques that didn't go where they were supposed to. I caught her kissing Phil. I hate people who're unfaithful.'

'When will you be coming back?'

'Are you missing me?'

'Yes.'

'I'm missing you, too. I never thought . . . well, anyway, I'll be glad to get back.'

'*When?*' Goodness he could be so vague about details and practicalities.

'That's the bad news, love. I think I'd better stay on for another few days. I want to see my mother and there are some things I can do better than Phil, practical things. See the sub-contractors, finish off this project. I thought Phil could cope with that, at least, but it's not been done as it should have been.' He broke off. 'Well, anyway, I'll sort it all out.'

She struggled for patience and repeated her question. 'So when approximately do you think you'll be coming back?'

'It all depends. A few days, give or take.'

'Right. Well, let me know once you *can* tell.' She wasn't going to turn into a dependent female, unable to settle to anything when her man was away.

His voice was gentle. 'I really am missing you, Meriel.'

'Mmm.'

'I can't think of anything else to say – I'm no good at nattering on phones – but I still don't want to hang up.'

She could feel her face softening into a smile. 'I don't want to hang up either. We're a pair of idiots, aren't we? I'm no good at small talk, either.'

'Well, I've a lot to do so I'll put the receiver down first. But Meriel – take care.'

The next day she received a phone call from one of the publishers who'd used her work before. Two more books to illustrate!

That took the emptiness out of her days – but not out of her nights.

A week later in the middle of the night Tina started growling and pacing up and down near the bedroom door. Meriel jerked upright, her heart thumping as the dog growled again. She slid out of bed quietly, her ears alert for the slightest sound, and picked up the baseball bat. Hardly daring to breathe, she stood listening, but could hear nothing. Tina was still fretting to and fro, however.

Suddenly she heard a faint sound in the distance. It took her a heart-thumping minute or two to work out that it was a car turning off the main road. Who would be coming here at this hour of the night? Adrenaline pumping through her, she crept through the darkness to the other side of the house and peeped out of the window. Tina pressed against her, growling.

She could see headlights on the side road now.

The car turned off up her drive and she began to wonder whether to ring the police, then realized she'd left her mobile in the bedroom. Running back for it she returned to her station by the window, fingers poised to dial for help. If the car hadn't come up to the house so openly, she'd have dialled already.

The car's headlights raked the shadows and settled on the driveway. Then Tina's barking took on a different tone and the moon came out from behind some clouds. Meriel sighed in relief and rushed to fling the front door open. 'What time do you call this, Elless, and why the hell didn't you phone to let me know you were coming? I thought you were an intruder.'

'Hey, don't hit me. I surrender!' Ben cringed back, pretending to be afraid of the weapon she was still clutching.

'Oh, you idiot!' She dropped the bat and allowed him to sweep her into his arms. Tina jumped up and down pawing at them and yelping a welcome, but Ben only gave her a quick pat and then began to kiss Meriel again.

'Did you really miss me?' he asked, when they both came up for air.

'Not at all.'

'Liar!' He swept her up into his arms and carried her through to the bedroom, slamming the door in Tina's face.

'Your limp's gone.'

'To hell with the limp. I want to see if you're still as beautiful as I remember.' He began to pull off her nightdress.

She had already started tugging at his shirt buttons. And all the time joy was running through her, joy that he was back, joy that he still wanted her . . . loved her.

In the morning they unpacked the boxes of papers that had only been delivered the day before, then Meriel began to go through them. What she found was like a jigsaw puzzle, and she took over the unfurnished spare bedroom so that she could lay the pieces on the floor in piles. She continued to work doggedly, sure that a pattern would gradually form.

Two days later she took Ben into his office and indicated several piles of papers and folders. 'Voilà!'

'What did you find out?'

She looked at him with sympathy. 'I think your partner has been carefully milking the company – and doing it for quite a while, years actually.'

He sighed. 'He swore he'd given up gambling.'

'You should have kept a closer eye on him, insisted on being informed about every single thing.'

'It can be difficult to insist when the person is a member of the family and his father has helped set up the business.'

She'd have insisted, she knew, but her Ben was a gentle person. She was only just beginning to understand how gentle. 'What are you going to do about it now? Let him take every last cent?'

'No. I'll take the evidence and confront him.'

'You should turn him over to the police.'

'His father's got inoperable cancer, is in his last few months of life. I can't do that to Rod.'

'You can't continue in the partnership, though. If Phil has to go bankrupt, they'll seize your assets too, including the land here.'

Ben gaped at her. 'Why would they do that for *his* debts?'

'Because that's how partnerships work.'

He swallowed hard. 'So the business is probably worth nothing?'

She nodded then went to put one arm round his waist, hating to see the desolate expression on his face, her heart going out to him.

He hugged her absent-mindedly, then said, 'I think better outside. I'm going for a walk.'

'Want some company?'

'Not this time.' He looked at her sadly and kissed her nearest cheek. 'I've made a mess of everything, haven't I?'

'Sounds to me like your partner's done that. The point is, how *much* of a mess has he made? How much do you stand to lose? And can you get free of him in time?'

Later Ben came back from his walk and joined her in the kitchen, his face set in grim lines. Meriel watched as Tina skittered out of the way of his feet for the second time. She'd decided to let him get to it in his own time.

But he didn't. He just kept pacing up and down, looking as if he had the weight of the world on his shoulders.

When she couldn't bear to watch any longer, she set herself in his path, arms akimbo. 'Spit it out, Elless!'

For a moment longer he hesitated, then said quietly, 'Let's go and sit down.'

She chose a chair opposite him, because if she sat close enough to touch, they'd end up forgetting to talk. 'Go on, give!'

'I hadn't realized that they might take all this from me.' He waved one hand around them. 'Even if they don't, I shan't be able to afford to develop things for a while. I can't bear the thought of them taking my property in Queensland after Sandy and I worked so hard. And . . . Well, I'd expected something at least from the business. So I'll have to try to *earn* more money. And the worst of it is that I won't be able to do that here, not the sort of money I need. All my business contacts are over east.'

Silence settled between them.

'Does it have to be a big development here?' she asked at last. 'Couldn't you start small again?'

'I suppose so, but the major earthworks won't come cheaply and the lake was to be the centrepiece. It won't be right without that lake, not on an inland site. So it'd make more sense to get that done first and work round it.' He sighed. 'You wouldn't fancy relocating to Queensland for a while, would you?'

She didn't want to leave. And yet, she didn't want to lose him, either. 'Give me time to think about it, Ben. We'll talk again tomorrow. We don't have to decide all at once, do we?'

The next day after breakfast, she cleared the table and sat down opposite him. 'How about we combine forces?'

'What do you mean?'

'I have some land. I could put it with yours and then you could start smallish.'

He looked at her. 'Thanks. If I've any money left . . . afterwards, I suppose we could consider it. But I'd not do anything till I was sure I was free of Phil. I'm not risking you losing your land if he drags me into bankruptcy.'

He was so subdued, so unlike his usual ebullient self it upset her. 'We'd not do it as a partnership in any case. We'd set up proper business arrangements. My share would be quite safe then. Do you have any paperwork about this development?'

He stared at her in puzzlement.

'You know, costs, estimates, projections, planning lists and figures. Tiny details like that.'

'Ah, well – I thought *you* could handle those. I've just got the image of it in my mind, how the lake would look, what plants I'd put round it – that sort of thing. It's quite detailed, I've been thinking about it for years . . . but I've not written it down.'

She rolled her eyes upwards, staring at the ceiling for a few seconds and praying for patience. She loved him, but she didn't trust him an inch where business was concerned, not because he was dishonest, but because he was impractical. 'I can't invest in anything until I know exactly what you're planning and how I'd be involved.'

'I thought we could just – make a start and see how we went from there. I'd do the drawings first, of course. I'm good at those.'

'Ben Elless, are you crazy? We have to start with working plans, not to mention contingency plans and detailed financial arrangements. If not, we could both end up losing everything we own. Is this how you always work?'

He shrugged. 'Sandy used to handle the business side of things and leave me to do the creative things. I admit I'm not the world's best numbers man, but I do have a flair for major landscaping, truly I do.'

She sighed. 'All I can say at this stage, then, is I'd be interested in looking things over, and potentially would consider committing some land to the project, but I'm not signing anything until I'm satisfied with the paperwork – and until you're clear of this Phil Hantley.'

'You'll still stay with me, though, won't you? I mean, you and I will still be an item?'

'Yes, you fool. It'll make no difference to our being together.' She wasn't sure she ever wanted to get married, though, and she was quite sure he would. Well, that was for later. 'Now, let's start working out the business stuff, Ben. I'm not going anywhere, I promise you.' She went to give him a hug and wound up just standing there in his arms for a while. It felt good. She definitely didn't intend to lose him.

When she moved away, he said, 'Let's go outside and I'll *show* you what I want to do. Put on some sturdy jeans and boots. We'll be pushing through the bush at times.'

Outdoors, Ben was much more impressive. He had wonderful ideas for landscaping and the ability to sketch a scene in a few lines on a notepad, then flesh it in with talk, so that you could almost see the way he'd shape the land, subtly, enhancing the natural flow and curves. He talked of rare wildflowers blooming, even, later down the track, rare native animals safe from harm in cat-proof enclosures.

She was more impressed than she'd expected to be by his vision and his instinctive grasp of how best to do what he wanted. He juggled alternative approaches in rough sketches that brought his words to life. He waved his arms around a lot, pointing, finding ways to minimize expense even as he built word pictures of his dreams.

Next time she wanted to talk figures, she'd bring him out here and jot down what he said on a pad. She'd get twice as much information in half the time, and better information too.

As they walked back to the house, she asked, 'Do you

have any skill with building chalets, or whatever it is you're going to put up here to house visitors?'

He shrugged. 'I've worked on residential developments, but I usually turn over the accommodation side of things to a builder – or to Phil.'

'I see.' Phil again, taking care of all the business details – and the finances – and keeping Ben in ignorance of half the things that were happening, but profiting from his creativity and vision. 'Have you ever thought of using kit homes?'

'Could do. As long as they didn't look too cheapskate.'

She would go and look at them herself first and take Ben along with her later if she found anything worthwhile. If they were going to become partners, they would each need to understand all aspects of the business, broadly at least. That seemed reasonable to her. None of this leaving things to other people – who might or might not deal with them properly, who might or might not take care of the finances and who might or might not be honest.

And she was still worried about who had damaged the old house. Had the would-be developers given up? Or were they prepared to harm Ben to get what they wanted? There could be big money involved. She didn't want to face dragons on two fronts.

No, her imagination was running wild. Deal with this Phil mess first.

She watched Ben stop to study a clump of plants and her heart twisted in her chest. She liked him better because he wasn't superman. She didn't even care now that he was good-looking, though of course the mutual attraction was crucial. What she cared about most was how good and kind a person he was. Too soft for his own good, but not too soft for her.

He and Grandpop would have got on like a house on fire.

Seventeen

The following afternoon Meriel took out the manuscript that had been couriered across to her from Sydney and began to read, marking passages of useful description which might provide a scene for the cover. The story was gripping and it was not until the light began to fade that she realized just how long she had been sitting there, or how many rough preliminary sketches she had screwed up and tossed into the bin. She sighed. Her worries about Ben were getting between her and her work.

Only as she went to join him in the living area did she look round and ask, 'Where's Tina?'

'I thought she was with you.'

'I haven't seen her since lunch time.'

'Nor have I, come to think of it.'

He put two fingers in his mouth and whistled loudly. Normally, the dog would have come running to hurl herself at him, but today there wasn't even the faintest bark or rustle of foliage in response.

'Where is she?' Tina never went far away and she always made some sort of noise when they called her.

They circled the house, finding no sign of the dog.

Meriel looked at him. 'There are snakes in the bush. She could have been bitten and . . .'

'Let's look round.' He put his arm round her shoulders and they walked along the path that led to his block. When they saw something lying half-hidden by a bush they both ran forward.

'Is she alive?' Meriel dropped to her knees, feeling a tightness in her throat at the sight of the usually lively animal lying so still.

'Let me. I'm used to dogs.'

Ben began to check Tina gently and Meriel watched, because clearly he knew what he was doing.

'Yes, she's alive, but only just. Her heartbeat is unsteady.

We need to take her to the vet's.' As he stood up, he studied the ground, stirring the mess with his toe. 'She's vomited and it contains pieces of raw meat.'

Meriel swallowed hard. 'We never feed her raw meat.'

'No.' His face was grim.

'Could she have found a dead animal and eaten that?'

'I doubt it. The lumps look too regular.' He was poking around in the mess with a stick. 'This is definitely butcher's meat. There's no sign of skin or bone or feathers.' He looked at Meriel and his voice was rough with emotion as he knelt down again and began to caress the dog's head. 'I think we have some more trouble on our hands here in the West, love. Serious trouble. Tina's been poisoned. And the only reason I can see for that was to threaten us – why?'

'To make us sell out and leave?' Meriel stood up and drew in a long, shaky breath. 'We'll not only call in the police but this time, Ben, we'll mention what happened at your uncle's old shack, too.'

'We can't prove anything.'

She looked at him in exasperation. 'No, but the police might be able to. It's all part of the same thing, I'm sure. This is far too serious to ignore.'

He sighed and as he leaned forward to pick the dog up, a man's voice called 'Elless!' from some distance away. He froze, making a quick shushing sound.

'Sell the land, Elless, and go back to where you belong!' the voice went on.

'Why the hell should I?' Ben yelled back.

'Because if you don't, your lady love might get hurt next, like your dog did.'

After that there was silence, then a short time later the sound of a car driving away in the distance.

Ben looked at Meriel and said in a low voice, 'Let's deal with poor Tina and later we'll go and see if they've left tyre marks. I'll carry her to the car then come back with a shovel and scrape up some of that mess for analysis.'

'No. Wait a minute. I'll fetch a shovel and we'll get our sample before we move away from here. I know we heard a car driving away, but we don't know that all the intruders were in it. You stay and keep guard.'

Before he could stop her, she'd darted off through the bush. Furious at her for taking risks, he could only wait for her to come back, listening intently the whole time. If he heard any other sounds, he'd leave the dog and go back to her . . . But whoever it was had driven off so surely she'd be all right?

He couldn't bear to lose another woman he loved. He'd do anything to keep her safe.

As Meriel ran, it was anger that fuelled her, not fear. Her peaceful asylum had been invaded and she wasn't having it. She carried the baseball bat ready, almost hoping someone would try to stop her so she could thwack the coward who'd poisoned an innocent animal. But nothing happened, no voice calling, no sounds of other people.

While Meriel drove Tina to the vet's, Ben stayed behind at the house. He found a vantage point outside from which he could observe the surrounding land and simply waited in silence. If anyone approached, he'd hear them. And if – *when* Tina recovered, he'd teach her not to eat from anyone's hands but his and Meriel's.

Didn't he have enough on his plate with Phil?

The police had still not arrived by the time Meriel returned. Ben ran across to the car. 'How is she?'

'Still alive. Just. They agree with our guess that she's been poisoned. And they're going to get the sample analysed for us.' Suddenly tears were running down her face.

He held her close, making low comforting sounds and rocking her slightly. 'What are her chances, could they tell?'

'Only fifty-fifty. They're keeping her under observation and if she lasts the night, they think she'll be all right.' She fumbled for a tissue and mopped her eyes. 'You get to love dogs, don't you?'

'Yes.'

She heard a gulp beside her in the darkness and realized he was near tears too, so gave him a rib-cracking hug. 'I love you, Ben.' It was the first time she'd said it to him.

He tipped her face up for a quick kiss, comforting not sexual. 'I love you too, Meriel.'

She leaned against him and they stood together looking

round at the quiet moonlit scene. 'Have the police been and gone already?' she asked after a while.

'No. They've not arrived yet. It's to be hoped we never have a real emergency.'

'What do you call this, Elless?' she demanded, thumping his chest for emphasis.

'Poisoning of a dog. And my shack was vandalism. Terrible for us, but not a major emergency in police books. Only . . . After this, I don't want you staying here on your own. And I reckon I'll have to go to and fro between here and Queensland for a while. I can't avoid that.'

She opened her mouth to say she could take care of herself, then closed it again. Someone had almost killed Ben and then nearly killed their dog. This was definitely more than she could handle on her own. 'I'll hire a bodyguard or get someone to stay with me while you're away. I'm not stupid. There are times to be independent and times to seek help. This time I need help.'

'Promise.'

'Yes, I promise. Now, do you want a coffee?'

He shook his head. 'No. I just want to keep watch till the police arrive.'

It was another fifteen minutes before they heard the sound of a car and saw headlights turn into their drive. When they'd explained to the young policeman what had happened, Meriel spoke up, since Ben hadn't said anything. 'You should know that there's been other trouble before this. Someone tried to injure Ben a few weeks ago.' She explained about the roof.

The policeman gaped at them. 'Why didn't you report it at the time?'

'No proof. Whoever did it came back and took away the sawn-off beams while Ben was getting treated. But the men who demolished the place can tell you that someone had been messing around with the place between the first time they examined it and the time they started work on it. Ben and I hadn't been near the place during that period. Well, he could hardly walk. I did keep one of the pieces of sawn-off beam, but we can't prove that it came from the old shack.'

'Can I see it?'

'Come inside the house.' She'd stood it at the back of her walk-in wardrobe in case Ben tried to throw it away.

The policeman examined it in the brightness of the kitchen, then turned to Ben. 'Who would want to hurt you?'

'I don't know.'

'And there was an arson attempt, too.' Meriel explained that to the young policeman, who was looking quite excited now.

'Don't you have *any* idea why this might have happened, Mr Elless?'

He shrugged.

'It might be someone who wants to prevent our development and do one of their own,' Meriel said, annoyed with his reluctance to speak out. 'We've both had generous offers for our land.'

The policeman swung round to her. 'Development?'

Ben glared at her. She glared right back. As far as she was concerned, lives were more important than businesses any day. Especially Ben's life.

'We're thinking of starting up a little tourist development here,' he explained reluctantly.

The policeman was clearly a countryman. If things hadn't been as serious, Meriel would have smiled as he immediately voiced one of the main concerns of inhabitants of small Australian towns. 'Why should anyone object to that? Tourism helps bring more people into the area and that's good for business, brings jobs to the town. There's too much money sitting in the cities. We've got higher unemployment out here in the country.'

'I'd – um – be grateful if you didn't tell anyone of our plans,' Ben said. 'If word gets around too soon, things can – you know – go wrong. Then there wouldn't be any development.'

'I'll certainly not make it public prematurely.' The officer put away his notebook. 'Look, there's nothing more I can do tonight. I'll be back in the morning to see what I can find. Don't go trampling on any evidence till I get here.'

When he had gone, they went to sit out on the back veranda, hand in hand, watching the moon slipping slowly down the sky.

'I hope that damned mutt's going to be all right,' Ben said at one stage.

'Me too.' Meriel scowled out into the darkness. If these people – whoever they were – thought they were going to drive her away from her home, they could just think again.

A short time later she woke with a start to find she'd been sleeping cuddled up to Ben.

'You snore,' he teased.

'I do not!'

He kissed her on the cheek then gave a great big stretch. 'I didn't dare move in case I woke you, Sleeping Beauty. Look, it's nearly dawn.'

'Want a cup of something?' she asked, standing up to ease her limbs.

While she was in the kitchen Ben walked up and down outside, studying the ground. 'There are some footprints,' he announced, when she came out to join him.

'How do you know those aren't yours?'

'I haven't walked over that patch.'

'How can you be sure?'

His voice was impatient. 'I just am. And besides, I don't have any shoes with that sort of sole.' He took a mug from her and slurped some tea.

She looked at her watch and sighed. 'It's too early to phone the vet's. They said not until eight o'clock.'

'I have faith in Tina's constitution. Labradors are hardy specimens.' He looked at her piteously. 'But if I don't get a couple of your banana pancakes for breakfast, I'm not sure I'll survive.'

'Honestly! I'm going to have to teach you to cook. I'm not spending the rest of my life waiting on you.' She broke off. Was she revealing too much, assuming too much?

His expression was suddenly very serious. 'I wouldn't expect that. Meriel, darling, I hadn't dared hope – well, not so soon, anyway, that you'd be thinking permanence.'

'Well, I am. I'm not a great believer in marriage, though, so don't get any ideas about that. A piece of paper doesn't make a relationship work, as I've seen in my own family. But I do want to stay with you.' It surprised her that she could even say that aloud. She wasn't the impulsive sort, had known him such a short time and yet – he was Ben, her Ben now. And she did love him.

He gave her a wry smile. 'Well, I'm all for marriage. I've seen it work well and I shall want to publicly declare that we're together for keeps.'

The world seemed to whisper to a halt around them. 'Are you – proposing to me?'

He nodded, his face still serious as he stretched out one hand to her. Then, as she clasped it, he began to smile. 'Mind you, some people might say *you* had proposed to me. You were the first to talk about the rest of our lives.'

She thumped his shoulder.

'But if you prefer it,' he dropped suddenly to one knee, 'we can be more traditional about it all. Meriel Ingram – dearest Meriel might sound better, what do you think?' He didn't wait for an answer, but continued smoothly, 'Will you do me the very great honour of becoming my wife?'

She didn't know what to say. She loved him, there was no doubt about that, and this was another of his utterly disarming gestures, but marriage . . . No, it was too soon for that. For her, anyway.

He moved to sit beside her, quietly watching her, not pressing her to answer. The sun had just risen above the horizon and a light breeze was ruffling the air. Magpies were crooning in the bush nearby, other birds were calling to one another.

She knew he was waiting for her answer, waiting with remarkable patience, but she just couldn't do it. Swallowing hard, she said shakily, 'Ben, I do love you. Very much. But – can't we just live together for a year or two first, get to know one another really well? Marriage isn't really necessary these days, you know.'

His smile vanished and a tender look replaced it as he took her hand and lifted it to his lips. '*I* think it's necessary, but I can wait until you do too. Whatever we do, there are no guarantees that things will last, darling – not for us, not for anyone.'

She could see from the sadness in his eyes that he was

thinking of his late wife and she kept hold of his hand, squeezing it gently. 'Bear with me, Ben? Give me time to – to get used to the idea?'

'As much time as you need, love. Oh, damn!' The phone started to ring and he rushed inside to answer it. She looked at her watch, saw that it was eight o'clock and raced inside after him.

'Yes. Oh, thank goodness!' He made a thumbs up sign at Meriel, who had followed him inside, and mouthed 'Tina' at her. 'Yes, we'll leave her with you for another day or two. Thank you so much for letting us know. Great news.'

He put the phone down, dragged Meriel into his arms and danced her round the kitchen. 'She's all right. Weak, but doing fine. Hey, it's all right.' He brushed away her tears with his fingertips.

'I've grown to love her,' she admitted.

'I'm pretty fond of her myself.'

When the phone rang again, a few minutes later, Meriel was still smiling as she picked it up and waited for the beeps that signalled a long-distance call to end. 'Hello?' She half-expected to hear Rosanna's voice, but it was a man. And her smile vanished as she listened, to be replaced by a frown. '*What?*' she exclaimed in a very different tone of voice and made an urgent beckoning motion to Ben, who was sitting eating his second pancake. He set down his knife and fork and hurried across to listen with her.

'You heard me, Meriel Ingram,' the man said. 'It was only a dog that got hurt this time. We don't want anything to happen to *you* next, do we, sweetheart? I'm sure you can find somewhere else to live, somewhere safer.'

Ben snatched the phone out of her hand. 'Look here—' The connection was cut and they were left with only a buzzing sound.

Meriel stood there, stunned. 'It's like something from a sleazy detective novel.' Anger began to replace the shock. 'How dare they? Do they think I'll just give in and sell my home?'

'Nonetheless—'

She thumped her fist on the surface. 'This is my *home*!

No one – *no one at all* – is going to drive me away from here.'

'I don't want you getting hurt. Maybe if you went somewhere else?' He looked down, saw her open her mouth to refuse and added quickly, 'Just for a while. I could stay here and keep an eye on things and—'

'Being careful is one thing. Running away is another. I won't do it, Ben!'

'I'm thinking about your *life*, dammit! I have to go back east again, soon. They're bound to find out.' His voice cracked. 'You'll be too vulnerable on your own out here.'

'You've got a point there, Elless. I have to concede that – with great reluctance, mind. I've already said I'll hire a bodyguard when you're away.'

'Hire a bodyguard! In a small country town like York! Oh, sure, there'll be plenty of those to choose from. Just put an ad in the paper and they'll be queuing up to apply.'

'There's bound to be someone who wants a job.' Inspiration struck. 'We'll ask Bill Lansome. He'll know if anyone will. He knows everything and everyone round here. And in the meantime we'll make sure that one of us is at the block at all times. With a mobile phone, so they can't cut us off from calling for help.'

'No. Sorry, Meriel, but definitely not.'

'What do you mean, "definitely not"?'

'I mean, it's very brave of you, but I'm not letting you take the risk.'

She poked her index finger into his chest, making him jerk backwards. 'Get one thing straight from the start, Elless! If we take any decisions about this, we'll do it together.'

'But—'

She poked him again. 'I mean it.'

The quarrel was short and sharp. After which they separated – to make a lot of busy noise in different parts of the house and garden. Her anger soon faded though. It was just that he cared about her. And he had lost his first wife, after all. But still, he had to learn not to give her orders. She'd had more than enough of those from her mother.

An hour later, having been ostentatiously avoiding one another, they walked into the kitchen area from opposite doors, caught each other sneaking a glance sideways and both burst out laughing.

The policeman didn't return until late morning, this time accompanied by a detective. Together they walked around the edges of the area Ben had marked off by sticks and string, studying it carefully.

'Those tyre tracks aren't quite clear enough for definite identification,' the detective said at last, sucking the inside of his cheek to promote thought. 'And we can't prove they were made last night. You're absolutely sure those are not your footprints, Mr Elless?'

Ben gritted his teeth. He had already been asked this twice.'Of course I am. I don't have any shoes with that pattern of sole. Nothing remotely like it. I've checked that out already. But you're welcome to go through my wardrobe, if you like.'

The detective produced a camera and took a few shots of the various dust-blurred footprints. After he had finished, he sucked the inside of his cheek some more then made another pronouncement. 'I don't hold out much hope of finding whoever it was.'

'There's been a further development. A man rang up a short time ago and threatened Meriel's life if we didn't sell up.'

'That does change things somewhat,' the detective informed her. 'I'll get a trace put on your phone. Any other motive they might have apart from your development clashing with theirs?'

'Nope.'

The detective referred to his notes, 'Mrs – er, *Ms* Ingram? Any,' he coughed gently, 'problems in your past? Anything you say will be treated in absolute confidence, of course.'

'No shady characters, no deadly secrets,' she informed him with a straight face, while Ben turned round to stare out of the window, shoulders shaking. 'I'm an accountant. And an artist. I illustrate books. I've never even had a parking fine.'

Ben turned round again. 'I hope information about my plans for a tourist development will also be covered by that absolute confidence you spoke of.'

When the two men had gone, she looked at him. 'I could always come with you to Brisbane and we could leave Tina at the vet's. He runs kennels as well as his practice.'

Ben shook his head. 'Thank you for the offer, but I still need to sort this out on my own if I'm to have any self-respect.'

Eighteen

The next morning Meriel tried to find a bodyguard while Ben went to bring Tina home from the vet's. The local security firm couldn't help them except to promise to drive past every hour or two, so Meriel contacted Bill Lansome, who told her to leave it with him.

He rang back a short time later to say, 'I may have found you some bodyguards – of a sort. You may not fancy them, though. They're a bit – er – eccentric. Call themselves neo-hippies.'

'Call themselves *what?*'

'Neo-hippies.' He chuckled. 'Don't know about neo, they seem exactly like the old-fashioned sort of hippie to me. There were plenty of them around when I was young and surfing on the Gold Coast. Long hair and beards, women with full-length Indian skirts. This bunch smell of incense, but I guarantee they're not on drugs. One of them's been a good friend of mine for years.'

'*Hippies?*'

'Yeah. I suppose they were before your time, but if you've seen pictures of the sixties, you'll know what to expect.'

A pause seemed to indicate that he wanted an answer, so she said, 'Er – right. Go on.'

'They've been caretaking a property outside town for a few months. Left it in excellent order when the owner came back, better than when they went there. But they couldn't find anywhere else to house sit, so they made camp temporarily on an empty block. Only the owner found out about it and they were asked to leave. Actually, it belongs to the guy who made you an offer for your block.'

'You know him well?'

'Sort of. He's always trying to set up a property deal. Hasn't had much success.'

'Is he the sort to poison a dog?' She explained about Tina. Silence, then. 'I don't know. I'm not an unbiased witness.'

'You don't like him?'

'Well, no. But I don't know that he's ever done anything illegal.'

'Go on about your hippies.'

'They've been to see me to ask if there are any properties where the owners would like them to act as caretakers. I checked out whether they'd be interested in helping you and they said yes.' He chuckled again. 'They've not opted out of technology, mind. They've got a mobile phone, a generator and a computer. Thing is, are *you* interested? You could let them camp on an unused part of your land. They'd not be in your way, but they'd have to stay there for a while, because they couldn't be upping stakes and moving camp every time Ben went away, now could they?'

She'd had something a bit different in mind for a bodyguard, but beggars couldn't be choosers. 'Tell me a bit more about them. How many are there?'

'Four adults, two children, one dog. Large. As in Irish wolf hound. Big white teeth. No fillings.'

She chuckled. 'The dog sounds attractive, anyway. Go on.'

'Two caravans. Two beat-up old cars. Except for Ria, they don't take permanent work, just do odd jobs. She's a psychologist. Well, Big Jim is past retirement age now, though you'd never think it to look at him. They tidied up my garden for me a few weeks ago. Made a damn good job of it, too. They'd like to be self-sufficient but can't afford to buy the right sort of land.'

She could hear him tapping his pencil on the blotter. She didn't know what to say. Neo-hippies, for heaven's sake! Get real!

'You could let 'em stay for a while, see how things pan out – but tell 'em it's not permanent just to cover yourself legally.'

'You're trying to persuade me to use them. Why?'

'Well, I like them – and let's face it, there's a touch of the old nostalgia. Besides, I doubt you'll find anyone else suitable round here.'

It was a no-brainer. 'OK, Bill. Send them out to see me. If I like your protégés, they can camp on the slope on the other side of the drive. If I don't take to them, no harm done.'

There was a mutter of voices, then, 'They'll nip out to see you in one of the cars.'

Ben, who had just come in, asked, 'Who can camp on the other side of the drive?'

'Some hippies who're looking for a place to squat for a while. Bill Lansome just rang. He thought they'd make good bodyguards.'

'You're joking!'

'No, I'm not.'

'Well, they'd not make good enough bodyguards for my peace of mind. So you're not—'

Here he was trying to tell her what to do again. 'You know,' she leaned back in her chair and eyeballed him, 'you have this nasty habit of dictating what I can and can't do. Get over it, Elless. I'm not a little dolly-girl to be protected and dominated. My Grandpop taught me to look after myself and if I can't do that, I'll be the one who says what help I need.'

He glared right back at her. 'The trouble with you is you're so bloody independent you don't even know how to be a couple.'

The words hung in the air between them.

'No, I don't,' she said quietly, feeling hurt by this accusation, which sounded as if he wanted her to be a clone of his wife. 'And if it means letting you dictate to me, then I never shall.'

He closed his eyes and exhaled loudly, then opened them again. 'I didn't mean to sound dictatorial, but hell, Meriel, a guy likes to look after his partner.'

'And this partner likes to be just that – a partner – as in equal.'

The silence had ice prickling through it. She took a deep breath. Perhaps she had been just a bit touchy. 'Look, all I've done is told Bill to send these people over to see us. I've not made any decisions yet.'

'Can I meet them too, then? Help make the decision? If we're going to be equal partners, it works both ways.'

'Of course.' But there was a coolness to the careful way they were talking. She knew it, could see that he knew it, too, and tried to lighten the mood. 'Come on, then,

Sir Galahad! Let's go and inspect the lawn while we wait for them.'

Ten minutes later a car jolted along the drive, an old Statesman, large and comfortable, with a purring, well-tuned engine, though the bodywork was in need of a paint job. From it piled two men and a woman, anachronisms in their dress, as Bill had said.

'Peace,' one of them said, holding up a hand in a kind of Indian salute.

Meriel tried desperately to think of some suitable response, but only came up with, 'Hi! I'm Meriel Ingram.'

'I'm Big Jim. This is Pete. And Ria.' He looked at Ben.

'This is my – er – friend, Ben Elless.'

'Fiancé,' said Ben, putting a proprietorial arm around her shoulders.

She sighed, but didn't shake it off or contradict him.

'Bill said you needed company, that you'd had intruders.'

'Yes. They poisoned my – our dog,' she looked down and found that Tina, who'd been very clingy since she came back from the vet, was wagging her tail at these strangers. That seemed like a good sign. 'They tried to set fire to some stored timber too.'

The woman spoke in a deep, melodious voice. 'Do you know who they are?'

'The police are looking into that,' said Ben, 'but in the meantime I have to go away. Which is why we need a bit of company round here. Temporarily.'

Ria inclined her head graciously. 'I see.'

Meriel gestured to the house. 'Come and sit on the back veranda and tell us about yourselves. Would you like a cup of tea or something?'

'Water would be nice – especially if it's cold. We don't use caffeine, though.' She grinned. 'And we don't smoke pot, either, in case you were worrying about that.'

Ben nodded. 'Good to know. Come out of the sun, then.'

'You may also be glad to know that I'm a black belt in judo,' Pete said as they walked. 'That might be useful if you're having problems. I don't start trouble, but I won't take shit from anyone.'

Ria was walking beside Meriel, studying the place. 'It's nice here. Peaceful. We can't stand much more of that public camping ground. Too noisy.'

The other two nodded agreement.

'Folk always playing radios,' Ria added. 'Never make their own music. Never try to listen to the birds singing. It's not our scene. And the children are picking up bad habits. Oh, and I'm a black belt, too, by the way. A girl has to know how to defend herself.'

'I couldn't agree more.' Meriel shot a triumphant glance in Ben's direction, feeling even better about their visitors. 'But I know that if there were more than one intruder, I'd be in trouble.'

'Even one intruder could be a problem,' Ben put in.

She set her hands on her hips and glared at him. 'And there again, perhaps not! I've been forewarned now, you know.'

'Yeah, well,' Ria looked round, 'we can see your point. Love those willows. Do you ever go and sit inside the foliage?'

'Yes. You get marvellous filtered light.'

'Mmm. I think it'd be a great place to meditate.'

The more they talked, the more Meriel liked them and within half an hour they had come to an agreement, even Ben seeming won over. The hippies were to move in for a month's trial.

Meriel stood watching the car purr away down the track. 'They're perfect.'

'I'm not sure—' Ben saw her face tighten and held out his arms in a gesture of surrender. 'Hey, I'm allowed to talk about it, aren't I?'

'Talk, yes. Dictate, no.'

'Were you always so prickly and independent?'

'I have been since I grew up. It's a bit hard to be inde-pendent when you're a kid, or a teenager even. And my mother didn't exactly encourage independence in her children.'

'Perhaps that's why you're so touchy.'

'Perhaps. No offence meant, but was Sandy a dependent type?'

He cocked his head on one side to give this his consid-eration. 'Sort of. She ran the office for us, dealt with a lot of the business details. She was a bit like you in that, a good organizer. But she was,' he hesitated, 'softer than you. Couldn't service a car or hammer in a nail. More traditional, perhaps. But she wasn't stupid.'

'I like the way you speak of her,' Meriel said quietly. 'You must have loved her very much.'

'I did. But I love you too. Make no mistake about that. I think I'm very lucky to have met two women I can love so much.'

She had to swallow hard before she said, 'I love you as well, Ben.' She walked into his arms and rested there quietly, wishing life wasn't so complicated.

The group of neo-hippies returned and set about making camp with extreme efficiency, Jim and Pete digging out the latrines with a fine display of muscle.

'We use an organic system,' Pete said laconically when Meriel wandered down to watch. 'There won't be any smells or pollution, I promise you. All right if we run a hose line down from your tap? We'll pay for whatever water we use.'

'No need to pay. Just help yourself. I know you'll use it carefully.'

The two women erected a large tent as a communal room. The children ran to and fro, humping gear, working with nearly as much concentration as the adults.

The large grey wolf hound answered to the name of Dylan. As the two dogs were released, Tina rolled over on her back and exposed her belly. After a quick sniff, he accepted her with a quiet woof and they ran round together for a few minutes, then he sat and observed everything with a regal air. It was he who growled first to signal the approach of a car.

The policeman was back with a few more questions. When he saw her new tenants, he took Meriel aside and asked, 'What are *they* doing here?'

'Staying for a while. Ben has to go over east and I don't fancy being on my own.'

'You're right about not being on your own out here, but they're a bunch of weirdoes. Why, they may even be involved in your troubles! You don't want to invite the foxes into the chook pen.'

'These aren't foxes and I'm not a helpless chicken.' Besides, she couldn't imagine Pete doing anything illegal, or even anything unkind. He was a gentle soul with the luminously happy eyes of someone at peace with himself and the world. 'Two of them have black belts in judo. They also own a very large dog.'

'Well, on your own head be it. But if my sergeant had his way, we'd have run them out of the district.'

'Why? For being different?'

'You can be a bit *too* different. They're probably growing marijuana somewhere.'

'They told me they don't use it.'

As he let out a huff of disbelief, she decided it was better to change the subject. 'Did you come back for a reason?'

'Yes. We found out someone's been seen nosing around near Ben's uncle's place – what there is left of it. Couple of fellows have stayed overnight a time or two as well. They're not in town at the moment, but,' he looked at her with an air of triumph, 'they were in town around the time Ben's house fell down.'

She let out a long, low whistle. 'You've done well to find that out so quickly.'

Ria moved forward. 'Would those be the two men I saw using surveying equipment on the property next to this?'

The young man stared at her. 'You saw them doing that in broad daylight?'

'I certainly did. More than once.'

'Strange, that. Did they do any damage? If not . . .' He shrugged and looked at his watch. 'Is Mr Elless here? I'd like to ask him a few more questions.'

'I'll call him.'

The officer repeated his tale to Ben, then warned, 'It's not proof, just because some strangers were here at the same time as you. And they seem to have gone now, so we only have names, probably false, plus a vague description. Seems they were very quiet, nothing special to look at. You sure you haven't remembered anything else?'

'No.'

'Tell me some more about the people you work with back east.'

Ben patiently went through his business set up.

'Known this Hantley for long?'

'Since my student days. He's my first wife's cousin. She was killed in a car accident a few years ago.'

'Do you get on well with him?'

'Well, there's been a bit of tension lately because I want to break up the partnership after we've finished this project. But I can't believe Phil would try to murder me. For all his faults, he's family. And anyway, he's in Queensland. It's a bit far to nip over for an hour or two, isn't it?'

'Bad eggs turn up in the best of families. Be sure to let us know when you're going to be away, so *we* can keep an eye on things here as well as on your *bodyguards.*' There was a distinct sneer in the detective's tone. 'My sergeant doesn't like things happening on his patch – we could be dealing with an attempted murder, you know.'

'I had noticed.'

The hippies lined up to wave the police officer goodbye with calls of, 'Peace, man!' and even, 'The force be with you.'

He didn't respond or turn his head to look at them again.

'You shouldn't goad him,' Meriel scolded after the car had thrummed away into the distance. But she couldn't help smiling.

'He started it a while ago,' Ria said. 'And you can't deny us a bit of fun. They've been hassling us every way they could to try to get us to leave the district. They've checked every inch of the cars, looking for something wrong to charge us with. But Jim used to be a car mechanic and our vehicles are in perfect order, even if they do need a paint job.'

Pete stared down the drive, then turned back to Meriel. 'Mind if me and Dylan go exploring? Always helps to know your territory.' He hesitated. 'Should have told you before, though perhaps you noticed. I'm part Aborigine.'

She shrugged. What did that matter? And actually he had such an interesting face, she'd like to sketch him one day.

'My uncle taught me a bit of bushcraft, though my people aren't from round here. It's nice to see land more or less untouched. I hope you aren't going to dig all the native plants up when you do your developing.'

Ben came up to them. 'What's that about native plants?'

Within minutes he had discovered a kindred spirit and the two of them went off to explore Meriel's bushland together, with Dylan quartering the ground around them.

Tina, who was still wary of going too far away from the house, chose to remain with Meriel, who enjoyed two blessed hours of peace in which she was able to work on her latest book cover.

A few days later Ben left for the Eastern States. He was now reconciled to the presence of Ria and her friends, but he punctuated his packing with so many warnings to Meriel about what she should or should not do that in the end they had another row and he left without them really making it up.

Again she felt lost without him. How quickly that had happened!

She rang Rosanna to discuss it and her friend listened intently, then said simply, 'Nothing is ever perfect, Meriel. But your Ben sounds great.'

'Do you and Karl ever quarrel?'

Rosanna chuckled. 'We've been known to disagree a time or two. Loudly, usually.' She hesitated, then asked, 'Why are you so worried about a little disagreement?'

'I think Ben's going to be around for a long time. I don't want him keeping things to himself.'

'Hey, I'm glad for you! I've got to come and check him out.'

'Not just yet, if you don't mind. Not till we've sorted all these nasties out. But as soon as it's feasible, I'll phone you.'

'You do that. And Meriel . . . Stop worrying. It takes time for two people to settle down together, you know.'

'Yes. I suppose so.'

That conversation was a great comfort.

In the middle of the night, Dylan woke them all up with a crescendo of barking and blood-curdling howls. Prompted by this, Tina voiced a few protests of her own. When Meriel went out to investigate, Ria came across to join her. 'Pete's gone to check things out.' She grinned. 'Native tracker. Him heap quiet, findum white man.'

Meriel couldn't raise a smile this time.

Ria's tone of voice changed. 'It's getting to you, isn't it?'

'Yes.'

'You're not on your own now – you've got us as well as Ben.' Ria gave her a hug, then strolled off again, leaving Meriel feeling relieved and comforted.

Pete returned. 'There was someone snooping around but they had a four-wheel drive parked over the hill. Couldn't keep up with that on foot. Tomorrow I'll hunt round and see if I can find any good tyre tracks or footprints, but I don't hold out much hope. It's been pretty dry lately and the wind blows the dust around.'

He yawned and patted Meriel's shoulder. 'You might as well go back to bed now. You don't need to worry. Dylan's an excellent watch dog and he's really taken to this place.'

She nodded. 'Thank you.'

She had an excellent night's sleep from then on. The next morning she looked out of the window at the small camp down the slope and found herself smiling. These people, weirdoes or not, had brought her peace of mind – and Rosanna had made her feel less anxious about her developing relationship.

She'd had such poor role models in her own family, she doubted everything. Herself particularly.

Nineteen

Ben arrived at Brisbane airport in a grim mood. He hadn't let any of the family know he was coming because he didn't want his mother or Sandy's parents involved. This was between him and Phil. No one else. He had to find out exactly how he stood, then see how much he could retrieve from this mess.

When he turned up at the office, the reception desk was empty but there was the sound of voices coming from the big corner office − Phil and a man.

Ben went into his own office, which was the smaller of the two because he wasn't here very often. He looked round and frowned. Something was wrong. Then he realized that some of his things had been moved. They'd been put back in roughly the same place and to an outsider it would look just the same. But he knew how he always lined up Sandy's photo with the edge of the bookcase, and how the piece of sea-sculptured wood always lay with one tip touching the other corner of the same bookcase top. So who else had been in here? Cleaners − or Sandy's damned cousin? Not cleaners. The waste paper basket hadn't been emptied.

He opened a few drawers and found papers disturbed, put back almost as he'd left them, but not quite. Few people had as accurate a memory for spaces and objects as he did. He supposed that was why he enjoyed landscaping. Well, there was nothing for anyone to find here except sketching materials, plant catalogues and diagrams that only he would understand. What the hell had Phil been searching for?

He moved back to the door to hear his partner pleading, 'Can't you give me a little longer? We're expecting the next payment on the project soon. I can let you have that on account. I'm sure Ben will soon give up this crazy idea of staying over in the west. It's only because he's met some woman over there that he's even contemplating it.'

'You've had plenty of time to pay, Hantley, only you didn't

start to pull out of debt, you dug yourself deeper. Your partner may or may not continue working with you, but we want as much of our money as we can get out of you now, so we're foreclosing while there's something to foreclose on. *He* still has money, even if you don't.'

'You can't do that. You're nothing but loan sharks and—'

The stranger's voice became very low and menacing. 'My employers wouldn't appreciate being called loan sharks. You took out the loans legally enough, you used the business as security and *they* charged you a legal rate of interest. You'll be hearing from our lawyers. Be very careful how you drive that fancy car of yours from now on. We'd be extremely annoyed if we lost its value.'

Ben listened in shock. The situation must be far worse than he'd expected. He stepped back inside his office and waited until the man had left, then went to see Phil.

His partner jerked in shock at the sight of him. 'When did *you* get back?'

'Not long ago. I couldn't help overhearing your conversation. How much do you owe them?'

'None of your business.'

'It is as long as we're in partnership here and anyway, that man was talking about *my* assets.'

'I'll sort it.'

'Have you asked your father for help?'

Phil shook his head. 'No. He said last time he wouldn't pay my debts again.'

'Well, I'm not getting involved. I'm breaking up our partnership before they try to get at me.'

'That won't help you! The debts were incurred while we were still partners, and I said they were for business development purposes, so you're legally responsible for them as well.'

Ben breathed slowly, willing himself not to let his anger take over, because it wouldn't help. But Meriel was right. He'd been foolishly trusting. 'Why did you do that?'

Phil shrugged. 'Because I'm not Mr Nice Guy like you. Because I get bored with all this plant crap.'

There was a long silence then Ben turned on his heel, leaving the business and going straight to his own lawyer's office to find out his exact situation when it came to debts.

He left his lawyer feeling sick to the soul. Meriel had been right.

He went next to the organization for whom he was doing the major landscaping project, to check out that nothing had been skimped. While he was there, he asked that the final payments be paid directly into his personal bank account. Not that they'd amount to enough to clear the debts, nothing like, but he hated the idea of Phil gambling them away. And since the business account had been raided, he could only assume that Phil was able to forge his signature.

He felt gutted. If the lawyer was right, there wasn't much to be salvaged now from the company he and Sandy had started with such bright hopes.

The thing that upset him most was that this would affect him and Meriel. How could it not? He'd be penniless – or worse, bankrupt.

He couldn't bear things to go so wrong, not when he'd only just found her. She'd said she'd live with him, but she hadn't yet committed to marriage and would be even less inclined to do so now, he was sure.

As for them working on his special project together, that was out of the question for a good long time. He could only be glad she'd had enough wit not to sign anything. At least she'd keep her land, whereas he'd probably be losing his. His inheritance from Uncle Johnny was what the loan sharks were after, the only real asset left.

And once that was gone – well, he was the sort for whom love included marriage and who expected to support his wife and family. He wouldn't like to be dependent on her for everything, even if they were in love.

He didn't know what he'd do after the dust settled. He doubted he'd find work in Western Australia and even if he did set up a new landscaping business in the west, York wasn't the place to do it from. Besides, it'd take years for it to start making serious money.

But if he was forced into bankruptcy, would he even be allowed to open a new business? He wasn't quite sure what was permitted . . . afterwards.

He could blame Phil for a lot of this, but not all of it. He'd known what Sandy's cousin had done in the past, so he should have kept better control of things.

He didn't deserve a woman like Meriel.

When Ben got back to Somerlee, the first thing he did was pull Meriel into his arms and kiss her. But he didn't take matters any further, just held her close.

Her voice was quiet, without that crisp edge to it. 'Something's wrong. I can sense it. Tell me.'

He hesitated.

'Ben, you have to tell me.'

So he took her to sit on the sofa and explained what he'd found. 'I still don't know exactly what Phil owes, though. I'd guess there will be other debts besides the main one. My lawyer is trying to find out.'

'Oh, Ben, what a dreadful mess!'

'I don't know what to do. I just – can't see straight about it.'

'We can't really do anything till we have more information.'

'No. I suppose not. I guess I'll go for a walk. I think better out of doors.'

She didn't try to stop him but held his hand to her cheek for a minute or two. 'Don't be too long. I've missed you.'

When he'd gone, she stayed where she was, trying to understand her own feelings. The thought that he was in trouble didn't make her want to head for the hills. On the contrary, she wanted to help him, comfort him.

She was changing, she knew. He was causing those changes, just by being there. The money side of things seemed to matter less and less. Even if he was bankrupt, he'd still be Ben. Her Ben. Marriage might not matter to her, but being together did. It mattered more than anything else ever had in her whole life.

And if he had to start up a new business she'd make very sure it was on a sound footing – and that it was here in York! She wasn't going to live apart from him.

He was addictive. In the nicest possible way.

★   ★   ★

As the days passed there were no more attacks of any sort – though whether that was because of the presence of their new friends and the watchfulness of the massive hound, or for some other reason altogether, was anyone's guess.

Then a call from Queensland had Ben tight-lipped and calling for Meriel. She went into his office to find him lining up a plane reservation on the Internet. 'What's happened now?'

'Phil's creditors have foreclosed. There are other debts, as I thought. The bank is refusing to pay our final bills. I guess this is where I find out if I have anything left from the company at all – and whether my other assets will be seized.' He let out a long, shuddering sigh. 'I can just about afford my plane fare.'

She put one hand across the doorway to stop him leaving. 'Let me come with you.'

'No. That hasn't changed. I don't want you involved in the muckraking and mess.' He looked at her pleadingly. 'You will stay with me afterwards, Meriel, won't you? Whatever happens.'

'Of course I will, you fool! I'm not a fair-weather friend, or a fair-weather lover, either. But I think you're wrong. I could be a valuable resource. You should use me! Bounce ideas off me at the very least and ask my advice. Let me be beside you for comfort and support, even if I can't do anything to help. Don't just clam up on me and then take off into the wide blue yonder.'

He set his hands on her shoulders. 'Look, darling – in the new project I'll tell you every detail, I promise, and account for every single paperclip – but I haven't changed my mind about this. My mess, my job to clear it up. I haven't told my family about you yet, except for my mother. This is not the time to introduce you.'

She felt hurt by that. 'I thought you'd have told them by now. After all, you've asked me to marry you.'

'I was going to tell them last time, only Sandy's uncle was rushed back into hospital – and I was busy with Phil.'

'I hate being shut out like this and I'm worried. You aren't the world's best businessman, you know you aren't. What you do now, any unfinished ends left over from this, could affect your next project.' She was too upset to watch what she said. 'I daren't put my money into your project unless you can convince me that there'll be no trailing debts from Elless-Hantley.'

Ben shut his eyes and clenched his fists. 'It seems to me that what it comes down to is you just don't trust me. I have consulted a lawyer, you know. I'm not in this on my own.'

There was a dead silence.

He held out his hands in the age-old gesture of appeal. 'Meriel, you have to let me do this myself.'

She grasped his arm, 'Ben, I trust *you*, but not them, especially this Phil. *Please* take me with you. Just as your accountant. I'll stay out of the way the rest of the time and—'

'*No!*'

She turned round and walked from the room. What if Ben lost every single thing he owned, his uncle's land as well? However hard the two of them tried, such a setback would affect their relationship, if only because it would hurt him deeply, perhaps scar him for life.

She waited for him to come and say goodbye but he didn't. When she heard a car start up outside, she ran to the window and watched in disbelief as he drove off down the drive.

He hadn't even said goodbye!

A tear trickled down her cheek and she brushed it away angrily, but another followed. Something nudged at her leg and she looked down to see Tina's anxious face. Dogs could always tell when you were upset. She squatted down for a moment to give her friend a cuddle – or maybe Tina was cuddling her – then stood up, summoned up enough anger to keep the tears at bay and went into her studio to flesh out her preliminary ideas for the cover.

She slept badly, of course, but at least no one tried to break in or damage her property.

The next day she had to throw all the previous day's sketches away. They were as full of anger as she was, nasty images that would put people off buying a gentle book.

She waited for a phone call from Ben all evening.

The following morning Ben still didn't call her, so she

decided to call him. She dialled his mobile number, but all she got was a recorded message saying, 'This number is no longer operational.'

She tried again, thinking she had misdialled.

'What do you mean by "no longer operational"?' she asked the phone when it repeated its tinny-sounding message. 'It's the same number as usual.' Then she pulled a face. He'd have forgotten to recharge his battery. Or a bill hadn't been paid.

She phoned the office of Elless-Hantley. The receptionist promised to pass on the message when Mr Elless came in. Meriel spent a frustrating afternoon expecting to hear the phone ring.

He still didn't call.

Her emotions see-sawed from anxiety to anger, to memories that brought a smile to her face, to others that brought a desperate need to her body. Of one thing she was certain, though. This was unlike Ben. Sure, he got angry at her sometimes, but he never stayed angry.

Nor did she.

She wasn't angry now so much as worried sick. Something was wrong, she was sure of it.

She couldn't concentrate on her art, didn't dare move too far from the landline phone, so baked a cake. The mere sight of it filled her with nausea and she went to beckon to Ria.

Her friend walked up to the house, took one look at her and asked, 'What's wrong? Don't pretend there's nothing, because your face gives you away.'

'It's Ben. He hasn't contacted me. His business over east is in financial trouble, because of his partner. I wanted to go with him to help sort things out, more as his accountant than anything else, but he refused. Insisted he has to clear up his own mess. But Ria, he's a baby where figures and paperwork are concerned. Those people could be walking all over him.'

'Maybe you should follow him anyway?'

'I would if I could be sure he was still there, but he may have moved on, may even be on his way home again.'

Ria gave her a wordless hug.

'I made a cake, but I don't want it, so I thought you'd like it.'

'Jim is already addicted to your cakes. Thank you.'

After her friend had left, Meriel fell back on painting the walls of the spare bedrooms. At least it made good use of her frustration.

When it began to get dark Tina, who had an infallible internal clock, started whining for her tea. Meriel cleared up the painting things and went to feed the dog.

And still the phone didn't ring.

The next day Meriel again called the Elless-Hantley office. 'Did you tell him I called?' she asked the receptionist.

'Oh, yes, Ms Ingram. I told him about an hour after you rang.'

'Did he say where he was going today?'

'I'm afraid not.'

'Do you have his home phone number?'

'I'm afraid I can't give that out.'

'Of course you can. I'm living with him, for heaven's sake!'

'If he'd wanted you to have it, he'd have given it to you already.'

'He forgot. Tell him to call me urgently.'

'Certainly. As soon as he comes back.'

Meriel put the phone down, feeling frustrated in every way. She'd tried directory enquiries and he had a silent home number. Besides, she knew Ben would phone her if he could. So something was stopping him. What?

The only explanation was that the receptionist wasn't passing on her messages. But that didn't explain why Ben hadn't rung.

If he didn't call that night, she'd go after him. She did have his home address, at least.

When the phone rang early that evening she pounced on it with a growl of triumph, but it was a stranger's voice, a man, elderly from the sound of it.

'Is that Ben Elless's residence?'

'Yes, but he isn't here. Can I take a message?'

'I think it's you I need to speak to, actually. Your name is Meriel Ingram, I believe? I'm Rod Hantley. I gather from

Ben's mother that you two are seriously involved. I'm so glad he's met someone. He may have mentioned me, perhaps?'

'You're Sandy's uncle.'

'More to the point now, Phil's father.' He sighed and fell silent for a moment or two.

She sank down on the nearest chair. This was the last person she'd expected to hear from. Had something happened to Ben? If so she'd rather hear about it straight away. Just as she was about to ask if there had been an accident, Mr Hantley spoke again.

'I think you should fly over here, Meriel. I'm trying to help Ben, I promise you, but I want him to have someone he can turn to if anything happens to me or I don't succeed in what I plan to do.'

'I was going to come anyway.'

'I'm glad. Don't tell him I called. This is my contact number . . .'

When Meriel put the phone down she felt better for having something to do. There was a lot to arrange and she wouldn't get much sleep tonight. First she got on the Internet and booked the early flight to Queensland the following morning.

When she looked out of the window, everything was dark in her friends' camp, but she had no alternative. She went and woke Ria to explain that she was following Ben and ask if they'd look after Tina and the house. Then she went to pack.

At just before three in the morning she set off to drive to Perth airport for the six o'clock flight to Brisbane.

She didn't know what Ben would say about her turning up unannounced and she didn't know what Rod Hantley intended to do. But she did know that she intended to be with Ben – whatever the outcome.

She gave a wry smile as she slumped back in her seat on the plane. She'd always been so careful about financial security, and yet where Ben was concerned, money was the least of her worries. It was his stupid pride that was coming between them.

She couldn't bear that.

Rod Hantley seemed to be on Ben's side, but he'd admitted

he was seriously ill and the implication was that he could die at any moment.

No way was she leaving Ben to face all the troubles alone. Whatever he said.

Twenty

Ben woke feeling deeply depressed. He hadn't heard from Meriel and when he'd tried to phone her from the office, the secretary said her line was engaged. So he'd tried to phone her from his mobile, but found he'd lost the damned thing. They made them too small these days. They fell out of pockets.

And his home phone had been cut off because the company hadn't paid the bill. If he couldn't get through to Meriel from the office today, he'd buy another damned mobile or ring her from his mother's.

He hadn't even had the satisfaction of a big row with Phil, who had gone to earth somewhere and was staying out of the way.

Well, today, Phil would be forced to come out of hiding because they were having a preliminary hearing about the partnership's bankruptcy. Ben would find out at last exactly how much his partner owed and whether there would be anything left for him from the business he'd worked so hard to build. His lawyer had offered to accompany him, but he'd refused in order to save money. This was only a preliminary not a court hearing and he'd been instructed on what to say and ask.

He found Phil in the waiting area. 'Ah!' He strode across, determined to find out as much as he could before they went into the hearing room.

Phil looked at him, face expressionless, saying nothing.

'Where have you been? Didn't you get my messages?'

'Nareen passed them on. I didn't feel like replying.'

'You'll have to reply in there, so you may as well talk to me now.'

'I think not.' Phil got up and went to stare out of the window.

Ben was baffled. Phil had changed so much in the past year he seemed like a stranger. He followed him across the room. 'What the hell's got into you lately?'

'Lack of money. Lack of a home, too. Cheryl's turned me out. I had to sleep in the car one night. Not that *you* would care about that, though this is all due to you.'

Ben's anger boiled over. 'What the hell do you mean, due to me? I'm not the one who's been gambling beyond his means.'

'I could have worked my way out of it if I'd had a guaranteed income, but no, you had to stop that.'

Ben gave up trying. 'There's no use talking to you. It's always someone else's fault and—'

'Elless-Hantley!' a voice called.

Ben swung round. 'That's us.'

'Please come inside.'

The formalities began.

'You've had all the papers relating to this case?'

Ben frowned. 'I've had the papers saying when the hearing would be. Were there others?'

'There have been three sets. They were sent to your office.'

'I've had only one small envelope, as I said.'

'He's lying. The others were all passed on to him,' Phil said at once.

Ben gaped at him for a moment, then said grimly, 'It's you who's lying.' He half stood up.

'Don't let him attack me!' Phil said quickly.

'Mr Elless, please sit down.'

'I wasn't going to attack him.' Ben slumped back in his chair. He couldn't believe this. 'I didn't receive any of the other papers. Can I please ask for an adjournment to study them?'

The woman looked from one to the other. 'I'll give you two days. I happen to have a cancellation for Friday morning at ten o'clock. I'll make sure my clerk gives you copies before you leave, Mr Elless.'

'Then I'll get back to work now.' Phil stood up.

Ben jumped up and took a step towards the door. 'Wait! We need to talk, dammit.'

'I'd be grateful if you'd see he doesn't follow me,' Phil called out. 'I'm afraid for my safety.'

She looked from one to the other. 'You'd better leave now, then. Mr Elless, please stay where you are.'

Ben watched in frustration as Phil hurried out.

'You can stay in the waiting area till your photocopies are ready, Mr Elless.'

He looked at her. 'I really didn't receive anything. Can you please make sure any future communications intended for me don't go through the office?'

'Yes. Do you have another address?'

He gave her his home address, plus Meriel's address in Western Australia. He didn't know where Phil was staying, so couldn't follow him. He'd go straight to his lawyer as soon as he'd studied the paperwork. He felt so ashamed of this mess, he didn't even want to see his mother.

He sat fidgeting in the waiting area until a clerk brought out a big envelope containing the various papers.

'If you'd sign for these, sir?'

Ben didn't read them till he got home. They contained a list of debts and claims, and these were for amounts so much greater than he'd expected that he could only sit there, shocked rigid.

When he saw his lawyer in an emergency appointment at six o'clock that evening, Ben listened in even greater horror as his situation was carefully explained to him. If the business couldn't pay the debts Phil had taken on, then as a partner, Ben would be made bankrupt too. That meant he'd be treated as if *he* had committed a crime, wouldn't be allowed to be a director of a company, to incur credit above a small, fixed amount, or to carry on business under a different name without disclosing that he was a bankrupt.

And the worst case scenario Meriel had described was about to come true: they were allowed to take everything away from him, his home, his investment properties, his uncle's legacy, even his car, because as a bankrupt he would only be allowed to possess a cheap vehicle.

If he couldn't start a new business, how would he support himself and a wife, how would he build a decent life with Meriel?

He couldn't ask her to marry him now.

He forgot completely about food, wanted only to get home and shut out the world. But when he got there, the place seemed to echo around him and he wished suddenly that he'd brought Meriel with him.

Why had she refused to return his calls? Was she so angry she intended to break up with him?

How could he live without her now?

Was he to lose another woman he loved?

He went to sit outside the back of the house, feeling as if he couldn't find enough oxygen indoors.

Meriel arrived at Brisbane airport late that afternoon, eastern time. She felt tired after eight hours of travelling, which had included an hour's wait at Melbourne. Why were planes always so stuffy? When she had to fly somewhere she arrived feeling lethargic and headachy until she'd got some good fresh air into her lungs.

She took a taxi out to Ben's home, but found the place in darkness. She wheeled her suitcase to the front door and rang the bell, rang it a second time, waited, then left the suitcase and walked round the house. If he was out, she'd just have to break in and wait till he got back.

But he wasn't out. He was sitting in the garden in the moonlight, shoulders drooping, misery in every line of his body. For a moment she watched him, her heart going out to him, then called his name softly.

He jumped in shock and turned round to stare at her.

'Meriel? Am I dreaming?'

'Oh, Ben, of course you aren't!' She ran across and flung herself into his arms, hugging and kissing, incoherent with love and worry for him.

He kissed her back and held her tight for a few minutes, joy on his face. Then he stiffened and pushed her away. 'I told you not to come.'

'I never did learn to obey orders. So sue me.'

'Meriel, it's a worse mess than I thought. You don't want to be involved.'

'I do.' She tugged him to sit down on the wooden garden bench and kept hold of his hand. 'Whatever it is, I won't let you shut me out any longer. That's the sort of woman I am. A bully. Get over it.'

He stared at her as if he'd never seen her before, then pulled his hand away from hers. 'There's nothing anyone can do to help, even you. You told me it was dangerous to form a partnership and you were one hundred per cent right. I'm ruined.'

She watched him close his eyes in pain. 'We still have my house and land, so we'll have somewhere to live.'

'*You* still have it, thank goodness. I think if I'd lost your land for you, I'd have thrown myself off the nearest cliff.'

She let him talk for a while, realizing he needed to get it out of his system. Then she put her hand over his mouth. 'Look, Elless, you're not going to turn all noble on me, are you? Because I tell you frankly, I won't have it.'

'I don't intend to be a burden on anyone, especially you.'

'Yeah, well, you're not riding off into the sunset, either. I need you – not your money, or your land, but *you*, Ben Elless, the man I love.' She put her arms round him. 'I love you so much.' She could see that his eyes were bright with unshed tears and her own eyes were also brimming over.

All the times she'd told herself she didn't need love, she'd been fooling herself. Everyone needed love. It was the most important thing in the world.

His hand came up to caress her cheek and he bent forward to kiss her other cheek. Then he drew back and his voice was husky. 'I think that's the most wonderful thing anyone ever said to me.'

They sat hand in hand for a few moments and she saw his stiff shoulders ease a little. When she judged that he was feeling a little better, she said, 'I hope this is an honest neighbourhood.'

'Why?'

'I left my suitcase outside your front door. I was going to break in if you weren't home.'

'You can break into my house any time. I'll go and get the case for you.' He came back a couple of minutes later and took her inside, leaving the case in a room near the front door. 'I'm sleeping in here at the moment. Or do you want to go to a hotel?'

'Of course I don't. This'll be fine.' She suddenly became aware of how hungry she was. 'Do you have anything to eat in the house?'

'Some bread and jam.'

'I'm feeling more like red meat and a luscious dessert. Let's get a shower and go out.' She could feel him tensing up again, moving away from her. 'What? What've I said?'

'I can't afford to take you out. The bank's cancelled my credit card.'

She pulled him close. 'Well, I can afford it and I'm not having any stupid heroics about who pays. Take me out and feed me, Elless, or there'll be major trouble. Hell hath no fury like a hungry woman.'

'All right. Just this once you can pay.'

But she could see his black mood returning and knew that nothing she said or did would dispel it completely. For the rest of the evening he put on a brave front and she went along with it, telling him about Ria and the others, chatting about her latest book cover.

When they were in bed, she tried desperately to stay awake, but a huge yawn overtook her, in spite of the time differences.

'Go to sleep,' he said. 'You've fought enough dragons for today.'

'You won't leave me, Ben?'

'No.'

'Promise.'

'I promise. I don't think I could leave you. I love you and need you.'

'Me, too.'

In the morning he got out the bread and jam, which were all he had in the house, then suddenly said, 'Wait! I've got some tomatoes growing wild on one corner and I think the passion fruit vine still has fruit on it.'

He came back with misshapen tomatoes and a pile of dark purple globes, which they cut open to scoop out the seeds and flesh.

She sighed blissfully. 'That's delicious. I've never had passion fruit freshly picked before.'

'I keep forgetting you're a Pom.'

'Watch it, Elless. Some people use that word as an insult.'

'Would I ever?' He pulled her close and said in her ear, 'Thank you.'

'What for?'

'Everything. Coming here. Helping me pull myself together. Loving me. When this is all over, I'll find myself a job and start again. If possible over in the west, if not, over here in Queensland. Will you put up with that?'

'I'll put up with anything as long as we're together. And if necessary, I'll sell up and move over here with you. I'm not letting go of you now, Elless.'

His smile was dazzling. 'When it comes to love, I'm the luckiest man on earth. Others think they are. I know it for certain. I'll get over the other stuff, but I don't think I'll ever get over you.'

'Good.'

'I'm going to ring my mother now. I want her to meet you.'

'I'd like that.'

He put the phone down a minute later. 'I forgot. It's not working.'

She got out her mobile. 'Here. Use this.'

He phoned his mother and arranged for them to meet that evening.

Meriel put her mobile back into her shoulder bag. 'What happened to your mobile, Elless?'

'I don't know. I think someone must have picked my pocket. I had it at the office on my first day over here and haven't seen it since.'

'That secretary probably stole it. She has mean eyes. She didn't pass on my messages, did she?'

'No. I caught her and Phil kissing one day, so I guess she's been aiding and abetting him. But she's going to be disappointed if she thinks he'll stay around once she's no use to him. He lets everyone down sooner or later.'

He stared at the ground for a moment or two, sighing as he added, 'You know, what hurts most is how naïve I've been, how I've let Phil use me and rob me blind for *years*.'

She took his hand and raised it to her lips. 'I like you exactly the way you are, Elless, naïve or not. I can be suspicious enough for the two of us from now on, so don't change on me.' She reached up to kiss his cheek. 'I think

I'll just check that everything's all right back at the ranch, then you can show me the town.'

'Shouldn't we be doing something in preparation for the hearing?'

'We have to go there and tell the truth. What's to prepare about that? Let's just chill out for an hour or two. You look like you need a break.'

So they went into the City and took the Riverwalk, stopping now and then so that Ben could explain how a piece of land had been modelled and once, with much gesticulating, he described what he'd have done instead. The sun was shining, there were cafés and displays of art, smiling people, and most of all, the two of them were together.

'We've never done this,' she said as they sat drinking cappuccinos outside a café.

'Done what?'

'Enjoyed ourselves away from home, relaxed, chilled out together.'

His smile had a hint of sadness. 'Making lemonade, huh?'

'Why not?'

'We did have dinner twice in York.'

'That was before we were together and I was very much on my guard. I was terrified at how attracted I was to you.'

That evening as she got ready Meriel admitted to herself that she felt a little nervous about meeting Ben's mother. It mattered so much that they got on, given how fond of her he obviously was.

But she needn't have worried. Louise was as warm and friendly as her son, looking far younger than her age. She hugged Meriel and took her outside to see her beautiful garden. She said immediately how delighted she was that Ben had found someone to love. 'My boy needs to love someone and be loved. He's not hardwired to be a loner.'

'No. I've discovered that.'

'And I gather you're the practical one. You know he isn't?'

Meriel rolled her eyes. 'Yes. I definitely found that out.'

'Good. He needs keeping on track about details. Sandy wasn't much like you, but she was very practical about everyday life. You don't mind me talking about her?'

'No, not at all.'

'I'll show you some photos of Ben as a boy after we've eaten.'

'I'd love that.'

'He was a delightful child.'

Meriel smiled. 'He's a pretty wonderful man, too.'

When they got back to his house, Ben hugged Meriel suddenly. 'I really needed you to make me see that this isn't the end of the world. Will you come with me to the hearing tomorrow?'

She hid her joy at this with a flippant, 'I thought you'd never ask.' But it seemed like another step on their path together, so she grinned and confessed, 'Actually, I was coming whatever you said or did.'

'Don't push your luck, Ingram.'

She grinned. 'You're all talk, Elless, but you're a pussy cat underneath.'

He purred then kissed her fingertips slowly, one by one. Who would have thought that such a small action could be so sexy? She sucked in air and dragged her hand away.

He gave her a smug look and mimed a meow.

Twenty-One

The next day, Ben grew very quiet as they got ready to go to the rescheduled preliminary hearing. Meriel kept an eye on him, but didn't try to cheer him up. He had a right to feel upset and worried. She was worried too.

She hadn't told him about Rod Hantley's phone call because she didn't want to raise any false hopes. Sandy's uncle might not be able to sort this out and then Ben really would lose everything.

She wouldn't let him be noble about it, though. They were together and they were staying together, whatever happened, wherever they wound up.

They had trouble finding a parking spot and were only just in time for the hearing. Phil was sitting in a corner of the waiting room. He looked across at Meriel with a scornful expression. 'Brought the blond bimbo along to hold your hand, have you?'

Ben stiffened and Meriel kept tighter hold of his arm, but fortunately a door opened just then and the same woman as before called 'Elless-Hantley. Ms Parnahan is ready for you'.

Phil sauntered across the room and pushed in first, so didn't see the outer door slide open and a man in a wheelchair enter. Ben did and stopped in his tracks.

The old man rolled forward, holding out his hand. 'I hope my son's behaviour won't come between us, lad.'

Ben grasped the hand, not only shaking it but clasping it in both his. 'Definitely not, Rod.'

By this time Phil had heard the voices and come back out to join them. 'Dad! Great to see you.'

Rod Hantley's whole expression changed and his voice became icy. 'It's not great to see you here, Philip. Your mother and I are bitterly disappointed in you. Now, let's go inside. We don't want to keep the hearing officer waiting, do we?'

Phil's mouth fell open in shock, then he snapped it shut, looking sulky.

When they were all settled, Rod took charge, and for all his frail looks, there was an authority in his tone. 'If you'd kindly outline the financial situation to me, Ms Parnahan, we can discuss what to do about it.'

Phil smirked at Ben.

Ms Parnahan read through a list of his liabilities, ending, 'Normally we would suggest that Mr Elless and Mr Hantley declare themselves bankrupt. The court would then arrange to take whatever assets they have, within the specifications of the law, to apply towards payment of the debt incurred by one partner.'

'Which seems rather unfair when only one partner incurred the debts,' Rod said quietly. 'And in this case, I believe I can help you come to a settlement without such drastic measures.'

'I can't let you do that, Rod,' Ben said. 'I was stupid and naïve. You shouldn't have to pay for that.'

'You can't stop me, Ben. He's my son, even though he's broken his promises in a multitude of ways. I'll feel better if I try to make amends. My wife and I will deal with our relationship with him on a personal level, but I'm not having you suffer financially because of his irresponsibility.'

'I could have worked my way through this if *he* hadn't tried to break up our business,' Phil said at once.

'Keep silent if you want my help, and stop blaming others for your own mistakes.' Rod's voice was as quiet as ever but sounded like fractured ice. He turned back to Ben. 'Phil isn't and never has been your responsibility. The family was wrong to persuade you to set up in business together, so we bear part of the blame. I doubt he'll ever change, so we need to rid you of him.'

He turned to Ms Parnahan. 'I'll give you my personal guarantee that all debts which need to be paid to release Mr Elless from any obligations will be paid. My lawyer,' he gestured to the man who had pushed the wheelchair in, 'will deal with this for me. I believe you and he are already acquainted?'

She nodded.

Rod turned to Ben. 'Will you wheel me out, please? My chauffeur is waiting to take me home afterwards, but there's a café nearby where we could discuss the rest of this. Phil! You'll need to be there too.'

Phil stepped forward quickly. 'Of course, Father. And *I'll* push you.'

'I don't want you to do that. In fact, after today, I don't want to see you again, ever. And I don't want you pestering your mother for money after I'm dead. I've left instructions on how that should be dealt with if you're stupid enough to try.'

Flinching as if he'd been struck across the face, Phil took a step backwards.

Ben glanced quickly at Meriel, who flapped one hand to urge him on. He didn't feel sorry for Phil, but he felt enormously sorry for Rod, as well as grateful to him. He was still trying to take it in that he wasn't going to lose everything, could hardly believe this wasn't a dream.

Taking hold of the wheelchair, he pushed it towards the lift. Meriel fell in beside him and Phil walked a short distance behind them, scowling.

By the time they were settled in the café, Rod was grey-faced with exhaustion, but he again took charge.

'What I have to say to you, Phil, is quite short, so don't bother ordering anything. I've changed my will so that this settling of your current debts will be considered your inheritance. Apart from that you'll get nothing from me.'

'You can't do that! What about Cheryl and the boys?'

'I've set up a trust fund for them, one you won't be able to touch. I haven't much longer to live so I won't be here to see the mess you make of the rest of your life.' He waited a moment, then continued, 'And I've arranged to deal with the people you paid to vandalize Meriel's property and try to drive her and Ben away. It sickens me that you'd descend to such a level. I've made a lot of money in business, but I've made it honestly and no one can say I cheated or bribed or threatened them in any way.'

He paused to draw breath, then looked at his son and spoke with such sadness that Meriel felt tears well in her eyes out of pity for this kind, decent man.

'And now that you understand that, Phil, I'd be grateful if you'd leave us. I don't want to see you again. I haven't long to live and I want to spend that time in peace with your mother. My lawyer will be in touch with you.'

'Dad, please—'

Rod beckoned and a burly man got out of the big luxury car waiting on the other side of the street and came to stand beside their table. 'My son is reluctant to leave, George. Will you help him on his way, please?'

Phil glared at Ben and left, shaking off the burly man's hand and striding down the street, radiating anger.

'I'm so sorry, Rod,' Ben said quietly.

'I've come to terms with it, as much as one ever can come to terms with losing a child, which is how my wife and I have decided to regard it.' He looked at Meriel. 'This is the new woman in your life, I gather? She and I have already spoken on the phone.'

'You have?'

'I felt she should be here.'

'And I agreed,' Meriel put in. 'Though I'd have come here anyway.'

Rod held out his hand. 'I'm delighted to meet you in person, Meriel. I hope you and Ben will be happy together. I wish I could get to know you properly, but I'm afraid that won't be possible now.' He sighed and beckoned to the burly man, who had watched Phil till he was out of sight then returned to the café. 'I'm afraid I'm tiring rapidly, so I think I'll let my attendant take me home and put me to bed. Please stay and have a meal here at my expense.'

'I think we'd rather go home,' Ben said. He went to bend and give the older man a hug. 'I wish . . .'

'No use wishing for the impossible.' Rod patted his arm, smiled at Meriel and nodded to his attendant, who wheeled him out of the café.

Ben looked at Meriel. 'Was I right about that? Do you want to go home now?'

'Yes. I'm not at all hungry at the moment. Oh, Ben! I'm so glad for you.'

He nodded and blinked his eyes furiously but a tear still

rolled down his cheek. 'Rod's a great guy, you know, doesn't deserve all this.'

As they walked down the street, Ben said in a husky voice, 'I still can't believe that I'm free of debt – and of Phil, too.' He suddenly picked Meriel up and swung her round several times. Passers-by stopped to stare so he grinned at them. 'She's just agreed to marry me.'

He accepted their congratulations and watched them walk away smiling, then turned to Meriel. 'I couldn't resist it!'

'I forgive you this once. It's been a fraught time.'

'Now that I'm free, we really can get married. How soon is the only question?'

'Let's discuss that when we get back. I was thinking. Do you have anything at the office that you want?'

'Yeah, there are some useful bits and pieces and some sentimental stuff, too.'

'Well, we'd better go back and pack them up straight away. I wouldn't put it past that louse to smash everything of yours. If ever I saw a man who'd like to harm you, he's it.'

'There's nothing much he can do now.'

There he went again, being an optimist. 'Humour me. Let's get your stuff, then go home.'

'All right. Are you sure you wouldn't like to go and choose a ring first?'

'No. We can do that later.'

Much later if she had her way. She wasn't into all the fuss and botheration of getting married, still shuddered at the memory of the pink meringue of a dress she'd had to wear to her sister's wedding – and from her mother's recent letters, it looked as if Helen's marriage was failing too, which didn't add to her confidence about the marital state.

No, marriage was unlucky, a stupid sort of institution. Either you wanted to stay together or you moved apart. No one should tie you forcibly to another person.

She wasn't going down that path, but she'd have to ease Ben into accepting that they didn't need marriage to make them stay together.

The outer door of the office suite was unlocked and after a shocked glance at Meriel, Ben hurried across to his room, cursing under his breath as he stopped in the doorway. The place had been ransacked and most of his professional drafting equipment smashed, as well as his mementoes and worst of all the portrait of Sandy.

'Stay back,' he told Meriel. 'I'm contacting the police. It's Phil who did it, of course, though we may never prove that, but this time I'm definitely bringing in the police.'

When he went to use the phone, it wasn't working.

'Here, take my mobile again.' Meriel fished it out of her bag. 'I'm going to buy you one of your own when we get back and chain it to you.'

He made the call, then gave a thumbs up. 'They'll be here in a few minutes. They've got a campaign on about inner city break-ins and burglaries, apparently. We haven't to touch anything.'

They wandered into Phil's office, which hadn't been disturbed, then Ben said, 'I think I'll just nip along to the toilet. I won't be long.'

When she heard footsteps, Meriel turned round, but it was Phil standing in the doorway, not Ben. And he was looking her up and down in a very offensive way.

'Well, well. What are *you* doing here?'

'Waiting for Ben.'

He moved forward towards her. 'Maybe we can think of some way to enliven your wait. A lovely woman like you should share yourself around a bit.'

She realized he was drunk and also, to her astonishment, that he was about to assault her. He must have poured the booze down to get drunk so quickly. Was the man utterly stupid? It appeared so.

With a foolishly confident smile on his face he reached out for her as if expecting her to stand there and wait for him to grab her. She stepped sideways, shoving him away from her hard. 'Back off, you idiot!'

But he laughed and moved forward again, arms outstretched to bar her way.

'I've taken self-defence classes,' she warned him, moving behind a chair. 'I don't want to hurt you, but I will if you don't leave me alone.'

He sniggered and let out a mocking, high-pitched, 'Oooh! I'm so scared.'

Well, she'd given him warning. In a rapid series of moves, she jabbed at him with the chair and when he grabbed it, as she'd known he would, she let go suddenly. While he was off balance, she darted forward and hurt him in a very private place.

As he yowled and folded up on the floor, she turned and saw two people standing in the doorway, grinning. Footsteps pounded along the corridor and Ben pushed them aside, stopping to gape at the sight of Phil, still curled up in agony on the floor. 'Are you all right, Meriel?'

She stepped back and mimed dusting off her hands. 'He tried to assault me so I had to protect myself. I did warn him to keep away. I'm afraid I've hurt him, well, I hope I have. You men have one particular weak spot. His is a little more tender than it was.'

Ben stood glaring down at Hantley. 'I'd like to punch him.'

The man behind him tried to turn a laugh into a cough but failed. 'Better not, sir. I'm Detective Constable Paganino, madam, and this is my colleague, Detective Constable Sterran.' He flashed an identification at Meriel and the woman with him did the same. 'We both overheard this man threatening to assault you, and you warning him to stay away. I think we'll make credible witnesses if he complains, don't you?'

'Couldn't find better.'

Ben dragged her towards him. 'You are,' a kiss landed on her nose, 'the most amazing,' another kiss landed on her cheek, 'woman I've ever met.'

She had had enough of this pussy-footing around, so she grabbed his head with both hands and pulled his face towards hers for a much more satisfying kiss.

It was interrupted by the female detective clearing her throat rather close to their ears. 'I wonder if you two could spare me a moment? The original complaint was about an office that had been burgled.'

They turned to look at the woman who had a distinct twinkle in her eyes. 'Spoilsport,' Meriel complained.

Ben led them into his office which looked as if a tornado had hit it. 'I suspect my ex-partner did this.'

'I deny that absolutely,' Phil said, still in a rather wheezy voice.

'We'll pursue our investigations later, sir,' the female detective said to Ben. 'But in the meantime this gentleman will be taken to the police station and questioned about the burglary. You'll need to make a statement too, Ms Ingram.'

'I'll be delighted to.'

When the police officers had left and taken Phil with them, Meriel looked at Ben. 'I was worried about you for a while back there, Elless.'

'I was worried about you, too, Ingram, when I heard someone cry out. I should have been there to look after you.'

She rolled her eyes at him. 'Here we go again. Look, Elless, I can deal with a drunk without any help from you. I *don't – need – protecting.*'

He sighed. 'It's going to take me a long time to get used to a wife like you.' He pulled her towards him with one arm and they began to walk towards the door. 'So I think I'd better get into intensive training.'

When they were sitting in his car, he looked sideways at her. 'Right, to get back to my original question – how soon can we get married? You didn't answer me.'

She took a deep breath. 'As I said before, I'd rather live together first, see how we go and maybe get married when the time's ripe to have children. And I'm *not* wearing one of those stupid white dresses when we do it, either.'

His voice was suddenly husky. 'But you will marry me one day? Promise.'

'Who else would have you, Elless? Besides, it's the only way I can keep you safe. And I'm warning you now – you'll not only have to promise to love me, but to let me vet all your contracts and do all your accounting.'

He gave her a fond smile. 'When we're married, you'll be an Elless, too, so you'll have to use my first name.'

'Oh, no. I definitely won't be an Elless!'

He stared at her in surprise. 'What do you mean by that?'

'You don't think I'm giving up my name and taking yours, do you?'

'It's usual.'

'Yeah, well, if you insist on us sharing the same name, you can change yours. Ben Ingram sounds fine to me.'

'Meriel—' He broke off and drew in a deep breath. 'You're having me on – right?'

'Not about the name. I'll seriously consider marrying you, Elless – one day, when we're ready to start a family – but I'm not changing my name and becoming Mrs Ben Ingram. No way.'

'We have to have the same name, for our children's sake.'

'Hmm. You have a point there. OK, when the time comes we'll toss for it – Ingram-Elless or Elless-Ingram. They can change their names if they want to when they grow up.'

The argument that ensued was cut short by their arrival back at his house.

'You know,' he said suddenly. 'Once we've completed all the necessary formalities, we could drive back to Western Australia. Take a couple of weeks, stop where we like. You could ring up your hippie friends. I'm sure they'd look after things for us.'

'I'll think about it. We'll see how long it takes to sort things out.'

He watched her stretch lazily, her body outlined by the light from the window behind her. 'If I wasn't so hungry . . .'

She grinned at him. 'Later. I'm hungry too.'

'The trouble with you, Ingram, is you've no romance in your soul.'

'Are you prepared to go without your food, Elless?'

'Well, now you put it like that . . .'

Later, as they lay sleepily entwined, all appetites temporarily satisfied, she remembered something. 'I've got some figures to show you tomorrow. I had an idea while you were away – about our new development.'

'Are you an artist or an accountant, woman?' he asked in mock anger.

He'd asked her that before and she'd been unsure of her

answer. Now, she had no hesitation in saying firmly, 'I'm both.'

Which wasn't a bad thing, she reckoned – especially with a guy like Ben Elless to look after. She snuggled against him, feeling happier than she ever had in her life before.

Epilogue

Two years later

'You're late,' Ben said thoughtfully. 'And you're not usually late starting your period. How long is it overdue now? Two weeks?'

Meriel lay in bed willing herself not to be sick.

A finger poked her in the ribs. 'Answer me, Ingram!'

'Yes. I'm late.'

'And you've rushed to the bathroom to be sick the last few mornings, even though you've tried to hide that from me.'

'What are you now, Elless, a detective?'

'I'm the man who loves you and wants to marry you. The man you've been refusing to marry for two whole years.'

She wriggled uncomfortably. 'There didn't seem to be any need. I mean – we were happy as we were.' The wriggle had been a mistake. She groaned, jumped out of bed and rushed into the en suite.

When she came out he was waiting, arms folded. 'I reckon you're pregnant.'

'So, sue me.' She still felt rather fragile, so walked carefully across to the bed and lay down on it again.

He came to kneel beside her. 'Would you like a cup of tea, love?' His voice was gentle.

She looked sideways. 'Oh hell, Ben, I probably am pregnant – and I'd die for a cup of tea. But no milk. I can't stand milk at the moment.'

He was back a few minutes later with two mugs of tea and a plate of biscuits. 'They say a dry biscuit helps settle the stomach.'

She hauled herself into a sitting position and took the mug from him, sipping thankfully, glad of the clean sharp taste. He went round to the other side of the bed and sat next to her. The silence was deafening.

'So,' he said when she'd put the cup down and picked up a biscuit, 'Do you want me to make an honest woman of you or not? Surely you don't want our child to be born out of wedlock?'

She nibbled on a biscuit. 'Oh, very well. I suppose we'd better get married now.'

He let out a growl of anger and pulled her round to face him. 'That is *not* the most enthusiastic response I've ever heard to a proposal of marriage.'

She could see he was really hurt. 'Oh hell, it's not that I don't love you, Ben. You know I do. But I hate all that marriage fuss. If we have to do it, we'll book a marriage celebrant and have a quiet wedding here in the garden and—'

'Nope.'

'What do you mean by that?'

'I mean I'm not getting married in a sneaky, hole-in-the-corner way. I want the works: fancy clothes, big party and all our relatives here with us.'

She slammed down her empty mug. 'Well, you can forget that – absolutely forget it. If you think I'm prancing down any aisles in a white dress like a sacrificial virgin, you can think again.'

He looked at her and grinned. 'Then I refuse.'

'What?'

'I refuse to get married. If you're ashamed of me, we'll just scrub the wedding.'

'You louse! You wouldn't dare.'

He folded his arms and tried to look plaintive. 'That's it. Call me names. No one respects unmarried fathers. I think I'll go and see how the breakfasts are going. Our guests like a bit of personal attention.'

She grabbed him as he pretended to get up. 'You're going nowhere until we've sorted this out, Elless.'

He turned and his face became very serious. 'I mean it, Meriel darling. I want to marry you in style to show the world how proud I am of you – and since you've kept me waiting this long, we may as well wait a bit longer and get it right.' Then he swung off the bed and went across to the en suite.

For the rest of the day she was very cool with him. Once

the morning nausea had passed, she was her old brisk self, working in her studio for a while, then going to check that all was well in the central complex. She could see Ben talking to the guys working on the second-phase units, then as he came back towards reception, stopping to talk to one of the guests, who seemed, by the smile on his face, to be fairly happy about something. He should be. He was being spoiled rotten here.

When Ben came up to her, however, he lost the smile. 'Thought it over, Ingram?'

'What's to think about? I'm not – repeat not! – having a big wedding.'

He shrugged and walked off.

She glared at his back and let him go.

By the following day, she was really worried. He was tender with her in the morning, bringing her tea and biscuits again, but not staying to share them with her. And he refused point-blank to discuss the situation.

'I mean it,' he repeated as they got ready for bed and she tried to reason with him. 'I want to do this properly, with all my family here and yours, too. Or else I'll not do it at all.'

She had never seen him like this, so quietly determined. They had argued, laughed, made wonderful passionate love, worked hard, done everything together for the past two years, and he had never, ever dug in his heels like this.

She grabbed his arm. 'Can't we come to some compromise?'

'No. Not on this. It's very important to me.'

She could feel tears welling in her eyes. She had never been so damned emotional in her life as she had lately.

He put out a fingertip and wiped a tear away. 'Poor darling. I don't want to upset you.'

'Then don't insist on—'

He started to pull away.

'Ben Elless, I'll look an absolute fool, dressed in white when we've been living together for two years and I'm pregnant!'

'You'll look beautiful – and I'm quite happy for your dress to be cream if you hate white, but it must be a beautiful dress and—'

She sighed and finished for him, '—and you haven't changed your mind?'

'No, and I shan't.'

'Ben, *please!*'

'You must be desperate to call me Ben instead of Elless. You usually only do it when we're making love.'

She shuddered. 'I *am* desperate.'

'There's a lot of fun involved in getting married.'

'My sister's wedding wasn't fun at all, believe me. My mother fussed so much that everyone was on edge the whole time and—'

'It means a lot to me to affirm our love and commitment publicly, Meriel. Maybe I'm kinky, but the only way I'm going to get married is with all the trimmings. Otherwise we can just go on living together.'

His voice was low and husky and he had never looked so handsome – or so loving. She stared at him and knew she'd have to give in. She'd been lucky in love, so very lucky, and this was a small price to pay for marrying Ben. But she still hated the thought of a fancy wedding. 'Oh, hell!'

Silence tiptoed around them as he waited, arms folded across his chest.

'You're a rat, Elless!'

'And?'

'And I'll do it your way. But don't expect me to like it.'

He picked her up in his arms and swung her round. 'You will. We're going to have the best damned wedding there ever was. Shall I ring my mother first or shall you ring yours?'

She shuddered. 'I'll get it over with.' She picked up the phone, took a deep breath and said brightly, 'Mum? Guess what . . . ?'

A month later a big four-wheel drive purred into the small country town of York, Western Australia. The sun was shining and the town looked dusty, the people hurrying from one patch of shade to the next. The vehicle didn't stop in the town centre but drove on through, following the new, elegant signposts that said SOMERLEE COUNTRY RETREAT.

The driveway was wide and neatly gravelled, with plants

and flowers all the way along the sides. They were still young, but had space to spread and many were already in bloom or displaying beautiful foliage.

The central complex of the small, exclusive development stood at some distance from the original house, in a spot overlooking the new lake.

All the buildings were in the old colonial style, with tin roofs and wide, fly-screened verandas. Behind the central complex, pathways led to the individual units, but the units themselves were also screened by blocks of vegetation, so that only glimpses of them could be seen from the entrance road.

Beyond the buildings, gleaming in the sun, was a lake, bordered on one edge by the line of original willow trees. A path circled the stretch of sparkling water, begging people to walk round it, and here and there were shaded seats in case anyone wanted to sit and commune with nature.

At one point there was a circular paved area, with stone seats built into the low wall that surrounded it. This was becoming very popular for weddings.

The owners' house was screened from the guests' area by a group of young gum trees and a low fence bore a sign saying PRIVATE. The vehicle turned that way, ignoring it.

As the visitors drew up, Meriel came hurrying out of the house, beaming, and the two women embraced. 'Rosanna and Karl!' She lowered her voice. 'Thank goodness you're here! My mother's been here for four days and I'm already dreaming of shooting her.'

'It's all looking great. You've done a lot since last time we came.'

'Wait till you see it when some of the fast-growing trees mature. Ben's done some lovely watercolours of what it'll be like. I've never seen a man so happy.'

'You don't seem unhappy yourself,' her friend commented. 'Whenever we meet you're bubbling over with enthusiasm for something.'

'I am happy, very – except for this wedding stuff, but Ben's lapping all that up. He even thinks my mother's amusing. Ha!'

'Where are your resident hippies? I'd like to catch up with Ria again.'

'They finished building their eco-house and live over the brow of the hill now. We've given them a couple of acres. They'll be with us for the wedding.' She paused and gestured to two dogs, who were sitting panting and grinning up at them. 'Dylan visits us regularly. He's a great favourite with the visitors and inspects them all carefully for us. Tina follows him around so closely I'm sure she's in love.'

She chuckled. 'Actually, the Back to the Sixties aspect of our resort is very popular indeed. People come here, buy flower people clothes, burn sticks of incense and really chill out. Ben's not the only one to have good ideas, you know.'

She looked out of the window proudly. 'Just think. This could have been a new housing development, with rows of houses, instead of a lake and the bush. I'm so glad we stopped the developers.'

Rosanna joined her at the window. 'What with them and Ben's cousin, you had to fight to keep this place as you wanted, didn't you?'

They stood for a minute watching the sunlight play on the rippling water then Meriel said, 'Well, that's all in the past now. I took the liberty of putting a bottle of champers in the fridge.' When she'd poured them a glass each and herself a thimbleful, she said softly, 'Here's to us!'

A voice from the doorway made them both jump. 'I knew you'd be into that champagne, Ingram, as soon as my back was turned. Are you an alcoholic or what?'

Meriel bounced to her feet. 'Look here, Elless. One quarter of a glass isn't going to hurt the baby and it's not every day Rosanna comes to help me get married, so butt out.'

He walked across and gave her a quick hug. 'I didn't realize I was marrying a secret drinker.'

Meriel pretended to slap the side of his face. 'I said watch it, you!'

He poured himself a glass and smiled at their friends. 'Tomorrow can't come too soon for me, but she's a bit on edge, so treat her gently.'

'Make that a lot on edge,' Meriel said sourly.

'It'll be all right,' Rosanna soothed. 'My wedding was great fun.'

Meriel just sighed and didn't waste her energy arguing. Everyone else was happy about all the fuss, but not the bride.

The next day dawned bright and clear, but fortunately not too hot for the overseas guests. Sunlight and laughter threaded the day.

Meriel wore a calf-length dress of ivory silk, her hair as simply styled as ever. On her head she wore a wreath of fresh flowers created by Ben and in her hands she carried a posy he'd made, as did her matron of honour, Rosanna.

And when the bride and groom made their vows, using words they'd written themselves, few people stayed dry-eyed, because love rang in every word, shone in every glance.

'Your piece was beautiful, Ben,' Meriel said as they had their photograph taken yet again.

'I meant every word, my darling. I really am the luckiest man on earth.'

Time hung suspended for a moment, then she dabbed at her eyes and smiled mistily at him. 'Look what you're doing to me. I don't usually do sentimental stuff.'

'You do now.'